THE FOOL DIES LAST

THE FOOL DIES LAST

Carol Miller

**SEVERN
HOUSE**

First world edition published in Great Britain and the USA in 2022
by Severn House, an imprint of Canongate Books Ltd,
14 High Street, Edinburgh EH1 1TE.

Trade paperback edition first published in Great Britain and the USA in 2022
by Severn House, an imprint of Canongate Books Ltd.

severnhouse.com

British Library Cataloguing-in-Publication Data
A CIP catalogue record for this title is available from the British Library.

ISBN-13: 978-0-7278-2303-8 (cased)
ISBN-13: 978-1-4483-0841-5 (trade paper)
ISBN-13: 978-1-4483-0840-8 (e-book)

All Severn House titles are printed on acid-free paper.

Typeset by Palimpsest Book Production Ltd.,
Falkirk, Stirlingshire, Scotland.
Printed and bound in Great Britain by
TJ Books, Padstow, Cornwall.

For Butchie and Babs

ONE

'I need to know,' Rosemarie Potter said. 'Tell me what you see.'

She thrust her chubby, suntanned arms across the table toward Hope Bailey. Rosemarie was one of Hope's regular clients, typically visiting the shop two or three times a week, always with her beloved pug Percy in tow. A gregarious woman in her mid-fifties, Rosemarie was fond of billowy flowered dresses and had her hair dyed an eye-popping shade of red. Hope took Rosemarie's outstretched hands into her own and turned up the palms.

'Well?' Rosemarie prompted after Hope had studied her right palm for a minute. 'Will I get married again?'

'Wasn't your divorce finalized only last week?' Hope murmured, shifting her attention to the left palm.

'It will be ten days from Tuesday,' Rosemarie replied cheerfully, without any hint of embarrassment or regret. 'That's why I need to know. Time to climb back on the horse, so to speak.'

'Assuming the horse plans on buying dinner,' Summer Bailey Fletcher chimed in, coming from the jewelry display case that she had been tidying to supply Percy with his usual pre-reading doggie cookie.

Hope and Summer were sisters – thirty-two and thirty-three years old respectively, separated by a mere fifteen months – and proprietors of Bailey's Boutique, a small mystic shop that sold crystals, candles, herbs, and the like. The shop was located on the ground floor of an old three-story brownstone that was tucked into an equally old and narrow side street in the historic district of downtown Asheville, North Carolina.

'A man has to be the sort to want to take you out for dinner and dancing,' Rosemarie concurred. 'Otherwise, there's no sense in it.'

'And fix things,' Summer added. 'He has to be able to fix things.'

'Speaking of fixing things,' Hope interjected, glancing up from Rosemarie's hands. 'Gram wanted me to remind you that she's still waiting for Gary to put together the new raised bed for the garden.'

The brownstone was owned by Hope and Summer's maternal grandmother, Olivia Bailey. She was the one who had originally started the boutique many years earlier when their mom had been no more than a toddler. Hope and Gram both still lived upstairs, while Summer had moved out to the suburbs when she had married Gary. At the rear of the property was a little green space that they used as a patio and garden. It supplied the herbs and many of the flowers and other plants for the boutique.

'Gary has been awfully busy,' Summer apologized on behalf of her husband.

'Still working on that big construction project?' Rosemarie asked.

'He was promoted to foreman,' Summer responded proudly.

'How exciting!' Rosemarie congratulated her. 'That must be good for him getting future jobs.'

'It's also good for giving him an excuse not to come home at night,' Hope remarked dryly.

'But it's a three-hour drive to the site,' Summer protested. 'It makes sense for him to stay at a motel during the week and only come home on weekends.'

Hope would have agreed, except for the past month Gary had supposedly been too busy to return even on the weekends. She knew that the project was behind schedule and, as a result, the whole crew was working on Saturdays, but she was beginning to have some doubts as to why Gary wasn't coming back on Sundays. A week or two was understandable. Four weeks seemed to be bordering on the suspicious to her. Summer, however, had full confidence in her husband, so Hope held her tongue.

'You and Gary have always made such a handsome couple,' Rosemarie gushed to Summer. 'Him so blond, and you with that beautiful dark hair. We're all waiting for you to make some beautiful babies.'

A deep blush spread over Summer's cheeks. She and Gary had

been married for three years, and for the last two Summer had been trying to start a family, without success. It was becoming an increasingly sensitive subject for her, understandably enough. Hope was about to jump in to deflect it when the wind chimes rang out at the front door of the store. A trio of laughing, chattering ladies entered, carrying a plethora of shopping bags, and Summer hurried over to greet them.

It was early May, and the tourist season was slowly beginning. The boutique had a loyal clientele, but tourists were also an important part of their business. That was especially true this year, because although Hope was still reading palms, she had stopped working with the Tarot in February. Before that, her Tarot readings had always been prodigiously popular, both with devoted regulars and walk-ins. The sisters had never earned much money, so the extra income was sorely missed. They were keeping their fingers crossed that the warming weather would bring plenty of vacationers.

'Enough about Summer's wonderful marriage. I want to know about *mine*.' Rosemarie wiggled her arms on the table like a pair of plump pink salmon struggling upstream. 'Tell me, Hope. Tell me.'

With a smile, Hope directed her attention back to Rosemarie's palms. On the outer edge of her hand, extending into the palm under the little finger, there were five small horizontal lines.

'Those are your marriage lines,' Hope explained.

'So I'll be married five times?' Rosemarie exclaimed.

The trio of ladies, who were in the process of trying on various bracelets, pendants, and earrings based on Summer's explanation of what the different semi-precious stones related to, glanced over with interest.

Smiling once more, Hope shook her head. 'Not necessarily. The lines show the *potential* for strong relationships. It doesn't mean that you'll get married each time. One – or more – of the relationships could end up being just a close friendship with lots of mutual attraction.'

'But *five*!' Rosemarie repeated with enthusiasm.

'You see how two of the lines are so fine, those other two are somewhat heavier, and that one is really clear and defined?'

Rosemarie nodded.

'That one also comes up strongly from the side of the hand. It shows that you'll have a very deep and stable relationship.'

An exhalation of joy escaped from Rosemarie's lips.

All four of the lighter lines curved slightly downward, indicating that four separations or divorces were also likely. But Hope knew better than to share that piece of information. Rosemarie had already been divorced twice, and Hope didn't want her to start off her next relationship with the assumption that it wouldn't work out, either. The possibility for self-sabotage was too great. Marriage lines, or relationship lines, could – and frequently did – change. They would appear and disappear, strengthening or fading like shifting dunes of sand with the passage of time, which made them generally informative but rarely definitive. Hope had learned that over many years of palmistry, along with sufficient personal experience.

She released Rosemarie's hands, and after another blissful exhalation, Rosemarie rubbed the five little lines with vigor, as though it might make a magic genie in the form of a marvelous new husband appear out of one of them. Suppressing a chuckle, Hope pulled open the drawer on her side of the table and reached into a bag for Percy's post-reading doggie cookie. Percy was very familiar with the standard order of business: remaining dutifully at Rosemarie's feet while in the shop and refraining from barking at customers equaled a treat.

As Hope presented Percy with his reward and added a bit of scratching under his harness, the trio of ladies approached the table. Hope wasn't surprised. In fact, she rather expected it. Customers in the boutique for the first time were often too shy or uncertain to ask about a reading, but once they saw somebody else getting one, they were usually hooked. That was particularly true if the current reading happened to involve the invariably intriguing topics of love, sex, or money. The table was set discreetly in one corner of the store, and Hope always kept her voice low to protect her clients' privacy. Rosemarie, however, was far from bashful and had spoken loudly enough to be overheard.

The subject of marriage lines was simply too fascinating to be ignored, and the ladies quickly decided that they wanted a reading, too. They were running late for the four o'clock wine-and-cheese at the nearby hotel where they were staying, but they made a triple appointment for the following afternoon, while their husbands were scheduled for a round of golf. Happily for all, Hope had the requisite time available. Summer finished with the ladies' jewelry purchases, and the trio departed laughing and chattering even more enthusiastically than when they had arrived.

Hope was about to start helping Summer straighten up after the ladies when Rosemarie gave a plaintive sigh. She was still sitting at the table. It was an aged, coffee-brown pine table with simple lines and little embellishment, in all likelihood the product of some local North Carolinian furniture craftsman a century or two earlier. The table was perfect for Hope's purposes. Over time the rectangular top had been worn soft and velvety smooth to the touch, with no chance of painful splinters. It was small enough to reach across for palm readings but still wide enough to cast the larger Tarot spreads, and the single drawer on one side was just the right size to hold all of Hope's supplies.

The table had been left in the attic of the brownstone by the previous owner. There was initially some question as to whether Hope should try to bring it downstairs. The attic – or, more accurately, the attic's spectral inhabitants – could get rather possessive of its contents, even aggressively so on occasion. But in the end, after a bit of bartering, the attic had given up the table without opposition. It had also relinquished custody of the four matching coffee-brown straight-backed chairs. Although as worn as the table, the chairs were still sturdy and surprisingly comfortable.

Leaning back in her chair and continuing to rub the lines on her palm – more slowly and thoughtfully now – Rosemarie sighed again. 'I wish that you could tell me something about him, Hope.'

'Your hand only talks about you,' Hope reminded her. 'No one else.'

'But how will I know who he is?' Rosemarie's voice warbled with anxiety. 'You said that it would be a deep and stable relationship. But what if I miss it? What if I miss him somehow, by accident?'

'You won't miss it – or him.' Hope spoke confidently, and she gave Rosemarie's arm a reassuring squeeze.

Hope was good at comforting her clients. It was one of the reasons they liked – and trusted – her so much. She had gained a reputation for being reliable, because unlike some in her line of work, she was honest. Hope didn't pretend to see things that weren't actually there, and although she was careful about how and when she dispensed bad news, she didn't automatically limit her readings to only happy information. People came to her looking for knowledge, and she didn't think it right to restrict that knowledge solely to nice and agreeable things. Life certainly wasn't always rainbows and sunshine. Pretending that it was didn't help anyone. Hope believed that the more information a client had, the better choices they could potentially make, especially when those choices might be difficult ones.

'You'll feel it when it's right,' she told Rosemarie, nodding at her encouragingly. 'And you know that you can come here any time if you're worried or having doubts.'

Rosemarie nodded back at her with gratitude. 'I do know, Hope. And I appreciate you always fitting me and Percy into your schedule, even at the last minute, but . . .' Shifting in her seat, she let the sentence trail away unfinished.

When a reading was over, there were some clients who promptly departed, while others – such as Rosemarie – tended to linger, either because they wanted to muse about what Hope had told them or simply to hang out and chat for a while. By its nature, the boutique was a social place. Friends and neighbors frequently dropped by, looking for a piece of advice or just to say hello and pass along a bit of gossip. Hope and Summer enjoyed the company and never pushed anyone out of the door, no matter how long they dawdled. After all, customers had to feel comfortable sharing their problems, and that couldn't be rushed.

'But?' Hope asked patiently.

'Well . . .' Rosemarie hesitated, clearly wanting to say something but reluctant to do so. Finally, the words tumbled out. 'I need to know more about him, Hope. I really do. Like his job. Or if he loves animals as much as me. Or what sort of personality he has.'

Hope didn't respond. She could guess what direction Rosemarie was headed, and she was not happy about it.

'Just a little something,' Rosemarie went on. 'A hint. Maybe his astrological sign? Or the color of his hair? I know my palms can't show any of that' – there was a slight pause as she shifted in her seat once more – 'but the cards . . .'

Summer set down the necklace that she had been returning to the jewelry display case and turned toward them. Hope didn't look at her or at Rosemarie. Knotting her fingers together beneath the table, she stared out of the front window of the shop.

Rosemarie cleared her throat awkwardly. 'It wouldn't have to be one of those big, fancy spreads. Just a few cards. One or two, even. Like you used to do when someone had a quick question.'

'You know that Hope doesn't work with the Tarot anymore, Rosemarie,' Summer interjected.

'But she could see so much,' Rosemarie entreated. 'And she was always so accurate. Everything would turn out just like she said.'

'Not everything,' Hope corrected her in a low tone.

'If you mean . . .' Rosemarie began. 'But you *couldn't* have seen that—'

Summer shook her head at her, and Rosemarie didn't continue. A heavy silence followed. Hope kept her gaze fixed outside, watching the people pass by on the sidewalk. A young mother pushing a stroller with a screaming toddler. Two middle-aged businessmen in dark suits engaged in an earnest discussion. A delivery chap steering a hand truck with a wobbling tower of cardboard boxes.

'How about an early dinner tonight?' Summer suggested after a minute. 'When we close up, instead of eating here, we could go across the square to the café with the good soup. It's Thursday, so they'll have that yummy potato feta.'

'Oh, I love that place!' Rosemarie exclaimed. 'And Percy loves their burgers. They allow dogs in the outdoor section. If you'll let us join you, it'll be my treat.'

'Of course you can join us,' Summer replied. 'What a nice offer. Isn't that a nice offer, Hope?'

Hope wasn't at all hungry, but she nodded anyway, knowing that the offer was Rosemarie's good-natured attempt at an apology. Except there was no need to apologize. Hope wasn't angry with her. It wasn't Rosemarie's fault. That's what happened when you read the Tarot, and everybody relied on you to read the Tarot, and then you suddenly stopped reading the Tarot. People tried to be understanding and accepting, but really they just wanted you to start reading the Tarot again. Summer was different. She didn't keep pushing Hope back to the cards. Instead, she tried to ply her with food, because food – especially creamy soups, biscuits slathered with gravy, and anything in the cheesecake family – was Summer's emotional fortification in times of distress, so she naturally assumed that it worked with Hope, too. But it didn't. Hope had lost her appetite back in February, and she hadn't regained it.

'Do you know if Megan is planning on stopping by today? If so, we could invite her along . . .' Summer paused as she saw Hope frown. 'What is it? Are you OK?'

'I'm fine,' Hope answered. 'But I don't think he is.'

She pointed through the window to a man crossing the street who appeared to be approaching the boutique. He was tall and lean, and walked with long, quick, purposeful strides. There was something clutched in one of his hands, while his other hand was curled into a tight fist. If it was an angry fist, it matched his face. The man's brow was heavily furrowed. His lips were pressed together hard. And his eyes were narrow and agitated.

'Uh-oh,' Summer said apprehensively. 'That looks like trouble. Do you recognize him? Is he a customer?'

'If he is' – Hope's frown deepened – 'I don't remember him.'

Rosemarie turned to look outside as well, and when she saw the man, she clucked her tongue in admiration. 'Well, you certainly wouldn't forget *him*. He's gorgeous.'

A moment later, the door to the boutique slammed open. The wind chimes banged instead of sang. The man stepped inside, glanced once around, and scowled.

'Which one of you tried to kill Betsy Hughes?' he demanded.

TWO

For a long minute, no one spoke. It was a glaringly bright and sunny day, and the inside of the shop was comparatively dim, so the man had to blink several times before his vision could adjust. It gave Hope the opportunity to take a better look at him. He was about thirty-five and well dressed, with tailored slacks and an expensive, stylish shirt. Even though his thick, sandy hair was ruffled from the wind, she could see that it was fashionably cut. He had a fancy watch and fancy shoes, and he wore it all with a natural ease. Scowl aside, it was clear that the man was confident and comfortable with himself. Too confident and comfortable, if Hope's initial assessment was correct.

'Oh, that chiseled jaw,' Rosemarie crooned under her breath. 'And those eyes. Just look at those eyes, Hope.'

The eyes in question circled slowly around the shop, scrutinizing it and its contents. When they came to Hope, they paused. They were a pale, frosty blue that reminded her of an ice-crusted lake. They surveyed her in turn, and if they liked what they saw, they didn't show it. The man's scowl remained.

'It's called a *boutique*,' he said brusquely. 'Doesn't that mean the place should sell clothes?'

'We have scarves,' Hope responded with equal curtness.

The chiseled jaw twitched slightly, betraying some degree of surprise. 'You're the owner?'

'I am. Along with my sister.'

Following the direction of Hope's gesture, the man glanced at Summer. After a brief examination, he appeared even less impressed than he had with Hope. 'You don't look related,' he remarked.

He wasn't wrong. Physically, Hope and Summer shared the same glossy dark hair, but little else. Summer was considerably rounder, both in her face and body, with generous curves. Even before losing her appetite, Hope had always been the more petite of the pair, with a naturally slender, deceptively delicate shape. Summer had a peachy complexion, with hazel eyes and a wide, pouty mouth. In contrast, Hope's skin was ivory, with emerald-green eyes and long black lashes. Neither sister had ever minded not looking like the other. Both as teens and adults, they had never attracted the same sort of men, which had helped to keep them close instead of turning them competitive.

'If there are two of you,' the man went on, 'shouldn't the name be *Baileys'* plural rather than *Bailey's* singular?'

Hope raised an eyebrow. He was obviously quick-witted – and a stickler for proper grammar and punctuation. He was also annoyingly critical. 'The shop is named after our grandmother, who was the original proprietor,' she told him, although as she said it, she wondered why she bothered with an explanation. The man was clearly not one of their customers, and so far everything about him was much too irritating to make him a potential friend.

'What kind of shop is it anyway?' The frosty blue eyes traveled once more around the interior before returning to Hope. 'What do you do here – other than try to kill gullible old ladies?'

'What on earth are you talking about?' Hope snapped, the color rising in her cheeks. She hadn't understood him before, and she still didn't.

While her agitation rose, the man's seemed to subside. His scowl faded into a calm, almost insolent expression as he leaned against the frame of the front door. Folding his arms across his chest, his shirt tightened, revealing a fit figure.

'Oh, those muscles,' Rosemarie murmured. 'Sweet heaven, look at those muscles, Hope.'

This time her admiration wasn't sufficiently under her breath, and the man responded with a rakish grin.

'If only I were twenty years younger' – Rosemarie heaved a wistful sigh – 'then he could be one of my five.'

'Consider yourself lucky that he's not,' Hope replied tartly. 'I'd wager that his version of a deep and stable relationship means staying for a whole night.'

The man threw his head back and laughed. For possessing such a cool exterior, it was an unexpectedly warm laugh. 'You must know some of my ex-girlfriends,' he chortled.

'I don't need to know them,' Hope countered. 'I know your type.'

The blue eyes flashed in amusement. 'Viper-tongued little thing, aren't you?'

Hope was about to prove him right when Percy gave a heralding bark. An instant later, Megan Steele glided through the open door of the boutique, a three-quarters-full carafe of wine in one hand and a half-empty platter of cheese and crackers in the other.

'Hello, hello, my darlings! I come bearing gifts, as usual. This afternoon's feature is an exceptionally mediocre rosé . . .'

Megan's voice trailed away as she noticed the man leaning against the frame. She stopped and gave him a long, inquisitive look. He responded in kind. Neither one blushed or turned away at the other's thorough examination. Megan was easy to admire, and she knew it. She had the sinewy legs and wild eyes of a colt, with a bob of baby-fine blond hair and a pert nose.

Although there was no question that she was an attractive woman, it was Megan's categorical disinterest in marriage that rather ironically drew men to her like big-game hunters to a mythical beast. In her teen years, Megan's parents had put her and her brother through an extraordinarily nasty, nearly decade-long divorce, in which the two children and a pair of prize-winning Dalmatians had been used as negotiating pawns. Megan had often joked that the dogs were more desired than the kids, and, sadly enough, there was a good deal of truth to it. Not surprisingly perhaps, the experience had left her unwilling to commit herself to any man in any meaningful way, and with many men that gave her an irresistible appeal, as though she must somehow be conquered or tamed. So far, none had succeeded.

'Well,' Megan purred to the man currently garnering her attention, 'aren't you a delectable morsel?'

'Right back at you, sweetheart,' he repaid the compliment smoothly.

'Nice choice, Hope.' Megan turned to her with a wink and a nod. 'I approve.'

Aside from Summer, Megan was Hope's oldest and closest friend. They were the same age and had gone to school together.

With her own family relations so strained, Megan had attached herself to the sisters and Gram in a surrogate fashion, and they saw each other on an almost daily basis.

Hope wrinkled her nose in reply. 'You've had way too much of that rosé if you think he's here because of me.'

'Hmm.' Megan's brow furrowed, and she turned back to the man. 'You're not here for Hope? I could have sworn from the way that you were looking at her when I came in . . . And I'm rarely wrong about these things.'

Megan prided herself on her quick – and accurate – assessments of people, both men and women. It was a function of her job. She was the Director of Activities at Amethyst, a luxury hotel and spa also located in downtown Asheville, only a few blocks from the brownstone. The clientele was correspondingly upscale and liked to be pampered. Megan was in charge of anticipating their wants and needs, and to her credit, she did it well. As part of her duties, she organized the four o'clock wine-and-cheese. It was her custom to bring the leftovers to the boutique shortly after five when she got off work. She and Hope – and sometimes Summer, depending on Gary's whereabouts – along with whoever else happened to be in the shop at the appointed hour, would then share a glass and their stories of the day.

'Hmm,' Megan repeated, gazing at the man more thoughtfully. 'You don't look like you're shopping on behalf of a wife or girlfriend. And I know that you haven't come in pursuit of dear Summer. She's much too dedicated to that shifty husband of hers to ever consider stepping out on him—'

'Gary is *not* shifty!' Summer objected indignantly. It was the first time that she had spoken since the man had stormed into the boutique. Up until that point, she had been too perplexed by his peculiar remarks to do anything more than stare at him.

Hope and Megan exchanged a glance, but neither one commented further on Gary's alleged shiftiness.

'So that leaves Hope,' Megan concluded to the man. 'You must want *something*' – her lips curled into a mischievous smile – 'from her.'

'You're right,' he answered. 'I do want something from her.' His face and tone were expressionless. 'If she's the one who made this.'

He held up the item that Hope had seen clutched in his hand as he had been approaching the shop. She recognized it instantly. It was a small, amber-colored glass bottle capped with a black eyedropper. The boutique sold dozens of them every week, except they weren't made by her. They were made by Summer. Or more accurately, the contents of the bottles were made by Summer.

Recognizing the bottle and eyedropper also, Megan's smile grew. 'Ah, one of Summer's famous tinctures. I hope that you made your selection wisely.'

'My selection?' the man questioned her.

'Summer offers quite an array of choices.' As she spoke, Megan walked over to the table where Hope and Rosemarie were sitting and deposited both the cheese-and-cracker platter and the wine carafe on it. 'There's one that I'm particularly fond of.' She gave a breathy, coquettish sigh. 'Gives a man great stamina.'

Hope couldn't restrain a laugh. 'If the nuns from our old school could hear you now . . .'

Megan laughed, too. 'I know. I'm such a dreadful disappointment to them. C'est la vie.' She shrugged, then started toward the rear of the shop. 'Are you staying?' she asked, glancing back over her shoulder at the man holding the tincture. 'Should I bring out an extra glass?' Before he could respond, she said, 'Never mind. I'll get one regardless.'

While Megan disappeared in the direction of the kitchen, the man turned to Summer. His scowl had resurfaced. 'So this concoction is yours?'

Summer squinted at him and the bottle in his hand. 'It might be,' she replied haltingly. 'I can't really tell without taking a closer look and knowing—'

'Knowing who you gave it to?' He cut her off sharply. 'You gave it to Betsy Hughes.'

The squint intensified. 'Yes, I know Mrs Hughes, but I don't know if—'

'If this is what you gave her?' he interrupted her again. 'Well, it is. I can assure you of that. I took it from her myself this morning.'

'You took it from her?' Summer echoed in confusion. 'Why would you—'

'Because it could have killed her!'

Summer's mouth dropped open, but not a syllable emerged.

'Don't be absurd,' Hope snapped at the man, tired of his imperiousness and preposterous accusations. 'Nothing in that bottle would kill Betsy Hughes. Or anyone else, for that matter. It's designed to help, not to hurt.'

'*Help?*' He gave a derisive snort. 'You're the ones who are being absurd. You don't help an elderly woman suffering from high blood pressure and high blood sugar with harebrained potions and salves. You send her to a doctor for medicine. *Real medicine.*'

With an audible clack, Summer's mouth clenched shut. Hope rose stiffly from her chair. Even Percy gave a low growl.

'Uh-oh,' Rosemarie said, shaking her head. 'Now you've done it.'

The man's gaze circled around, and he found four sets of hostile eyes – canine included – glaring at him.

'Now you've done it,' Rosemarie repeated. 'Now Hope is going to put a curse on you.'

'Did you say a *curse?*' The man snorted a second time. 'That really is absurd.'

He looked around once more, and when none of them blinked, a small crease spread across his brow. He straightened up from the door frame. Hope concealed a smile. For all the man's high-handedness, even he could be made a touch uneasy by the mention of a potential curse.

'I don't do curses,' she remarked equably.

'But you could,' Rosemarie rejoined, helping herself to a large chunk of cheddar from the platter.

Hope offered an ambivalent shrug. 'Curses can be messy. They have a habit of turning out differently than expected. Karma's sticky.'

'You could look at his palm,' Summer suggested, coming over to the table for her share of the snacks, 'and tell him about something bad you see in his future. That would serve him right.'

'Oh, yes! Do that!' Rosemarie agreed excitedly, clapping her hands while simultaneously stuffing another piece of cheese into her mouth. 'Tell us about him, Hope. Tell us something *bad.*'

The crease in the man's brow deepened. Hope could see that he was struggling with what they were saying. He understood the words, of course, but he didn't fully grasp the conversation, and he wasn't sure whether they were being serious or not. That wasn't too surprising. The mystical world was an enigmatic and exotic territory for many, even a little frightening for some. Although she was still annoyed at his arrogant attitude, Hope decided to be generous and go easy on the man.

'If you had let my sister finish speaking instead of continually interrupting her,' she told him, 'Summer would have explained to you that she had no intention of treating Betsy Hughes's high blood pressure or blood sugar. She gave her a simple tincture of lemon balm.'

'Lemon balm?' the man said.

'Lemon balm,' Summer confirmed in between bites of cracker. 'It's a bushy, sweet-scented herb in the mint family. I can show you an example of the plant if you want. We grow it here ourselves' – she gave a wave of the hand – 'in the garden at the back.'

'I know what lemon balm is,' he replied. 'But I don't know—'

It was Summer's turn to cut him off. 'You don't know why I'm sharing this information with you? Well, I don't either. Frankly, it's none of your business what I give – or don't give – to Mrs Hughes. You haven't explained to us who you are or how this is any of your concern. And furthermore, I think that you've been rather rude, not just to us, but particularly to poor Mrs Hughes. For some incomprehensible reason, you took away her tincture, which she needs for her stomach.'

'Her stomach?' A second crease appeared in the man's brow.

'Mrs Hughes has a nervous stomach,' Summer responded. 'Not that her stomach is any more your business than my tincture,' she added with unconcealed resentment. 'Her doctor put her on so many pills – so much *real medicine*, as you would call it – that it upset her stomach to the point that she couldn't eat and she couldn't sleep. I gave her a *harebrained potion* – also your words – consisting primarily of lemon balm. And guess what? Her stomach stopped hurting. Now, thanks to you, without the tincture, it'll start hurting her again. Worse than ever, in all likelihood.'

'You're wrong,' the man tossed back tersely. 'It is my business, because *I'm* her doctor.'

There was a momentary silence. If he was expecting an apology or a resultant degree of deference, he was in error. Rosemarie shifted her attention to the sweating carafe of rosé and subsequently toward the kitchen in an effort to determine what was keeping Megan from returning with the promised glasses. Summer glowered at the man like an irate lioness in strident defense of her cubs. She put her heart and soul into trying to help people who couldn't find relief for their suffering from the conventional medical establishment, and she was ill-disposed to having her efforts – or her clients' ailments – belittled. Hope gave him a hard look. He was Betsy Hughes's doctor? That couldn't be right.

The boutique's phone rang. Summer answered it, and an instant later, both Betsy Hughes's stomach and her doctor were forgotten.

'It's Gram.' Summer's hazel eyes were wide, and her voice came out as a ragged whisper. 'There's been an accident.'

THREE

Hope remembered the last time there had been an accident. It had left a heavy, jagged scar that would remain etched in her memory forever. February – the winter storm that had covered the entire region with ice – the bewildering phone call and the awful words. *Automobile fatality . . . Nothing could be done . . . Very sorry for your loss.*

Thankfully, this accident wasn't like the other, and Gram was all right. Or at least the fact that she had been speaking on the telephone to Summer allowed for the assumption that she was all right. She hadn't answered any of Summer's anxious questions. She had only said that there had been an accident and that Hope needed to come immediately. Gram didn't drive, so it couldn't have been a road accident. While she technically still possessed a valid license, she preferred to have someone else transport her. Gram's eyes weren't the best after dark or in the rain and fog. Her hearing tended to be selective. And her left hip gave her enough trouble that she walked with a cane, although Hope knew that she used it more as a stage prop than for actual support.

Asheville was blessed with a user-friendly public transportation system, and, cane in hand, Gram nearly always opted for the bus. If the snow and ice became too thick on the sidewalks in January or the heat and humidity grew too oppressive in August, Hope would insist on taking her wherever she wanted to go. Otherwise, Gram liked to be independent and choose her own schedule and itinerary. Today – as usual – she had headed over to the community center for afternoon bingo, which was invariably followed by the Thursday spaghetti supper.

Driving as quickly as she could from the boutique to the center, Hope tried to surmise what sort of an accident might have occurred during bingo and supper. The majority of the participants were affable retirees who came mostly to socialize and share photos from their latest cruise and the growing grandkids. How bad an accident could it really have been? A sprained wrist in too eager a pursuit of the five-dollar prize money? A giant spilled pot of pasta and sauce? Except neither of those possibilities explained why Gram had been so adamant that she come to the center immediately. Hope was neither a nurse nor a caterer, and Gram certainly wasn't the panicky type who needed consolation or hand-holding over minor misfortunes. It also wasn't late in the evening. The buses were still running, so it couldn't be that Gram had no other way of getting home.

When Hope turned into the parking lot and saw the ambulance – without flashing lights or visible paramedics – standing at the front entrance of the center, she immediately revised her theory. The trouble was probably heart palpitations or an acute case of indigestion. According to Gram, both were common among the community-center crowd. Some of the folks were in their eighties and nineties. A few had even crossed the century mark. A bit too much excitement or one too many pieces of spicy garlic bread, and an especially vigilant member of the group had decided to be safe rather than sorry by calling for medical assistance. Although that still didn't explain why Gram wanted her there.

After debating for a minute whether to park in a regular space or pull up behind the ambulance, Hope decided on the latter. She had barely climbed out of the car when Morris Henshaw greeted her.

'Hello, Hope. Olivia asked me to keep an eye out for you.'

Although friendly, Morris's tone was grave enough that it caused Hope some concern. 'Is Gram all right?' she said hastily.

'Of course she's all right. I can't remember a time when she wasn't all right. Your grandmother is a fine woman.'

Hope restrained a smile. It was no secret that Morris Henshaw was sweet on Olivia Bailey. The two had been good friends for many years and shared most of the same interests and activities. Gram would often spend the night at Morris's house, and the two frequently went on extended weekend trips. But although Morris was eager for greater commitment, for some reason Gram hesitated at marriage or formally moving in together. When asked about it by Hope or Summer, she would only say – laughingly – that she didn't want to rob the cradle, which was utter nonsense considering that Morris was a mere five years her junior, and their respective ages were sixty-nine and seventy-four.

Walking toward him, Hope noticed Morris's stiff posture and the thick brace supporting his middle. 'How's your back feeling?' she asked.

'Better than before the surgery, but not as good as I'd like,' he responded amiably. 'The experts say that I should be pleased with my rate of recovery. I wish it were faster.'

'But didn't you only recently get out of the hospital? Isn't it a little quick for you to be up and about, especially outside the house?'

'Fiddle-faddle. You sound just like Olivia, and that's the same thing I told her: *fiddle-faddle*. If I don't move around, I'll get stuck permanently in a chair like some decrepit potted plant. Got to get the muscles strong again. How else will I keep up with your grandmother? She races about as though she's got a jetpack strapped on. I can't lag behind. And I have to get back to work. My patients are counting on me.'

As to his patients, he wasn't exaggerating. They did indeed count on him, in a way that few physicians could honestly boast. Morris Henshaw was a family doctor from a different era. He didn't rush through appointments, no matter how pressed for time he might be. He still volunteered for – and enjoyed – house calls. He didn't proclaim a specialty, because he knew something about nearly everything. And he truly cared for the people who came to see him, because he considered each and every one of them a neighbor and a friend.

Morris's office wasn't located in a glossy professional complex with a long list of other medical practitioners. It was in another old brownstone just down the street from the boutique. The man bore some resemblance to an old brownstone, too. He was tall and thin, with a narrow, angular face topped by wispy white hair. Although his demeanor was earnest – as could be expected from a trusted physician – he had a warm laugh that was instantly infectious. Like the aged building in which he worked, time had given Morris his share of spots, lines, and wrinkles, but to the right eye, they could both still be deemed attractive.

'So where's Gram?' Hope asked.

'Inside.' Morris gestured toward the center.

She waited for him to elaborate. When he didn't, she in turn gestured toward the ambulance. 'What kind of an accident was it? I hope nothing too serious.'

He hesitated a moment, as if unsure himself, then he said, 'Do you know Roberta King?'

'Roberta? Yes, I know her – a little. She comes into the shop once in a while to buy presents for her nieces.'

Morris nodded, after which he hesitated again.

'Was Roberta in an accident?' Hope pressed him, finding it odd that he was having such a difficult time explaining. 'Is she OK?'

Chewing on his lip, Morris replied, 'You had better come see for yourself.'

As she followed him to the entrance, Hope wondered why Gram would telephone her – accident or not – in regard to Roberta King. Hope didn't know the woman all that well, and as far as she was aware, although Gram and Roberta went some ways back, they weren't particularly near and dear.

Hope halted in surprise the instant that she stepped through the panel of sliding doors. The community center was a modern, spacious facility, with numerous rooms of varying sizes leading off the main hall like arms spreading out from the body of a large octopus. There were so many classes and clubs and activities and organizations using the building from early in the morning until late in the evening that the place was in a constant chaotic bustle. Except now. Now there was nothing. No people and no noise.

'Where–where is everybody?' Hope said, her voice sounding eerily loud in the empty space.

'The police moved them all into a different room,' Morris told her.

'The police?' she echoed, her surprise growing. 'But there weren't any police cars out front.'

'They came in from the back. It's closer.'

'Closer? Closer to what?'

'Where it happened.'

Hope frowned, but before she could ask any further questions, a policeman in uniform appeared at their side.

'You're not supposed to be wandering around out here,' he admonished them.

'Detective Phillips sent me to wait for her arrival,' Morris explained.

'Oh' – the policeman turned to Hope – 'so that means you're the granddaughter?'

Hope responded with a slight nod, too astonished to do much else. Why did the police move everyone into a different room? Who was Detective Phillips? And how on earth did any of it relate to her being the granddaughter? She had a sudden terrible feeling that something had actually happened to Gram, and Morris was trying to keep the truth from her for as long as possible. Only he didn't look upset. If something bad had happened to Gram, then surely he would have looked upset.

'Come with me,' the policeman directed.

He led them down the hall past one tightly closed door after another until they reached the last room on the right. Having been there before, Hope knew that it was one of the larger rooms at the center and frequently used for bingo and the spaghetti suppers. The policeman turned the handles on the double doors simultaneously. As he swung them open, Hope held her breath, fearing what she might find on the other side.

She needn't have worried – at least not about Gram. The first thing that she saw was Gram standing in the middle of the room, looking as hale as always. Gram was evidently also as chipper, because when she saw Hope in return, she gave her a jolly smile and waved her cane in greeting.

'There she is!' Gram declared to a man wearing tan slacks and a white, button-down shirt who was standing next to her. 'I told you that she'd come lickety-split. You can always count on Hope. And you can always count on Morris, too,' she added sweetly, switching the smile to him. 'Thank you for making sure that Hope got to the correct room, Morris.'

'It was my pleasure.' Morris cleared his throat, visibly gratified by the praise. 'It's a difficult time. I want to help.'

'You've been extremely helpful, Doctor Henshaw,' said the man next to Gram. 'Although I must warn you that I will likely have more questions for you in the future.'

'Whatever I can do,' Morris replied earnestly. 'However I can be of assistance.'

As she and Morris moved toward Gram and the man, Hope noticed that there were a dozen or so other people in the room. Based on their age and demeanor, they appeared to be there in an official capacity – law enforcement or related – as opposed to bingo and spaghetti-supper participants. Whatever it was that had happened, it must have occurred some time ago, because they all seemed to be concluding their business rather than beginning it. Bags and cases were being closed. Papers were being organized and put away. There was calm, quiet talking in small groups or pairs. No flurry of fresh activity.

'Hope, I would like you to meet Detective Nate Phillips,' Gram said, introducing the man next to her. 'Detective, this is my younger granddaughter.'

Detective Nate Phillips had a solid handshake and a thick, somewhat rough palm. He was in his thirties, with a round, youthful face and closely cropped, medium-brown hair. Neither chubby nor lean, the detective had a short, sturdy physique. Although his expression was pleasant enough, his eyes were by far his best feature. They were a deep chocolate brown – intelligent, open, and sincere. They reminded Hope of a faithful hound.

'I've heard a lot about you,' Detective Phillips said to her. 'And your sister.'

Hope gave Gram a quizzical glance. First the policeman in the hall and now this detective. Everybody seemed to know about her – and Summer also, apparently – but she knew nothing of what was going on.

'I want to thank you in advance,' the detective continued. 'Any information that you can give us would be greatly appreciated.'

Gram nodded. 'I told him that you were the one to ask, Hope. I told him that you would be the one who'd know.'

'No question about it,' Morris agreed. 'Hope's the person to ask.'

'I'd like to ask how she got here so damn fast,' a new voice said.

Startled by the interruption, the group turned around. Hope's jaw dropped as she saw the man who had spoken. It was the same man with the arrogant attitude and frosty blue eyes who had stormed into the boutique and claimed to be Betsy Hughes's doctor.

'Oh, Dylan!' Morris exclaimed. 'I'm awfully glad you made it! I wasn't sure about the directions I gave. I was afraid that I might have gotten you terribly lost. What a relief. It makes me so happy you could come!'

Hope's surprise at seeing the man from the boutique was almost eclipsed by her surprise at Morris's reaction to him. It wasn't just that he obviously knew the man. It was his enthusiasm at knowing – and seeing – the man, whose name was evidently Dylan. Morris tended toward the somber, not the euphoric. Hope didn't think that she had ever heard Morris so excited in all the years that she had known him, except once perhaps, a few months earlier, when – after considerable cajoling – Gram had finally agreed to accompany him to his upcoming fiftieth-year high school reunion in the fall.

'The directions were fine,' Dylan replied. 'Although if I had realized that we were going to the same place, I would have followed her' – he motioned toward Hope – 'and saved half an hour.'

'You've met?' Morris said, now looking surprised also.

'Briefly,' Dylan told him, not offering any details.

'I'm awfully glad!' Morris exclaimed again, with even greater joy and relief. 'Now you can all finally get to know each other. I do wish the circumstances were better; nevertheless, it's been far too long. Happily, the time has come at last.' He turned to Gram. 'Olivia, you've always listened so patiently while I talked your ear off about him. This is Dylan, my son . . .'

Although Morris went on speaking, Hope didn't catch much of it. She was too astonished. She knew a lot about Dylan Henshaw. She had been hearing stories about Dylan Henshaw for as long as she could remember. Tragically, Morris's wife had died shortly after Dylan's birth. Too grief-stricken to properly care for an infant and only just settling into his medical career, Morris had been persuaded to relinquish custody of his son to his wife's parents in California, on a temporary basis. But days had quickly become weeks, and weeks had turned into months, and soon Dylan's grandparents were unwilling to part with their only grandchild.

In the beginning, there were plenty of promises regarding visits and vacations. They grew more and more infrequent, however, and by the time Dylan had started elementary school, they ceased almost entirely. With an incessant string of manu-factured excuses and impediments, the grandparents had made it exceedingly difficult for Morris to visit his son, and Dylan was never permitted to go to his father. Although there was talk of litigation at various points over the years – especially early on – Morris had been too worried about what sort of traumatic effect it would have on Dylan, having already lost his mother. Eventually, it became too late to make a change. According to Gram, not raising his son himself was Morris's greatest regret.

'. . . Dylan has been a saving grace,' Morris continued to gush. 'When I told him about my back surgery, he insisted on taking a leave of absence from his job in California to fly out here and help. He's employed at a very prestigious university hospital, you know.'

'Of course I know,' Gram returned politely, smiling.

She did indeed know. Hope knew, too. Morris was tremen-dously proud of his son's achievements, and he shared them with everybody who would even half listen. There had been honors in college, followed by more honors in medical school. All sorts of fellowships and awards and appointments to desir-able positions had ensued. It was no secret that Dylan Henshaw had many professional accomplishments, particularly for his relatively young age. What had been a secret, however, was the fact that he had come to Asheville. Or if it wasn't an actual secret, Hope couldn't recall ever hearing that he was there.

Now that she knew who the man was, she could see the family resemblance, at least physically. The striking blue eyes, the tall height and slim build, the good looks, even the warm laugh. But that was apparently where nature and nurture parted company and went their separate ways, because while the father was compassionate and unassuming and indisputably pleasant, the son was flashy and conceited and indisputably annoying.

'Dylan has been seeing and treating my patients while I've been recovering,' Morris said. 'That's another reason why I have to keep moving and build up my strength as quickly as possible,' he added toward Hope, in relation to their earlier conversation. 'I can't saddle him with all my work for too long.'

Hope nodded, more to herself than to him. That explained how Dylan had suddenly become Betsy Hughes's doctor. It also explained the woman's sudden maladies. When she had been Morris's patient, Betsy Hughes had never come to the boutique complaining of stomach problems from all the pills that she had been given.

Dylan turned to Hope with a triumphant expression as if to say, *Ha! I told you so.*

Hope responded with an agitated frown. Too pleased with his son's return and the long-awaited introduction to Olivia, Morris didn't notice the exchange. Gram did, however, and she looked curiously between Hope and Dylan.

'When exactly did you two meet?' she asked.

'Yes,' Morris chimed in. 'How do you know each other?'

Before either of them could reply, Detective Phillips cleared his throat with authority. 'I'm sorry to interrupt the happy reunion and such, but we really do need to get down to business here. There is a dead body.'

FOUR

Hope took a startled step backward. A dead body? And then she realized that the possibility should probably have occurred to her earlier. Gram had been so urgent on the phone with Summer. There had been the empty ambulance at the front of the center, along with all the police and other official-looking people in the room. But somehow she had continued to think that it was just a minor bingo-and-spaghetti-supper accident, not a death.

If Dylan was as surprised as she was by the detective's announcement, he didn't show it. Instead, he cast a sharp glance at Hope. 'You didn't mention a body at the boutique.'

'That's because I didn't know about a body at the boutique,' she returned with matching sharpness.

'It's my fault,' Detective Phillips said. 'I asked your grandmother not to give out any details when she called you. We haven't yet been able to contact the deceased's relatives, and I didn't want to take the chance that word would inadvertently reach them beforehand.'

Morris sighed. 'I don't envy you, Detective. I've had to break my share of bad news over the years, too. Speaking with Roberta's family won't be an enjoyable task.'

Hope gave a strangled gasp. 'Roberta King is dead?'

'I'm afraid so, dear,' Gram confirmed.

'But–but how?'

Gram looked expectantly at Morris, who in turn looked at Detective Phillips.

'Go ahead,' the detective told him. 'With the understanding that the medical examiner will make the final determination, of course.'

'Of course,' Morris agreed. He hesitated a moment. 'And should I . . .'

'Go ahead,' Detective Phillips said again. 'If either of them is going to be of any help, then they have to see what we've got.'

'Yes. Yes, certainly.' Standing a bit taller and assuming a slightly more formal tone, Morris turned and started walking toward the rear of the room. 'If you will follow me, please.'

Dylan, Gram, and Detective Phillips immediately accompanied him. Hope hung back. Were they going to look at Roberta's body? She didn't really want to see Roberta's body – or any dead body, for that matter. She was also having difficulty understanding why she was there. Morris was a doctor. Dylan was also a doctor. And Gram must have witnessed the event, or been the last to talk to Roberta before it happened, or something similar. But none of that explained why Hope had been called to the scene.

The group – with Hope reluctantly bringing up the rear – stopped next to a long table that was lined with an equally long row of disordered folding chairs. The table was decked with a navy cotton cloth. On it were pitchers of water and soda, Styrofoam cups with coffee, and numerous plastic plates holding pasta and sauce, garlic bread, and chocolate chip cookies. Roberta's death had evidently occurred toward the start rather than the conclusion of dinner, because the plates were more full than empty.

'Before I make any comments,' Morris said, 'I'd like you to take a look at her, Dylan. Give your first impressions without influence from me. See if we draw the same conclusions. That's why I asked you to come.'

'All right.' Dylan took a step forward.

Hope intended on hanging back again, figuring that there was no need for her first impressions or drawing conclusions in regard to poor Roberta. But it didn't do her any good, because instead of Gram and Detective Phillips also stepping forward, Morris moved back, giving the whole group all at once a clear view of the deceased.

Roberta King lay on her side on the gray speckled carpeting, and it didn't take a medical degree to realize that she had died in considerable pain. The woman was curled up in a ball, with her knees drawn toward her chest and her hands clutching at her stomach. But her hands no longer looked like hands. Instead, they were two large, misshapen, flesh-colored lumps. And Roberta no longer looked like Roberta. In fact, if Hope hadn't been told that the person on the ground in front of her was Roberta King, she might not have recognized her. It wasn't because there was so much blood, or heavy bruising, or ferocious wounds. It was the extreme swelling. Like her hands, Roberta's head had become a bulging, distorted lump, only much redder in hue. Her eyes and nose were swollen shut. Her lips and mouth were swollen into her face, which was swollen into her neck.

'Anaphylaxis,' Dylan declared. 'No question about it. The flushing of the skin. The facial swelling. Hives, too.'

'Your father said the same thing,' Detective Phillips told him. Morris nodded.

'So, then, you're both reasonably confident that the throat swelling closed is the cause of death?' the detective asked.

'No,' Dylan corrected him. 'I'm sure the throat is swollen, as is undoubtedly the entire lower airway, but that isn't what killed her.'

Detective Phillips looked at him questioningly.

'In cases like this,' Dylan explained, 'it isn't the lack of oxygen that kills. It's the sudden, dramatic drop in blood pressure. That's why it's called anaphylactic shock and not anaphylactic suffocation.'

His tone was cold and clinical, as if he was discussing tire pressure in a hunk of rubber rather than blood pressure in a fellow human being. Taken with his attitude toward Betsy Hughes, Hope found the man's bedside manner abysmal. But although she doubted Dylan's benevolence toward his patients, she didn't doubt his medical knowledge. There was a level of confidence and acumen in the way he spoke that convinced her Dylan Henshaw knew his business.

'The question,' Dylan continued, more to his father than to the rest of them, 'then becomes the trigger.'

Morris nodded again.

Dylan studied Roberta's body a minute longer before surveying the surrounding area. 'Considering the severity of the reaction, I would ordinarily suspect either insects or latex. But there don't appear to be any wasps, bees, or fire ants in the vicinity, and I don't see sufficient latex to produce such an aggressive response. Which leaves us with the next most likely culprit: food.'

In unison, the entire group turned toward the table with its plastic plates and Styrofoam cups.

'Good heavens,' Gram exclaimed. 'I'm the one who brought Roberta her supper!'

'Were you? Excellent,' Dylan said. 'Then you can tell us what she ingested.'

'What she ingested?' Gram's brow furrowed. 'I'm afraid I can't answer that. I didn't watch her eat it. I just brought it to her.'

'What exactly did you bring?'

'Well, it was the same thing as everyone else. Spaghetti and bread and cookies.'

'You're certain?' Dylan asked.

'Yes.' The furrow in Gram's brow deepened. 'I think so, at least. I can't honestly say I paid that much attention. I went to where they were putting it all together.' She gestured toward the far corner of the room where a makeshift buffet was set up. 'I took a plate with the pasta. Then somebody – Marilyn Smoltz, I believe it was – put a piece or two of garlic bread on the side. And—'

'And I added a cookie,' Morris concluded for her.

Gram smiled at him. 'That's right, Morris. You so kindly volunteered to hand out the dessert.'

There was a pause as Dylan looked from his father to Olivia and back again. An expression of comprehension glided over his pale blue eyes. Regardless of what he might have supposed before, it was clear that Dylan now realized some sort of a relationship existed between the pair. Hope watched him, curious how he would react to the discovery. Both Morris and Gram were well liked in the community, and no one – at least as far as Hope was aware – had ever voiced any disapproval of their intimacy. A long-absent son who had been raised by his maternal grandparents might take a different view, however.

Whatever his thoughts were on the subject, Dylan kept them to himself. He returned instead to the more immediate issue.

'How many plates did you bring?' he asked Gram.

'Only one,' she replied, with some surprise. 'Although it might be difficult to see now, with her as bloated as she is, Roberta wasn't the type to gorge herself. Granted, we weren't especially close, so we didn't share that many meals, but I don't remember her ever eating more than a normal-sized portion. I suppose *normal* can be somewhat relative depending on age and body type and—'

'No, no,' Dylan interrupted her. 'I didn't mean how many plates you brought to her specifically. I meant, did you serve all the food, either to everyone in the room or to this particular table?'

Hope thought he said it in a manner that implied Gram was part of the hired help for the occasion, which many women in her situation would not have viewed kindly. But Olivia Bailey wasn't one to easily take offense.

'Serve all the food?' Gram burst out laughing. 'Gracious, can you imagine? Back and forth a hundred times with heaping plates? My cane would be all worn out!'

Morris laughed along with her, also taking his son's remark as a joke. Hope, however, wasn't amused, and she gave Dylan a resentful look. He frowned, visibly irritated by the laughter.

Gram must have noticed the frown, too, because she suppressed any further chuckles at his expense. 'Aside from my own,' she informed Dylan equably, 'the only plate that I served was to Roberta.'

The frown remained, but it became less irritated and more thoughtful. 'Why hers?' he asked. 'You just said that the two of you weren't especially close.'

'I was coming over for some reason or other . . . oh, yes, I was going to talk to Sylvia Norquist. Sylvia was seated down there.' Gram gestured toward the end of the table. 'As I passed by, I saw that everyone had their plate and cup, and was merrily chewing and chattering away, except for Roberta. She wasn't talking or eating, which was odd all in itself, because usually everyone who stays for supper, eats supper. Those who aren't interested in having dinner leave immediately after the bingo.'

'True. Very true, Olivia,' Morris confirmed.

'Roberta looked pale,' Gram said, 'and she was sitting kind of funny, leaning against the table with her head propped up in her hands. I stopped and asked her if she was feeling all right. She told me that she was dizzy and somewhat faint. I thought that maybe it was hunger. I get a little dizzy myself on occasion if it's been too long since I've eaten. My doctor' – she winked at Morris – 'tells me that it's low blood sugar.'

'True. Very true, Olivia,' he repeated earnestly.

'So I offered to get Roberta her supper,' Gram went on. 'When I came back with the plate, she was flushed instead of pale, and she seemed so drowsy that I almost thought she might fall asleep. I suggested that she eat to get her energy up, and she started to push the food around a bit. How much of it she actually ate, I don't know – as I said before – because that was when I turned to talk to Sylvia. Sylvia was in the middle of a most interesting discussion with Kirsten Willport, and Roberta began—'

'I will need to confirm the spelling of all these names,' Detective Phillips interjected, scribbling in a notepad.

Morris pulled a pen from his shirt pocket. 'I would be happy to write them down for you, Detective.'

As his father and the detective exchanged sheets of paper, Dylan tapped his foot impatiently. '*And Roberta began . . .*' he pressed Gram.

She nodded. 'And Roberta began to complain about the heat. To be frank, I didn't think much of it. The room was warm – as it usually is – filled with so many people all afternoon. Then she started to cough. I assumed that it was some crumbs from the garlic bread that went down the wrong way, so I gave her a cup of water. She tried to drink it, but she couldn't. She was coughing too hard.'

Dylan nodded back at Gram, encouraging her to continue.

'Roberta couldn't stop coughing,' she said, 'and she was sweating profusely. She was dripping wet like she had just stepped out of the bath. That was when I realized it was more than crumbs in her throat or the warm room. Something was seriously wrong. I was about to get Morris to come and help, but all of a sudden, Roberta stood up. She grabbed her stomach, and a moment later, she collapsed on the floor. She convulsed a couple of times, and then' – Gram swallowed hard – 'nothing.'

Everybody's gaze went once more to poor Roberta King lying on the gray speckled carpeting.

'I should have done something else,' Gram chastised herself. 'When she first began wheezing or her face started to swell.

But at the time . . . I didn't really understand . . . It all went terribly fast.'

'Don't blame yourself, Olivia. You did what you could.' Morris wrapped a sympathetic arm around her shoulders. 'It's difficult to anticipate the best course of action when everything happens so quickly—'

'Too quickly,' Dylan said, cutting short his father's soothing sentiments. 'Which means that it wasn't the food.'

Detective Phillips glanced up from his notepad. 'Not the food?'

'Not *this* food.' Dylan pointed at the pasta and bread. 'If she was exhibiting signs of dizziness and flushing before she got her plate, then her body was already having a reaction. So it must have been something that she ingested earlier. Some other food – or drink.'

'Any idea what?' The detective studied the remaining items on the table. 'Not the water, obviously. How about the coffee?'

'It's unlikely,' Dylan told him. 'Shellfish is a common offender. Kiwi fruit, also. And nuts, of course.'

'So it could have been an appetizer.' Detective Phillips turned to Morris and Gram. 'Were there any nut mixes available during the bingo?'

'Roberta wasn't allergic to nuts,' Hope said.

The group looked at her with a collective expression of surprise. Not having spoken in so long, Hope had the impression that the others had forgotten she was there.

'How do you know that?' Dylan's tone was dubious. 'You can't just guess on something like this.'

'I'm not guessing,' Hope responded tersely. 'I know that Roberta wasn't allergic to nuts, because I've watched her eat a bowl of them and walk away without any need of medical treatment. Last December, during our annual holiday open house at the boutique, Rosemarie Potter and Roberta got into a tiff, because Rosemarie caught Roberta picking all the cashews and pistachios out of the nut dish and leaving everything else.'

Gram chortled. 'I can see Rosemarie getting upset about that. She is awfully protective of her snacks.'

'Rosemarie? Is she the chatty redhead with the pug?' Morris said.

Hope nodded. 'Percy.'

'And was this Rosemarie here today?' Detective Phillips asked, once again scribbling in his notepad.

'No. As a matter of fact, she was at the boutique this after-noon.' Remembering how Rosemarie's admiration for Dylan's fit figure and chiseled jaw had been superseded by a desire for her to find something bad in a reading of his palm, Hope raised an amused eyebrow in Dylan's direction. 'You can confirm that. You met her.'

He evidently remembered also, because the chiseled jaw twitched with annoyance. 'Forget the nuts. Let's talk about your herbal nonsense instead.'

Hope's gaze narrowed. Maybe Rosemarie was right. Maybe she should read his palm and tell him something bad about his future.

'You and your silly sister with your stupid concoctions!' Dylan snapped. 'Did you give this woman one of your home-cooked remedies? Is she dead because of you? Is that why you're here?'

Hope's eyes flashed with anger, but before she could lash out at him, Gram spoke.

'Herbs aren't nonsense. They have been used in every culture around the world for thousands – probably tens or even hundreds of thousands – of years. And I would appreciate you not calling my granddaughters silly or stupid—'

'I didn't call *them* stupid,' Dylan argued. 'I called their supposed remedies—'

Gram didn't let him finish. 'Summer's tinctures are not why Hope is here.'

'She's here because of this,' Detective Phillips said, holding up a small, clear plastic evidence bag.

Inside the bag was a single card. A Tarot card. The Fool carrying his sack on a stick, whistling a merry tune in the sunshine, his little dog barking at his heels as he walks blithely off the edge of a cliff.

FIVE

'Roberta had a Tarot card?' Summer looked up in surprise from the box of scented candles that she was unpacking on the floor of the boutique. 'Just one?'

'Only the Fool,' Hope said.

'How odd.'

'Apparently, Roberta's handbag has one of those open front pockets where you can slide in a pair of sunglasses or a phone, and the card was sticking out of it.'

'How very odd,' Summer amended.

Hope nodded. 'Odd enough that Gram thought I should see it, and she convinced the detective likewise.'

'What did the detective say when you explained the card?'

'Not much, because I couldn't explain much to him. I kept getting interrupted.'

'Typical.' Summer rolled her eyes. 'I'm sure that he knows nothing whatsoever about the Tarot, and therefore automatically assumes that it's all rubbish.'

'Surprisingly enough, the detective was fine,' Hope told her. 'He asked if he could come by the shop today to get more information. The guy who kept interrupting me – and I'm glad that you're already sitting, because this will really throw you for a loop – was the same guy who marched in here yesterday and accused us of trying to kill Betsy Hughes with a tincture of lemon balm.'

'What! Why was *he* there?'

'That's the mind-boggling part. It turns out that he was telling the truth. He actually is Betsy Hughes's doctor. Temporarily at least, until his dad's back heals. The guy is none other than the illustrious Dylan Henshaw, only son of Morris Henshaw.'

Summer gaped at her.

'My reaction exactly,' Hope said. 'And in case you're wondering, the younger Henshaw – unlike the elder – doesn't improve one bit on further acquaintance. He was just as cocky and full of himself at the community center as he was here. And you should have seen Morris beaming at him with such paternal pride while Dylan was pouring forth his medical knowledge and enumerating potential allergy triggers.'

'Allergy triggers?' With a frown, Summer returned to unpacking the box in front of her. 'They think what happened to Roberta was due to an allergy? I don't remember Roberta ever mentioning any allergies. Granted, she only came in occasionally, but I always ask about possible sensitivities before— For criminy sake!' she exclaimed, abruptly interrupting herself. 'They shorted us!'

'Oh, no.' Hope groaned. 'Are you sure?'

'I ordered twenty candles. We *paid* for twenty candles. This box is designed with twenty slots, and see' – Summer held open the lid and tilted the box toward Hope – 'sixteen slots are full and four are empty. Four candles short. *Again.*'

'You called them up and complained to them the last time it happened, didn't you?'

'Yes, and they acted like I was a liar and trying to cheat them,' Summer replied indignantly.

'So let's try someone new,' Hope proposed. 'Megan mentioned to me the other day that one of her guests was expounding the virtues of an all-natural beeswax candle company just over the border in South Carolina. When I go to the hotel later for those palm-reading appointments that I have scheduled with the three ladies who came in here yesterday, I'll ask Megan if she remembers the name of the place, and we can give them a shot instead.'

'Good, because I'm done with these swindlers. What's that old saying? *Fool me once, shame on you. Fool me twice, shame on me.* Well, we are *not* being fooled a third time. It's ridiculous. We're a small business. We can't afford repeated losses like this. Plus' – Summer lifted a candle toward the light to take a better look at it – 'the quality is terrible. There are so many visible imperfections. We can't possibly sell these at the regular price. We'll have to put them on the clearance table or use them ourselves.'

Hope sighed. The boutique's finances were already tight since she had stopped working with the Tarot. Every little hiccup of this sort made them even tighter.

Inhaling the candle's scent, Summer's face wrinkled with disgust. 'Forget any hope of the clearance table. We won't be able to *give* these candles away. They smell horrible. Absolutely horrible!'

Climbing to her feet, Summer was about to hand the candle to Hope, so that she too could partake in the horrible smell, when the chimes rang out at the front of the shop and Detective Nate Phillips walked through the door. Seeing Hope first, he started to greet her, but he didn't get out more than two words before Summer stepped into his path and thrust the offending candle toward him.

'Does that smell like *Beach Breeze* to you?' She waved the candle beneath his nose. 'Not unless the wind is whipping through a pile of rotting fish and doggy doo-doo!'

The detective stared at her.

'What are we supposed to do with sixteen poo-scented candles!' Summer continued, unabashed. 'You want to tell me that?'

His mouth opened, and a slight gurgle emerged.

Hope swallowed a laugh. The man had come to the boutique on official police business, and instead of cogent answers in aid of his investigation, he got Summer shoving a scented candle in his face and comparing it to putrid fish and dog waste.

'Well?' Summer demanded. 'Are you just going to stare at me or are you going to speak?'

Another gurgle. Hope took pity on him.

'Detective,' she said in introduction, 'this is my sister, who you heard about yesterday from our grandmother. Summer, this is Detective Phillips. He's the one looking into Roberta's death.'

Summer squinted at the detective for a moment, then she gestured toward the box of candles on the floor. 'If you're with the police, then surely you can do something about fraud and the sale of faulty merchandise.'

'You . . .' Detective Phillips cleared his throat in an effort to find his voice. 'You could always return them.'

'That's no help! Do you have any comprehension what the return shipping on a box of this size and weight will cost us? And then there will be the hours of argument and aggravation trying to get a refund or a credit. Forget it!' Summer tossed the offending candle back with its brethren.

'Tea,' Hope suggested calmly.

'Excellent idea,' Summer agreed. 'Tea?' she said to the detective.

It was his turn to squint at her.

'My heaven' – Summer shook her pretty head – 'it's a simple enough question. Would you like a cup of tea?'

Still squinting, Detective Phillips struggled to produce an affirmative response. Hope swallowed another laugh. This was clearly not the interview that he had been expecting. No doubt in his line of work, the man had encountered more than his fair share of unusual characters, but under the right circumstances, someone like Summer was still able to flummox him.

'So what can I do for you, Detective?' Hope asked, as Summer headed to the electric kettle and stack of mugs in the corner of the shop.

He appeared stumped for a moment longer, then recollected his purpose in coming to the boutique. 'I have a few things that I'd like to know – about the Tarot – if you have the time for some questions.'

'Fire away,' Hope said, settling herself in her customary chair at the palm-reading table.

Detective Phillips pulled out his notepad and thumbed through the pages. 'Is it common for someone to carry a single Tarot card? I mean, people don't ordinarily carry a single club or diamond from a standard deck of playing cards.'

'We were just discussing how odd that is!' Summer called from across the room. 'Right, Hope?'

'It is unusual,' Hope replied. 'And when somebody does carry a lone Tarot card, then typically it's one of the Minor Arcana, not the Major Arcana.'

'The major – minor – what?' the detective said.

'It would probably be easier if I showed you. Have a seat if you'd like.' Hope gestured toward the empty chairs at the table, then she opened the drawer on her side and took out a small wooden box.

'Oh, a demonstration!' Summer exclaimed in delight. 'Don't start without me! I'm almost done with the tea.'

A second later, she came bustling toward them, clutching a trio of mugs with the steaming liquid sloshing precariously close to the rim. But she managed to reach her destination without incident and safely deposited her cargo on the table. Green mug for Hope, yellow for herself, and red for the detective.

'Hurry up and sit down,' Summer said to him, taking a seat herself. 'Hope explains it all so beautifully. I love it when she talks about the Tarot.'

Although Hope appreciated the kind words, she felt compelled to remind her sister that the demonstration was going to be limited. 'I'm *only* explaining, not doing a reading.'

'Yes, yes,' Summer responded cheerfully, blowing on her tea to cool it.

The response was a bit too cheerful – suspiciously so – and this time, instead of swallowing a laugh, Hope swallowed a sigh. Summer had always been good about not pushing her back to the Tarot, but Hope was beginning to have the feeling that, like Rosemarie Potter and so many others, Summer was growing increasingly impatient for her to return to doing her readings.

With a nod, Detective Phillips accepted a chair and the red mug. 'Your grandmother mentioned something about that yesterday. You used to work with the Tarot, but now you don't?'

'That's correct,' Hope answered, and before the detective could make any additional inquiries on the subject, she removed the inlaid lid of the wooden box and lifted out a brightly decorated silk scarf. She unfolded the edges of the scarf to reveal a well-worn deck of Tarot cards nestled inside.

'Suffice it to say,' she told the detective in response to his quizzical expression, 'that there are a lot of rules, traditions, and superstitions when it comes to the Tarot. It's been around for many centuries, acquiring a level of complexity and depth of meaning that make it impossible to explain quickly or with easy succinctness. There are entire secret societies dedicated to the study of the Tarot's mysteries.'

'Really?' Detective Phillips leaned forward with interest. 'Actual secret societies?'

Hope's lips curled into an enigmatic smile. 'The Tarot deck consists of seventy-eight cards. Fifty-six of those cards belong to the Minor Arcana. The Minor Arcana has four suits, similar to a standard deck of playing cards: Wands (which are like clubs), Cups (which are like hearts), Swords (which are like spades), and Coins or Pentacles (which are like diamonds). Also similar to a standard deck of playing cards, each suit has ten number cards, but the Tarot includes a fourth member of the royal family. So along with the king, the queen, and the knight, there is also the page.'

To show the detective an example, Hope cut the deck in half and lifted the first two cards from the bottom portion. The King of Swords and Two of Wands appeared. In spite of herself, she frowned.

Seeing her reaction, Summer's hazel eyes widened. 'What does it mean? Is it him?'

Hope shook her head. 'It's just a coincidence.'

'Baloney. We both know full well that in the mystical world there are no such things as coincidences.'

'That might be true *if* I had intended to read the cards, which I didn't. Drawing cards willy-nilly means nothing.'

'Baloney,' Summer repeated. 'That only applies to novices and acolytes. For someone as experienced as you, the cards *always* mean something. And that card is him.'

Detective Phillips looked between the sisters. 'What card is him? Who?'

'The first card that Hope turned,' Summer said. 'The King of Swords. It's you.'

'*Me?*' the detective exclaimed. 'That isn't possible. I'm not any sort of royalty. My family comes from Florida. We're blue collar, not blue blood. And I don't own a sword.'

Summer burst out laughing. 'Not an *actual* king with an *actual* sword, silly!'

A tinge of red crept up the man's cheeks.

Doing her best to repress her own chuckle, Hope responded mildly, 'Of course you aren't a king, Detective. The cards are representational, not literal. The Tarot was originally devised during the feudal period in medieval Europe – hence the images depicting the fixed stations in society at that time, such as the cobbler working at his bench or the knight charging into battle on his loyal steed. They're symbols of—'

'And that's why you need someone like Hope,' Summer interjected, 'to properly interpret the symbols and explain how they apply to you and whatever situation you're in. If you attempt to read the cards yourself, without really understanding them and how they fit together, you're going to see the wrong things and get it all screwed up.'

'Thank you, darling.' Hope smiled at her sister for the compliment.

'It's true,' Summer told the detective emphatically. 'Lots of people *try* to read the Tarot, but most of them are just playing with pretty pictures. Hope is the real thing. She's the best there is. Ask her anything, and she can tell you everything.'

It was Hope's turn to blush. 'I think that you're exaggerating my talents somewhat.' Before Summer could argue, she continued to the detective, 'So, no, you're not in fact sitting on a mighty throne, wearing a golden crown, holding a sword. But the King of Swords does often refer to leaders and authority figures, such as police officers—'

'Ha!' Summer interjected once more. 'I was right! The card *is* him. How about the second card? What does that one mean?'

Hope was about to reiterate for the umpteenth time that there could be no meaning in either card without an intended reading, but then she decided that it would be easier just to go along with Summer. Considering that the second card was the Two of Wands, there could be no harm in it, and it might help the detective understand better when she later discussed the Fool with him.

'The Two of Wands' – Hope pushed the card forward slightly – 'shows a man looking out over the sea from his estate, the world in his hand. It signals the start of a new venture, and the person involved is planning, working carefully and deliberately, taking the first steps on the road to a – hopefully – favorable result.'

Nodding enthusiastically, Summer turned to the detective. 'You see, don't you? It's your situation exactly. The cards apply perfectly.'

His brow furrowed.

'You,' Hope explained, pointing first toward the King of Swords, then at the Two of Wands, 'have a new venture. It's the start of a new case. You're working to find out what happened to Roberta King.'

There was a momentary pause as Detective Phillips studied the cards. 'Fascinating,' he murmured. 'Absolutely fascinating.'

Summer gave him an approving look. Rather than assuming that it was all rubbish, as she had initially accused him of doing before he had even entered the shop, he was actually paying attention and – perhaps to a degree – believing.

'Simply put,' Hope said, deciding that now was the time to move on, before the detective believed too strongly and asked her to draw additional cards for greater details about himself, 'the Minor Arcana represent the affairs of daily life. In that sense, they're not *minor* at all, because our daily lives naturally shape the whole of our lives. They depict the aspects of our everyday existence. Our health, our work, our family, our money – or the lack of those things. They symbolize who we are, how we get to where we want to go, and the people and situations that we encounter along the way. That's why I said if somebody has a single card, it's usually one of the Minor Arcana, because they deal with us and our fortunes directly, so to speak. A person might carry a particular card to manifest a wish, as a way to feel balanced and grounded, or even in an attempt at magic.'

'I do see,' the detective remarked earnestly, still gazing at the cards before him. 'I think I understand.'

Hope picked up the cards and returned them to the deck. 'That brings us to the remaining twenty-two cards, called the Major Arcana. The Major Arcana are what you most often find on television and in the movies, primarily because their images are so dramatic. The Lovers and the Devil, for example. They're always popular, for obvious reasons. Hollywood makes money on sex and the incarnation of evil. But in reality, the Major Arcana aren't quite that exciting. They're broad concepts, not necessarily specific persons or events. Individually, they don't mean much, because they can't provide the critical details. They need other cards – specifically, the Minor Arcana – to define and clarify them. Which is why, as intriguing as they might appear at first glance, it's unlikely that anyone with a serious understanding of the Tarot would carry a lone card of the Major Arcana.'

'And the card that Roberta King had in her purse?' Detective Phillips said. 'The Fool. It's one of the Major Arcana?'

'It is,' Hope confirmed.

'Very good, Detective!' Summer lauded him.

The tinge of red crept back into his cheeks. 'Can I then also assume that Roberta King didn't know much about the Tarot?'

'I think that it's a safe bet,' Hope replied. 'Roberta never mentioned the Tarot when she came into the boutique, and in my experience, when people have some knowledge of what we do here – even just a little – they typically tell us.'

'So she didn't get the card here?'

'That's a question I can't answer. I don't remember Roberta ever buying a deck. Do you, Summer?'

Summer shook her head.

'But that doesn't mean much,' Hope continued. 'We sell *a lot* of Tarot cards. If Roberta's card had come from a fancy, or unusual, or antique deck, then I would be able to tell you more, but her Fool was from one of the most commonly available decks on the market. She could have bought it here. She also could have just as easily bought it elsewhere.'

'From A to W,' Summer chimed in.

'A to W?' Detective Phillips asked.

'Amazon to Walmart,' Hope told him. 'Both sell Tarot cards. So do some bookstores and craft shops. And used decks frequently pop up at garage sales and flea markets. Not that I would recommend for anyone to purchase used Tarot cards.'

'Heaven, no.' Summer shook her head again, more fervently this time. 'Not without proper cleansing.'

The detective frowned, not understanding.

'Another story for another time,' Hope said, glancing at her watch. If she didn't leave for the hotel soon, she would be late for her palm-reading appointments with the trio of ladies. 'And it doesn't apply here anyway, because Roberta's card was from a new deck. Based on what I could see through that bag you showed me yesterday, her card had barely been handled. It looked slick and shiny, with no bent edges or signs of wear. If I were to guess, Roberta's Fool had never been shuffled or cast in a spread.'

'I've said it already, but I'll say it again.' Summer clucked her tongue. 'It's odd. Very odd.'

'I hope that I've been able to help you, Detective.' Hope wrapped the scarf carefully around the cards in her hands. 'But now, if you'll excuse me, I have another appointment.' She placed the deck back into the wooden box, closed the lid, and returned it to the drawer in the table.

With a thoughtful expression, Detective Phillips took the last sip of tea from his mug.

'Would you like a refill?' Summer asked him.

'Well, um, yes. If you don't have an appointment also. I have to confess that I'm not normally a tea drinker, but this is really tasty.'

Summer smiled at him sweetly. 'Thank you, Detective.'

The color in his cheeks darkened a shade. 'Please, call me Nate.'

'All right, Nate. Another cup for both of us, then.'

Rising from the table, Hope had to bite her tongue not to grin. Together with his flushed face, the detective's chocolate-brown, faithful-hound eyes were fixed attentively on her sister. No knowledge of the Tarot, palmistry, or any other form of divination was required to see what was happening. Nate Phillips had developed a crush on Summer. Unfortunately for him, she was attached to the shifty Gary.

SIX

With its circular cobblestone drive, bubbling cherub fountain, and verdigris copper trim, the exterior of the hotel had a warm, old-fashioned charm that fit perfectly into the surrounding historic district. The interior of the building, on the other hand, was cool and modern, with crisp lines and stark stylishness. From the walls to the windows, the whole place was decorated in some combination of black, silver, and – as was to be expected from a place named Amethyst – purple.

Hope found the trio of ladies waiting for her excitedly on the metal and leather sofas in one of the nooks off the lobby, chattering and laughing even more loudly than they had been the day before at the boutique. Rather than individual appointments, the three decided to share their time as a group. That was fine with Hope, because she could tell that they were more interested in amusing parlor tricks than serious palmistry. As soon as she showed them their heart and life lines, they promptly began comparing them to one another, after which they spent the next three-quarters of an hour recounting tales of loves lost and roads not traveled.

Thrilled with their entertainment, the ladies tipped Hope generously on top of her regular rate. As an added bonus, she discovered that the guest who had mentioned the beeswax candle company to Megan was part of the trio. Not only did Hope learn the name of the company, but she also got the proprietor's contact information, which boded well for the future acquisition of higher-quality, better-scented candles. That would certainly make Summer happy. And the detective, too, assuming that he preferred sipping tea with Summer to having her shove rotting-fish candles under his nose.

With the alert ear of an experienced social director, Megan appeared in the nook just as the ladies were preparing to depart, heading toward the hotel bar for their next round of recreation.

'Oh, we had such a fun time!' they gushed.

'We'll tell all our friends about you!'

'This city has the most wonderful hotel and local shops!'

Hope and Megan exchanged a pleased glance. Satisfied customers were repeat customers who gave good recommendations.

'So how was the reading?' Megan asked her, tidying up the nook after the trio had gone. 'Anything interesting come out?'

'It wasn't much of a reading at all,' Hope answered. 'Mostly just gossip between themselves. But I'm glad that they chose the hotel for the appointment. Sometimes there is such a thing as too loud and enthusiastic. It can drive away other customers, especially in a little place like the boutique.'

Megan nodded. 'That's what happened in the restaurant here last night. I heard from the sommelier that the wine flowed heartily during dinner, and the ladies and their husbands got pretty boisterous, annoying the other patrons to the point that some of them actually got up and left.'

Having finished straightening the furniture, Megan proceeded to straighten herself. She was dressed in her standard work attire: wide-legged linen trousers with a matching trim linen blazer. Today's ensemble color was cornflower blue. When she originally started at the hotel, she had worn mostly skirts. But then she discovered that her job – although not part of the official description – included wrangling unruly dogs, unruly children, and occasionally even unruly husbands. High heels and exposed legs were not conducive to such activities. Now it was solely flats and slacks.

Hope watched Megan fuss with her clothing. 'What's wrong?' she asked.

'Huh?'

'You're *hotel perky* as always, but I can see that something isn't right.'

Megan wavered a moment, as if deliberating how to respond. She popped her head into the lobby, checked once around, then returned to the nook, taking a seat on the arm of a purple sofa. Hope sat down across from her.

'Have you ever heard' – Megan lowered her voice discreetly – 'of a Mystique Monique?'

'No, I don't think so. What is it?'

'A person.'

'Named Mystique Monique? Seriously? That's sounds like a carnival act with a crystal ball.'

'My first thought was an exotic dancer.'

That made Hope smile.

Megan smiled, too, but it faded quickly. 'Earlier today, I was asked by a guest to book a pair of spa treatments for him and his wife. Hot stone for him. Facial for her.'

Hope nodded. Amethyst's spa was arguably its best – and most popular – feature. It offered a wide array of luxury treatments that many locals enjoyed along with the hotel guests. The services were expensive, however, so the Bailey sisters were not frequent visitors.

'While I was checking the appointments calendar for openings,' Megan said, 'I also looked at today's bookings. One – this afternoon – is for a couples massage under the name Mystique Monique.'

'Do you think that it's a fake appointment? A joke of some sort?'

'No, the appointment is real. The name is too – unbelievable as it may seem. The massage is linked to a hotel room reservation under the same name, and the credit card on file for both matches. *Ms Misty Monique.*'

'So not a carnival act or an exotic dancer then. Too bad.' Hope chuckled. 'That could have been interesting.'

Megan's expression remained grave. 'Ordinarily, I wouldn't have paid much attention to it, except with a couples massage, both parties are supposed to be listed. That way, if they come separately, each person can check in and begin using the spa facilities without having to wait for the other person to arrive.'

'Makes sense.'

'But with this booking, only Mystique – or Misty, if we go by her credit card – is listed. The hotel room is the same way. Reservation for two, but just Misty's name. Then I checked the number of keys authorized for the room. Also two. And that's where it gets sticky . . .'

There was a pause. Megan shifted on the arm of the sofa.

'Sticky?' Hope prompted her after a minute.

'Sticky,' Megan repeated unevenly. 'For security purposes, the hotel has a policy that every digital key must be linked to a specific person, whether a staff member or a guest. So if a guest wants multiple keys – for the wife, kiddies, Grandpa Joe, or Cousin Susie, for example – each extra key has to be registered in the wife's, kiddies', Grandpa Joe's, or Cousin Susie's name . . .'

Again she paused and shifted on the arm of the sofa.

Hope frowned. It wasn't like Megan to be so nervous, especially about everyday work issues. It was starting to make her a little nervous, too.

'So I looked at the keys for Misty's room,' Megan continued at length. 'One key is registered to her, of course. And the second key' – there was a final hesitation, then the words came rushing out – 'is registered in the name of Gary Fletcher.'

Stunned, Hope stared at her.

'I am so sorry.' Megan groaned. 'I hate having to be the bearer of such sordid news. I mean, I've never liked Gary. You know that. I always thought Summer was far too good for him. But I didn't imagine that he was such a lousy husband as to do something like this. That he'd stoop so low.'

'You're sure about the name?' Hope asked. 'Absolutely certain? It couldn't be a mistake?'

Megan shook her head. 'Definitely *Gary Fletcher.* I checked three times.'

'Maybe it's a different Gary Fletcher? There must be more than one in the world. It's not a particularly uncommon name.'

'Maybe.' Megan's tone was doubtful. 'I wish that you were right. But after I saw it, I went back and took a closer look at the previous room reservations and key registrations. Misty Monique and Gary Fletcher have been here every weekend for the past month.'

'And Gary hasn't been home for the past month,' Hope said. 'What are the chances that it's an innocent coincidence?'

'Summer doesn't believe in coincidences. She reminded me of that just this morning at the boutique.'

A heavy silence followed. Hope put her head in her hands. How on earth was she going to tell Summer? This was going to break her heart. Worse still, it was going to humiliate her. Summer had been so confident that Gary's weekend absences were due to work commitments. When everyone else had raised a questioning eyebrow, Summer had defended her husband without a shred of doubt. And now, instead of a much-desired baby in the family picture, there was a Mystique Monique.

Hope sighed. 'Well, before I do anything else, I have to be one-hundred-percent positive that it's him. When was the couples massage scheduled for?'

Megan checked her watch. 'It's supposed to be right now, actually.'

'Lovely,' Hope muttered, standing up.

'Consider it fortuitous timing,' Megan said, with a sardonic shrug. 'This way, you can catch him while he's still in the spa, instead of afterward in their room, whatever they might be doing then.'

Hope grimaced. 'Good point.'

Together, she and Megan headed through the lobby, down the gleaming silver staircase toward the spa located on the lower level of the hotel. The spa shared Amethyst's color scheme, and in front of its double-door entrance stood a black marble table with a humongous purple orchid in full bloom. The orchid had at least a dozen flower spikes, each a foot or more in length, covered from base to tip with iridescent blossoms. In spite of the unpleasant task before her – or perhaps because of it – Hope stopped to admire the plant.

'Wow. That's spectacular.'

'Impressive, isn't it?' Megan agreed. 'I was down here when they brought it in; the wine order for next week was being delivered at the same time. Speaking of which' – she looked at her watch again – 'I'm afraid that I will be a bit tardy for the four o'clock wine-and-cheese this afternoon.'

'Just get me into the spa and point me in the right direction,' Hope said, 'then go and do what you need to. Don't get in trouble because of me.'

'It wouldn't be because of *you*,' Megan corrected her. 'It would be because of Gary not being able to keep his pants on – in more ways than one if we include the massage. But I won't get in trouble, regardless. The kitchen staff puts together the cheese platters, and the bar staff takes care of the carafes. All

I do is smile, sashay around, and repeatedly confirm that every guest is having a *marvelous* time.'

'Setting out a couple of platters and carafes is easy. You've got the hard part.'

'Ain't that the truth,' Megan said. 'Pretending to be interested in all of the guests' boring stories is exhausting. But I anticipate an excellent turnout today. Let's not forget the trio of lovely ladies who were already heading to the bar for a head start. They'll be able to entertain each other and the rest of the participants just fine until I get there and make sure that nobody has gone crazy with the Gouda.'

'I'd like to have some Gouda right now. I'd like to throw it at Gary's face.'

Megan grinned. 'I must say that you're handling this remarkably well. When I first saw that he had a key registered in his name, I practically started hyperventilating with anger.'

Hope shook her head. 'I'm not handling it well. It's just false hope. Maybe there's been a gross misunderstanding. Maybe it's not really Gary. Maybe Mystique Monique is actually a new construction project that he's been hired to work on.'

'A construction project with a credit card in the name of Misty, who's also booked a couples massage?'

'I told you: false hope.'

'It's a sign that you need wine, not cheese. To drink, not throw.'

'Ain't that the truth,' Hope replied, echoing both Megan's earlier words and her grin.

'As soon as we're done here, we'll grab one of the carafes,' Megan promised. 'It's a Pinot Grigio today, slightly better than usual—'

She cut herself short as a man exited the spa. Megan held the door for him, smiled politely, and asked if he had enjoyed his visit. He said that he had. Twice-weekly acupuncture treatments. Greatly reduced the pain in his knee from an old snowboarding injury. Megan nodded, smiled some more, and wished the man a good day.

Still holding the door, she turned to Hope. 'Ready?'

'Not in the least,' Hope answered honestly.

They entered anyway. Unlike some spas that were so loud

and chaotic that they ended up being more enervating than rejuvenating, Amethyst's spa was pleasantly quiet and calm. The subdued lighting was gentle on the eyes. The serene sounds of nature played softly in the background: a bubbling brook, the rustle of autumn leaves, the twilight melody of a songbird. There was a refreshment table full of healthful fruits, dainty cookies and crackers, and a bulbous pitcher of lemon water with fresh-cut citrus slices floating on top. There were also lots of plush velvet chairs and loungers spread around invitingly – all in varying shades of purple, to no surprise.

A young woman in her early twenties looked up from the oval reception desk. Her long hair was pulled back in a tidy bun, and she wore a doctor's lab coat, except the coat was black rather than the traditional white and considerably more slim-fitting than generally seen in medical settings.

'Hello. And welcome to our oasis,' the woman greeted them in dulcet tones. 'We hope that we can make your day *truly amazing*. Anything that you need while you're here, please don't hesitate to ask. I'm Lisa, and I—' She stopped abruptly. 'Oh, gosh. Sorry for the song and dance, Megan. I didn't see that it was you.'

'Hey, Lisa. How are things today?'

'OK, I guess.' The dulcet had been replaced by something a bit more nasal. 'Some easy folks. Some hard folks. You know how it is.'

'I do indeed,' Megan commiserated. 'Lisa, you've met Hope before, haven't you?'

There was a momentary hesitation as Lisa studied Hope with a crinkled brow, then her face brightened with recognition. 'Of course! I'm in your boutique down the street all the time. You have the most fantastic crystals. I bought a tiger's eye there just last week. The other woman – she's your sister, isn't she?'

'Yes, Summer—' Hope began.

'Yes, Summer,' Lisa repeated excitedly, not waiting for her to finish. 'I was looking for something to help me with my exams. I was terribly worried and nervous about them. Summer said that tiger's eye would be just the thing. And she was right! I had the stone with me each day, during every test, and I felt so much more confident and focused. I think that my grades will be really good this semester. Maybe even good enough for the college to award me a small scholarship. Fingers crossed! I'm awfully grateful. Will you tell Summer how well it went, and thank her again for me?'

'I most certainly will,' Hope said. 'She'll be thrilled to hear it. She loves helping people. And right now any happy news' – she glanced at Megan – 'is very welcome.'

Megan sighed. 'Poor Summer.'

The crinkle returned to Lisa's brow. 'Poor Summer? Has something happened to her? Is she all right?'

It was Megan's turn to glance at Hope, wanting to make sure that it was OK for her to spill the beans. Hope nodded, albeit reluctantly. She wasn't eager for Gary's possible – or, more likely, probable – indiscretions to be broadcast publicly, especially before Summer herself was made aware of them. But she could see what Megan was thinking. If they told Lisa, Lisa would gladly help them find the right room, and then they would know exactly what Gary Fletcher and Mystique Monique were up to.

'Summer is the reason we're here actually,' Megan explained to Lisa. 'Her shifty husband . . .'

Hope didn't hear the remainder of the story, because a voice suddenly called out her name.

'Hope! Hope Bailey, is that you?'

Startled, Hope turned to find a woman walking toward her. She was coming from one of the adjoining corridors with the treatment rooms, and she was clearly in the middle of a spa appointment. Dressed in a terry-cloth robe with purple trim, the woman's face and neck were slathered with neon-green mud. The coating was so thick and covered her skin so completely that only her eyes were visible. They looked like a pair of bulging frog's eyes peering out from beneath fluorescent pond algae.

'Yes, it is you,' the woman confirmed aloud, nodding to herself. 'It's such a surprise to see you here, Hope. How are you?'

'I'm fine. Thank you,' Hope replied, trying not to gape at the woman's lime-colored face, which looked as though it were under attack by some alien fungus.

'You don't recognize me, do you?' The woman gave a little snicker. 'It's Marilyn. Marilyn Smoltz.'

Even without the subsequent name, the snicker would have revealed her identity. Hope wasn't personally close with Marilyn Smoltz. She knew her mostly through Gram. But she was sufficiently familiar with the woman's snicker. Marilyn snickered a lot. It was not an attractive quality.

'Oh, hello, Marilyn. With that mud mask, I didn't quite . . .'

'French green clay. Isn't it fabulous?'

'Well, um . . .'

'*Fabulous*,' Marilyn repeated, in a tone that brooked no dissent. 'Sylvia Norquist told me about it. Apparently, she heard about it from Kirsten Willport. Have you seen Kirsten's skin lately?'

Hope shook her head.

'She looks twenty years younger, at a minimum. Although the clay can't take all the credit for that.' Marilyn snickered. 'Kirsten's had so much work done. Her plastic surgeon has probably been able to buy another vacation home from her business alone. Not that I'm one to gossip, you know.'

On the contrary, Hope knew that Marilyn loved to gossip. Gram had warned her about it more than once.

'But nips and tucks aside' – Marilyn snickered again – 'Kirsten's skin really is divine. So when Sylvia told me about the clay yesterday, I insisted on getting an appointment here today. The funeral will be coming up soon, and since everybody will be there, I have to look my best for it.'

Hope frowned at the shallowness of the remark.

Marilyn mistook her frown for confusion. 'You do know that there will be a funeral, don't you, Hope? I had assumed that Olivia told you about what happened at the community center. About Roberta King's death?'

'Yes. It's very sad.'

'It's been ghastly for me,' Marilyn said. 'I barely slept a wink all last night because of it. I talked to Roberta during the bingo, and every time I think about it, my stomach turns into knots. It's so stressful having a person die just after you've spoken to them.'

Hope was tempted to respond that it was probably more

stressful for the person who actually died, but she restrained herself.

'Can you imagine keeling over in front of everybody like that?' Marilyn started to snicker once more but ended up coughing instead. 'One minute you're sitting at the table, eating your supper, and the next minute you're curled up on the floor, gasping your final breath!' She coughed harder. 'Get me some water, won't you, Hope?'

As Hope headed to the refreshment table and poured a glass – along with an obligatory slice of lemon – from the bulbous pitcher, she looked at Megan, who was now standing on the other side of the reception desk, studying a computer screen with Lisa. With any luck, they were making progress locating Gary and Mystique's room.

'Is it warm in here?' Marilyn asked, when Hope had returned with her glass.

'Not especially.'

'Are you sure?' Marilyn took a large drink. 'It seems awfully warm to me.'

'Maybe it's from the clay?' Hope suggested. 'Or the heavy robe?'

Marilyn gave the lemon slice a desultory poke with her finger, then she took another drink. 'I'll tell you what it's from: the horrible stress of Roberta's death.'

It took Hope some effort not to roll her eyes. The woman hadn't yet managed a single word of sympathy for Roberta. All she did was talk about herself and her own supposed suffering – and snicker obnoxiously.

'I'm getting tired. I should have a rest,' Marilyn said, sinking down on the nearest plush velvet lounger.

'That's a good idea,' Hope replied absently, looking again toward the reception desk. She was beginning to worry about how much time was passing. The couples massage might be over before she even found Gary, let alone had the chance to confront him.

'The more that I think about it' – Marilyn dabbed at the perspiration along her hairline with the sleeve of her robe – 'the more annoyed I am. All this horrible stress, and for what purpose? Why was it necessary for the police to be called to the community center? Why did they have to herd us around like cattle? If you ask me, the entire situation was ridiculously overblown. Just a desperate need for attention.'

Hope squinted at her. 'You think that Roberta died to get attention?'

'No, no. It was from asthma or whatever. I'm referring to Morris Henshaw, of course. Why else would he contact the police? Why would he insist on keeping everyone away from Roberta's body until they arrived?'

'Aren't the police automatically contacted whenever there's a call to emergency services—'

'So Morris could be important, that's why,' Marilyn interjected brusquely, dabbing at more perspiration. 'He was putting on a show for his son. Dylan is visiting from California, you know. Morris called him yesterday, too, after the police. I didn't see Dylan myself – I had already been forced out of the room – but I know that he came to the center, looked at Roberta, and talked to the authorities. My sources gave me all the details.'

Hope suppressed a smile. Marilyn's sources weren't too reliable, evidently, because they had failed to mention that she had also come to the center, looked at Roberta, and talked to the authorities.

'When I have more energy' – Marilyn slumped against the back of the lounger – 'I'll speak to Olivia about it. It's not fair for the rest of us to be subjected to such stress. This shouldn't be allowed to happen again.'

It wasn't clear to Hope what exactly Gram was supposed to do about it; in any case, there seemed to be little chance – thankfully – of another death happening during Thursday afternoon bingo and the spaghetti supper.

'When you next see Olivia, you'll tell her, won't you, Hope? Tell her that I need to speak with her urgently—'

Hope was saved from having to continue the conversation by Megan's shouts.

'We found them, Hope! They're in room nine. Hurry!'

Megan didn't have to tell her twice. Hope immediately spun around and headed toward the adjoining corridors with the treatment rooms.

'It was nice to see you, Marilyn,' Hope called over her

shoulder. 'Best of luck with the clay. I hope that your skin ends up looking divine, too!'

'You must tell Olivia!' Marilyn hollered after her. 'These Henshaws need to be reined in.'

SEVEN

B ased on her experiences with him so far, Hope doubted that Dylan Henshaw was the sort of man who could be *reined in*, but she gave it no more than a fleeting thought. All her attention at that moment was focused on what might be happening in room nine. The same tranquil music was playing in the corridor as had been in the reception area of the spa. It didn't help Hope, however. She wasn't tranquil in the least. Her emotions kept jumping between rage at Gary, concern for Summer, and a remaining bit of wishful thinking that the whole thing really was a gross misunderstanding.

Midway down the corridor, Megan halted her quick pace and turned to a door on the left. 'This is it,' she whispered when Hope caught up to her.

'You're sure?' Hope whispered back.

With a demonstrative gesture, Megan pointed to the large figure nine on the door.

'I mean, are you sure that it's Gary's room?' Hope said. 'The only thing worse than barging in on him wearing nothing but a towel is barging in on some shocked stranger wearing nothing but a towel.'

'It's his,' Megan confirmed. 'But it was difficult to find him. He and Misty switched rooms – twice. That's why it took so long to track down the right one. Lisa said it was as though they were deliberately trying to keep anyone from knowing they were here.'

Hope sighed. So much for it being a gross misunderstanding. A gross confession was more like it.

'What's the plan?' Megan asked her. 'Go in with a bang and eviscerate him in front of the girlfriend? Or just peek in to verify that it's him, without letting him realize that we've seen what he's been up to? I vote for the former, of course – always a fan of evisceration – but I can't help wondering if maybe Summer would prefer the latter?'

It was a good question. Would Summer want them to keep the egregious discovery quiet until she herself decided how to handle the matter, or would she want them to let Gary know right then and there that his secret weekend rendezvous weren't secret anymore?

'Uh-oh.' Megan looked down the corridor. 'That's not a promising sign.'

Following her gaze, Hope saw a man coming toward them. He was stocky and muscular, wearing a black Amethyst logo T-shirt and pushing a small housekeeping cart. The cart was stacked with freshly folded towels, clean linen, and an array of lotions, oils, and other spa essentials.

'Sorry for the rush, Sean,' Megan said to the man in a low, hurried tone, 'but time is of the essence. Do you know if the couples massage in room nine is done?'

'Sure, Megan,' Sean responded amiably. 'Bettina and I finished with them just a few minutes ago. I had the guy; she had the girl. I was about to do the clean-up.'

Megan groaned in frustration. 'Then we're too late.'

'Trying to get a message to them?' Sean asked.

'Trying to catch them in the act,' Hope muttered glumly.

Sean had no difficulty understanding her. 'Looking for a cheater, eh? I could pretend and tell you that it's rare around here, but it isn't.' He shrugged at Megan. 'You get 'em upstairs, and we get 'em downstairs.'

Megan nodded.

'So which one is the cheat?' he said. 'The guy, the girl, or both?'

'The guy.' Hope frowned, realizing that she knew nothing about Ms Misty Monique. 'But she could be also. I have no idea.'

'She did seem sort of nervous,' Sean remarked. 'Bettina had a hard time getting her to relax. The guy was much more laid-back. He spent most of the appointment admiring the girl. Not that admiring her is hard to do.' He grinned. 'She's a real looker. All the right parts in all the right places, if you know what I mean.'

Megan gave a little snort. 'That doesn't surprise me about Gary,' she said to Hope.

'He always was an ogler. When he and Summer got engaged, the first thing Gram did was warn her that Gary's eyes might get him into trouble one day.'

'It isn't Gary's *eyes* that are the problem,' Megan replied dryly.

Sean's grin grew. 'Is his wife in the hotel? Does she know what her dearest is up to?' He began to laugh. 'It reminds me of the Nellens.'

Megan burst out laughing with him, but a second later – looking chagrined – she clamped her hand over her mouth. 'That was way too loud.'

'No worries,' Sean told her. 'The walls are solid. You can't hear anything in the rooms when the doors are closed.'

Although more restrained this time, Megan laughed again. 'I'll never forget the Nellen incident.'

'The way he looked – and smelled! It was one of the funniest things that I've seen in all the years I've worked here.' Sean chortled so hard that he hiccupped.

Despite the rotten reason for her being in the spa, standing in front of room nine, their profuse laughter made Hope smile. 'Who are the Nellens?' she asked.

'Jeff and Joan Nellen,' Sean said. 'How long did they stay at the hotel, Megan? I know that it was quite a while.'

'Nearly six months,' Megan answered. 'Jeff was an executive with some big paper company in Wisconsin. They were setting up a new pulping plant on one of the rivers coming out of the Smokies. His wife, Joan, would fly down to Asheville for the weekends, then return home – to Green Bay, if I recall correctly – during the week, while Jeff would remain here and work. For the first month, it was fine. Jeff dined alone in the restaurant most evenings or with an occasional business associate. The second month he must have started to get lonely, because he rarely ate by himself and the associates were more often female than male. Come the third month, the dinner companions also frequently became breakfast companions. And by the fourth month, Jeff had settled on one permanent companion: his temporary secretary.'

Hope raised an eyebrow. 'You must be joking. The boss from headquarters hooks up with the local secretary while traveling? That's one of the worst clichés ever.'

'Cliché but true.' Megan smiled wryly. 'They shared a room in the hotel every night, Sunday through Thursday. On Friday, Joan would arrive. Husband and wife would spend the weekend in wedded bliss, until Sunday afternoon when Joan would fly back to Wisconsin. By dinner time, boss and secretary were back together.'

The eyebrow went higher. 'And this went on for months without the wife having a clue?'

Megan shrugged. 'Joan was pretty obtuse. In her defense, Jeff was a fast talker. Every time I saw him, he was spewing baloney about something to somebody. He probably told her one tall tale after another, seemingly explaining away all the inconsistencies, and she believed him.'

'Just like Gary. A grand master at spinning yarns. Summer trusts his every word and lets him talk his way out of anything.' Hope cast her unhappy gaze toward the door of room nine. No doubt Gary would try to talk his way out of this, too. If only she had managed to catch him red-handed.

'Until one day the yarn unravels . . .' Sean began, interrupting himself with a hiccup.

'And then the truth is revealed in all of its pungent, pineapple-and-coconut-scented glory,' Megan finished for him.

Hope squinted at her. 'Its *what*?'

Instead of responding directly, Megan continued her story of the Nellens. 'Eventually, Jeff's birthday rolled around. That Friday, Joan took an earlier flight to Asheville than usual. Wanting it to be a surprise, she didn't tell him of the change. As another surprise, she asked me to book a couples massage for them—'

'Remind me never to sign up for a couples massage,' Hope said.

'Likewise,' Megan concurred. 'So Friday afternoon, Joan meets me in the lobby, and we go down to the spa together. I get the room number for the appointment from the reception desk. Unbeknownst to me, however, there is a second room reserved in the name of Nellen: one for the boss and the secretary.'

'Yikes.'

Megan nodded. 'Without realizing it, we head to the wrong

room. Joan wants to know if it's possible to have a bottle of champagne brought in during the massage. I start giving her the speech about alcohol being prohibited in the spa for liability reasons. She doesn't listen; she's too excited about the whole weekend. Before I know it, we're at the room. Joan opens the door, and, lo and behold, her husband is already in the middle of a couples massage – with Sean doing the honors. Except in Joan's place, there is the secretary.'

'Double yikes.'

This time Sean nodded. 'It didn't take long to grasp the situation, and we all just stood there, with everybody staring at everybody else, not quite sure what to do next. Then, in this sort of slow motion, Joan walks over to me. I had a cart by me like this one' – he gestured toward the little housekeeping cart that he had been pushing down the corridor – 'because the room was low on supplies. Joan picks up a refill bottle of massage oil from the cart. She goes to the table with her husband on it—'

'Jeff starts stammering and spluttering,' Megan chimed in, 'no doubt trying to conjure up some half-baked excuse and explanation . . .'

'But Joan doesn't give him the chance and promptly proceeds to pour the entire gallon bottle of tropical-scented oil right over the top of his head,' Sean concluded.

He and Megan broke into peals of laughter.

'The man looked like a wet cat that had fallen into a rain barrel,' Sean told Hope in between guffaws. 'But instead of dripping off as water would have, the oil stuck to his skin. He was coated from nose to toe. And it stank! There was so much oil in the bottle, and it was so concentrated. The odor spread through the spa like a cloud of noxious, perfumed gas. First the room, then the corridor, and finally all the way out into the reception area. The entire place smelled as though a giant pineapple-coconut bomb had exploded.'

'The best part,' Megan added with gusto, 'was that no matter what Jeff did, he couldn't get rid of it. He tried to rub it off with towels. He tried showering, repeatedly. He even tried the sauna, sitting there for hours, sweating buckets. But none of it worked. The man reeked to high heaven – and he continued reeking. All through the weekend, anytime he went anywhere, everybody would stare at him because he smelled like a walking bottle of Malibu Rum.'

'And Joan?' Hope inquired, now laughing also.

'She left immediately. My guess is that she flew straight back to Green Bay to consult with a divorce attorney.' Megan grinned. 'Jeff departed the following week. Considering his stench, he probably wasn't allowed to get on an airplane before then. We never saw either of them – or the secretary – again.'

'But we'll always remember the smell!' Sean began to hiccup once more. 'The scent of pineapple and coconut lingered for weeks. Whenever a new guest would walk into the hotel, they would stop, sniff, and look around, as though expecting to find somebody handing out complimentary pina coladas at the door.'

'What a funny story! I have to tell it to Gram. She'll laugh herself silly . . .'

The sentence was left unfinished as the handle from the door to room nine began to jiggle. In unison, Hope, Megan, and Sean turned toward it. A moment later, the door swung open, and a giggling, cuddling couple appeared. Neither group expected to see the other standing abruptly in front of them, so there was a moment of startled silence all around.

To the casual bystander, the couple emerging from room nine might have looked happy and committed, but to Hope, her brother-in-law's simpering smirk was that of a cheater and a louse. There was no misunderstanding of any sort. Gary's arms were wrapped around a woman, not a new construction project. And Sean hadn't exaggerated his admiring description of her. Mystique Monique was indeed a looker. She was a thin, leggy, runway-model type, with saucer eyes set in an angular face. She was also fairly intelligent, apparently, because when she looked at Sean and his cart before her in the corridor, she realized that he was intending to clean their room.

'I'm terribly sorry,' she said to him. 'We've stayed far too long. And now we've probably thrown off your schedule for the rest of the afternoon. If there's a charge for the additional time in the room, I certainly have no objection to paying it. Just add it to my credit card . . .'

Hope didn't hear the remainder of the apology. She was too busy glowering at Gary, appalled at his gall. How dare he do this to Summer! And so publicly, too. Marilyn Smoltz was probably still lounging in the reception area. She would see Gary and Misty upon their exit, as would everybody else who happened to be wandering about the spa or hotel at that time. Summer deserved more respect, to be treated with more dignity, than having her shifty husband parade his sleazy behavior for all and sundry to witness.

As soon as his pea-sized brain recognized Hope and Megan and processed what that meant for the future of his marriage, Gary started to hem and haw. It reminded Hope of the story that she had heard just a minute earlier, about Jeff Nellen from Green Bay, Wisconsin, stammering and spluttering, trying to conjure up some half-baked excuse and explanation as to why he had been caught in the middle of a couples massage with someone other than his wife. And in that instant, Hope knew exactly what to do. She turned to Sean's cart, picked up the largest bottle from the bottom rack, flipped open the top, and poured the contents over her brother-in-law's head.

Gary was too stunned to react quickly, and by the time he jumped away, more than half of the bottle had been emptied on to him. Having selected the bottle based on its size rather than its contents, Hope didn't know what product she was coating the man with. The scent swiftly revealed itself, enveloping them in the same noxious, perfumed cloud of gas that Sean had described in relation to the Nellens, but instead of tropical pineapple and coconut, it was floral rose and jasmine. A light touch of the oil would have been rich and sensuous. By the quart, it was a sickly-sweet combination, so overpowering that the entire group immediately began to cough and wheeze at the smell.

Pinching her nose, Misty wasted no time in heading toward the ladies' dressing room. Gary – covered with oil and swearing like the proverbial sailor – grabbed some towels from Sean's cart and stomped angrily in the direction of the men's dressing room. Laughing and hiccupping in between coughs, Sean took the remaining towels and threw them on the floor to soak up as much of the spilled oil as possible. Also in between coughs,

Hope and Megan asked him how they could help with the necessary clean-up.

Sean waved them away with a grin. 'No worries. I'll take care of it.' Then he winked at Hope. 'You got him good. He'll be stinking for days.'

Hope returned the grin. 'It serves him right. And now he won't be able to pretend that nothing happened.'

'I think this calls for some wine, don't you?' Megan said to her. 'A carafe of Pinot Grigio is waiting.'

'Excellent idea.' Hope linked her arm in Megan's as they turned down the corridor. 'I'll need a boost before seeing Summer and sharing the news.'

They made it only half a dozen paces before an ear-splitting scream echoed through the spa.

EIGHT

Startled by the noise, Hope and Megan halted.

'Is it coming from the reception area?' Hope said.

Megan nodded. 'It sounds like Lisa.'

'She couldn't be that upset about the smell, could she?'

The scream continued briefly, then it faded away in a sad sort of whimper. With quick steps, Hope and Megan reached the reception area a moment later. The scent of rose and jasmine was just as intense there as it had been in the corridor. Lisa had left her desk and was standing by the refreshment table, her face florid and her eyes watering. Hope's first thought was that the odor of the oil was affecting her more than the rest of them, but then she saw Lisa pointing in horror toward the floor.

As Hope had supposed earlier, Marilyn Smoltz was still in the reception area. Except she was no longer resting on the plush velvet lounger, sipping her glass of lemon water, eager to gossip about whomever and whatever she might see there. Marilyn was now lying on the ground, her eyes wide open and her limbs rigid.

Although quieter than Lisa's, Megan let out her own shriek. 'Good God! Is she . . . She's not . . .'

Approaching the motionless figure, Hope knew the answer without Megan concluding the question. Marilyn Smoltz was dead. She didn't blink and she didn't breathe. She was curled up in a ball on her side with her knees drawn toward her chest and her hands clutching at her stomach. It was the same position that Roberta King had been in on the gray speckled carpeting of the community center. Unlike Roberta, however, there was no swelling or disfigurement. Marilyn's hands still looked like hands, and Marilyn was still recognizable as Marilyn. Her face, mouth, and neck all appeared normal, albeit covered with neon-green mud that was now heavily smeared.

'What the hell happened here?'

Not expecting the voice next to her, Hope jumped in surprise. She had been so focused on Marilyn that she hadn't noticed the main doors of the spa open and Dylan Henshaw enter.

Dylan bent down over the body and checked for a pulse. Shaking his head, he stood back up. 'Has anyone contacted the police?'

There was no immediate response. Hope stared at him. Megan stared at Marilyn. And Lisa wiped her eyes with a napkin from the refreshment table.

'The police?' Dylan repeated, more loudly.

'I'll call them,' Lisa murmured, blowing her nose and heading to the phone at the reception desk.

Dylan turned to Hope. 'This seems a bit familiar, doesn't it?'

'What–what are you doing here?' she said.

'I was on the stairs, heard a scream, and figured that it might be a good idea to see if everyone was OK. What are *you* doing here?'

'I . . . we,' Hope amended, motioning toward Megan, 'were in the corridor and heard the scream, too. But why are you at the hotel?'

'I'm staying at the hotel,' Dylan told her.

'Not at your dad's house?'

'No. I need my own space. And I assumed my dad felt the same way, especially while recovering from surgery. Now that I know about his' – there was a slight hesitation – 'relationship with your grandmother, it's clear that I made the right decision for all involved. Speaking of which, is Olivia really your grandmother?'

'Huh?'

'Olivia Bailey. The woman I met yesterday while standing over a body very much like the one before us now. Is she your actual grandma, or do you just call her that as a term of endearment?'

'She's my biological maternal grandmother. Why do you ask?'

'Her age and your age,' Dylan said. 'They don't fit quite right.'

Hope nodded. 'You aren't the first one to mention it. Gram had my mom while she was in college, and my mom had

Summer and me right out of college, hence the smaller-than-usual age gap.'

Dylan nodded back at her. 'And the surname you all share? Did Olivia or your mom never marry, or do the women in your family simply love keeping the name Bailey?'

She raised an eyebrow. 'You're awfully curious. Or perhaps I should say, nosy.'

'You could view it that way, but I consider it as being judicious. My father appears to have taken a tremendous liking to your grandmother. I want to know who exactly he's getting into bed with.'

Hope cast him a sharp look. Dylan's pale blue eyes were inscrutable. Whether he had meant the remark figuratively or literally, she wasn't sure. But she was sure that if he so chose, he could – being Morris's son – cause considerable turmoil in their lives. She was also sure that her initial assessment of Marilyn Smoltz's last words to her were correct. Dylan Henshaw was not the sort who could be reined in with the snap of a finger.

'For your information,' Hope remarked coolly, 'my sister has taken her husband's name.'

'But I doubt it will be for much longer,' Megan interjected, finally overcoming her shock at seeing Marilyn's lifeless body and joining the conversation. 'Not now that we've found out about shifty Gary spending all his weekends here in the amorous company of Little Miss Mystique.'

It was Dylan's turn to raise an eyebrow. 'Shifty Gary has been caught with his hand in the cookie jar?'

Hope couldn't help smiling at Dylan's adoption of the *shifty Gary* moniker.

'He has,' Megan confirmed. 'And when Summer learns all the dirty details, I can't imagine that she won't drop the name Fletcher like a rotten potato.'

'While we're on the subject of moldy produce,' Dylan said, sniffing and wrinkling his nose, 'am I the only one who thinks that it smells like a rancid greenhouse in here?'

Hope and Megan exchanged a grin.

'As a matter of fact, the scent is rose and jasmine,' Megan told him. 'And it comes to you courtesy of Hope, who just a few minutes ago poured a giant bottle of floral-scented massage oil over shifty Gary's head.'

'Seriously?' Dylan chuckled. 'I would have enjoyed seeing that.'

'Well, at last sighting – and smelling – Gary had fled to the men's dressing room, presumably in the hope of removing some of the stink. If you're lucky, he may try to leave this way, and then you can . . .'

No sooner were the words out of Megan's mouth than other spa guests began to emerge from their treatment rooms. Still standing at the reception desk, Lisa turned to Megan for some suggestion as to how to handle them. Megan shook her head, not sure herself.

'You should make a list of their names and contact information,' Hope advised. 'And then do what you can to get them to leave through the back. There is a rear exit from the spa, isn't there?'

'Yes.' Lisa nodded. 'Down the far corridor.'

'Having them go out the back is a good idea,' Dylan agreed. 'Otherwise, they'll all just crowd around here, pointing and gawking, which won't help anyone. And the list will give the police a record of who was in the spa and how to get in touch with them if necessary. Very smart,' he complimented Hope.

His unsolicited praise surprised her. It made Hope wonder if maybe she had been a little too hasty in her judgment of Dylan. Maybe he wasn't quite so full of himself, after all.

As the guests appeared in the reception area, Lisa sprang into action. Pen and clipboard in hand, she promptly intercepted them, cutting off their path to the refreshment table and just as swiftly turning them around. The nasal quality in her voice disappeared, replaced once more by the dulcet tones. It turned out that Lisa had the natural herding instinct of a Border collie. More or less nipping at the guests' heels, she succeeded in driving every last one of them back down the corridor without causing a stampede or even a lone bolter, calmly making a record of names and phone numbers as she went.

When the reception area resumed its former quiet state, Hope's gaze returned to Marilyn Smoltz. 'It seems wrong to just stand here,' she mused. 'I feel as though we should be doing something.'

Megan sighed. 'I was thinking the same thing.'

'There's nothing we can do but wait for the police,' Dylan responded. Then he added a moment later, 'At least there isn't anything *I* can do. I only handle the living, not the dead. You're the one into all the mystical mumbo jumbo. Maybe you can resurrect the dear departed with voodoo or something.'

Hope frowned at him. Presumably, he meant it as a joke, although he wasn't smiling. In any case, she wasn't amused. His compliment from a minute earlier was forgotten. Her original appraisal of Dylan stood – with renewed strength.

'Rather irreverent, don't you think?' Megan said, frowning also.

'Are you referring to me or her?' Dylan rejoined. 'I'm not the one who peddles potions and palm readings.'

'Then you should know to be extra careful,' Megan snapped. 'Because it's a short step from potions to curses.'

Dylan looked at her with cold eyes. 'You're the second person to warn me about a curse in just as many days.' The stony gaze switched to Hope. 'Is that why your sister is having romantic troubles? Too many curses?'

Megan let out a venomous hiss. 'You miserable—'

Fortunately for Dylan, she was interrupted by the arrival of the police. Detective Nate Phillips stepped through the main doors of the spa. He halted mid-stride when he saw Hope standing in front of him.

'This is a nice surprise,' Nate said, smiling at her warmly. 'I left your sister at the boutique just a few minutes ago.'

Hope returned the smile. He had spent the entire time at the boutique? His budding crush on Summer must have gained ground.

'You know Summer?' Megan inquired, giving Nate an appraising look.

'We had tea,' he replied cheerfully. 'She makes the most wonderful tea.'

Her lips curling with a hint of a grin, Megan glanced sideways at Hope. Hope knew what she was thinking, because she was thinking it, too. The attentions of a pleasant man would do

Summer's confidence a world of good when she learned how dreadfully her husband had been deceiving her all these weeks.

'If you like Summer's tea,' Megan told Nate, 'then on your next visit, you should try one of her tinctures. They're even better.'

Dylan coughed. 'Better for killing old ladies.'

He said it in such a muffled tone that only Hope – who was nearest to him – heard him. She glared at him.

'I didn't realize that it was so late!' Megan exclaimed, looking at her watch. 'The wine-and-cheese must be more than done.' She pulled a business card from the pocket of her linen blazer and handed it to Nate. 'Here's my card. All my information is on it. I'm employed by the hotel, and I was with Hope the entire time, so she can tell you everything for both of us.' Not waiting for approval or even an acknowledging nod from the detective, she blew Hope a hasty air kiss and then hurried toward the double doors. 'If you want help breaking the bad news to Summer, call me!'

Her exit was so abrupt that Nate started to shout after her, but Megan's parting words to Hope stopped him. 'Bad news to Summer?' he echoed, turning toward Hope with a furrowed brow.

'Just a little hiccup,' Hope responded lightly. She had no intention of reciting the whole sordid story to him or the two uniformed police officers who had arrived with him and were standing within earshot just outside the spa doors. 'Nothing to worry about.'

Dylan coughed again and, in the same muffled tone as before, said, 'Au contraire. Shifty Gary has plenty to worry about.'

The remark would have made Hope smile, but she was still too irritated with him for his previous commentary.

As the furrow in his brow eased, Nate proceeded to the more immediate subject before them. 'I'm here because we received a call that someone had . . . Well, I'm glad to find that it was a mistake.'

Hope shook her head grimly. 'It's not a mistake. Marilyn Smoltz is over there, on the other side of that lounger.'

Having stopped just inside the reception area, Nate couldn't see the floor behind the lounger from where he was standing.

He moved quickly forward, and when his eyes found Marilyn, his expression grew grave. For a long moment, no one spoke as they all gazed at the body curled up on the ground.

Nate broke the silence first. 'This seems a bit familiar, doesn't it?'

'I said the same thing,' Dylan replied.

'And yet there are some differences . . .'

'No hives. No flushing of the skin. No facial swelling.'

'What is that on her face?' Nate asked.

'French clay,' Hope answered.

Nate squinted at the remnants of the neon-green mud mask. 'And it's intentional?'

She nodded. 'It's currently quite popular at the spa. At least according to Marilyn, who heard about it from Sylvia Norquist, who heard about it from Kirsten Willport, who apparently has the most divine skin . . .'

'Wait a minute. I've heard those names before, haven't I?' Pulling out his notepad, Nate flipped through the pages until he found the correct one. 'Yes! Yesterday – at the community center – from your grandmother.'

Hope nodded again.

'So this is Marilyn Smoltz?' he said. 'According to my notes, she was the one handing out the garlic bread at the supper. She's on my list to be interviewed.'

'Not anymore,' Dylan remarked drolly.

'True.' Nate slapped the notepad shut. 'And that concerns me. I don't like losing potential witnesses.'

'For what it's worth,' Hope told him, 'I don't think that Marilyn would have been much help to you. She and I spoke about Roberta King this afternoon – while Marilyn was sitting on the lounger, in fact – and all she did was complain about how stressful and overblown the whole situation was. It had her so agitated that she was determined to talk to Gram about it.'

'And did she talk to her?' Nate said.

'No. Marilyn didn't leave the reception area. When I went down the corridor, she was still sitting on the lounger, and when I came back . . .' Hope gestured toward the floor.

'What was Marilyn like on the lounger?' Dylan asked her.

'Gossipy and grumbly. Pretty much the same as always.'

'How was she *physically*?'

'Fine. She had on the spa robe and the mud mask and . . .' Hope paused, reflecting. 'No, looking back on it, Marilyn wasn't fine. She said that she was warm and tired. She was perspiring heavily. And she was coughing, too. She asked for some water, and I brought her a glass.'

Nate inspected the empty glass that was lying beside the body. 'So the glass came from you. Where did the water come from?'

'The refreshment table in the corner. I poured it from the pitcher.'

Both Nate and Dylan looked at the table and the pitcher, then they looked at each other.

'What do you think?' Nate asked him. 'Same cause of death?'

'Possibly,' Dylan answered. 'Allergic reactions can present differently, so it's best not to draw too many conclusions from a few hives, or a lack thereof. It's the similarity in the positions of the bodies that I find interesting. And how quickly both women fell ill. Then there's also the timing – a mere twenty-four hours apart. Those are considerable coincidences.'

Nate nodded. 'I like coincidences. They show me where to take a closer look.'

'Don't tell that to Summer,' Hope murmured under her breath.

'And while we're on the subject,' Nate continued, turning to Hope, 'it's rather coincidental about you and your grandmother, isn't it?'

She frowned, not understanding.

'Your grandmother supplied the dinner to the deceased yesterday,' Nate explained. 'And you supplied the water to the deceased today.'

Her frown deepened. 'What exactly are you suggesting?'

'The facts speak for themselves,' Dylan responded. 'We have two bodies, and you and Olivia were the last to provide the food and drink to both of them.'

Hope's eyes flashed with resentment – and confusion. Was he serious? Did he and Nate honestly think that she and Gram could be involved in Marilyn and Roberta's deaths?

'What do we have here?' Nate said, seeing something

protruding from the pocket of Marilyn's robe. He leaned down to examine it. 'Now we're getting really coincidental. And a bit *too* familiar.'

He pulled the item from the pocket and held it up for Hope and Dylan to see. It was a Tarot card. The Fool.

NINE

'I don't understand it,' Gram said, walking toward the polished pecan dining table. Her cane was in her hand, but it didn't touch the floor. 'How can Marilyn be dead? I saw her only the day before yesterday at the center.'

'No one lives forever, Olivia,' Morris reminded her from the kitchen. 'Sad as it may be, death is a fact of life.'

'Yes, of course, dear. I'm seventy-four, not seven. I know perfectly well that we are not immortal beings. And thank heaven for it, because otherwise I would be stuck with this on-again, off-again hip for all eternity.'

Hope set the salad bowl down on the table. 'So you hadn't heard of Marilyn being ill recently, or having any particular ailments?'

'No,' Gram answered. 'As far as I was aware, she was as fit as a fiddle. Marilyn Smoltz may have been a grouser, but she was a tough old bird.'

'Witty,' Hope said, noting the fowl references.

Gram smiled and seated herself. The dining table was an antique behemoth, with twelve matching intricately carved pecan chairs. Four place settings had been laid. Saturday-evening dinner at Morris's house was a regular event for Hope, Summer, and Gram. Similar to Gram's left hip, Gary was an on-again, off-again participant. He hadn't appeared for the past month, and considering the episode with Misty and the massage oil at the hotel the previous afternoon, there seemed to be little chance that he would be appearing tonight.

'People can look outwardly healthy,' Morris continued from the kitchen, 'but not all illnesses are evident to the eye. There are numerous silent killers. Coronary artery disease, cerebro-vascular disease, cardiomyopathy. And let's not forget the host of potential complications arising from diabetes, hypertension, hepatitis infections—'

'Thank you, dear.' Gram cut short the depressing catalogue

of maladies. 'I didn't mean that Marilyn *couldn't* be sick and *couldn't* die. I meant that it's strange she should die *now*, only one day after Roberta's passing. Both of them going so suddenly and in more or less the same manner. It's curious, isn't it?'

Hope nodded in agreement. 'Dylan and Detective Phillips talked about it, too. The similarity in the position of the bodies and the timing of the two deaths.'

Gram nodded back at her. 'It feels like a pattern to me.'

'Dylan is excellent at spotting patterns,' Morris called out.

Hope was tempted to respond that Dylan excelled to such a degree, in fact, that he had also spotted the pattern of her and Gram being the last to provide the food and drink to Marilyn and Roberta. She wisely restrained herself, however. Sharing Dylan's remark would only upset Morris and Gram, and Hope couldn't help wondering whether that had been precisely Dylan's purpose in saying it. He could be trying to cause a rift between the pair.

Gram didn't respond to Morris, either, but for a different reason. She was absorbed in her own thoughts.

'There's something about it,' she mused. 'A connection between them . . .'

'A connection?' Hope asked her. 'Beyond that Marilyn and Roberta knew each other?'

'They went way back,' Gram replied absently. 'We all go way back.'

Hope nodded once more, sympathetically. Losing old friends and acquaintances was never easy.

'There's something about it,' Gram said again. 'Only I can't quite . . . I can't seem to put my finger on it. It's like trying to remember a neighbor's name when you run into them at the post office or the grocery store. You know it – it's right there on the tip of your tongue – and yet you can't grasp hold of it.' She shook her head in frustration. 'The aged brain is getting foggy, I guess.'

'Your brain isn't foggy in the least,' Hope rejoined. 'Whatever it is that you're trying to think of, I'm sure that it will come to you—'

'In the middle of the night,' Morris chimed in, simultaneously opening the oven door with a loud bang.

'What was that, dear?'

'One night either this week or the next, this month or the next,' Morris told her, 'you'll wake up for no reason at all, and there it will be. Like lightning striking from out of the blue, you'll suddenly remember your cousin's birthday, where you left the key to your gym locker, the phone number for the handyman who cleans the leaves out of the gutters . . .'

Gram tapped her cane against the leg of the dining table impatiently. 'I'm thinking about poor Marilyn and Roberta,' she muttered, 'and he's thinking about the handyman who cleans the leaves out of the gutters.'

Hope had to bite her lip not to smile.

The oven door banged a second time.

'Do you need any help, Morris?' Hope asked. 'I would be happy to lift or carry something for you.'

'No, I'm fine. It's all fine.'

'Are you sure?' Gram pressed him. 'Don't forget about your back. You aren't supposed to bend too much or pick up anything heavy right now.'

'Fiddle-faddle,' was his reply.

Gram tapped her cane again. Hope understood her impatience and concern. Supportive brace or not, Morris's surgery was barely behind him. He could easily overexert himself and cause serious, permanent damage to his back. But when Morris prepared dinner, he didn't like having extra hands in the kitchen, even if they were only there to assist in taking down plates from the cupboard or moving heavy pans around the stove. Ordinarily, no one objected to Morris's possessive attitude toward his kitchen on Saturday evenings. He greatly enjoyed cooking, and he was good at it. Eschewing commercial recipes, Morris preferred instead to craft his own menus from scratch, and it was the rare creation that didn't turn out well. He claimed to have northern Italian ancestors, and although his surname and family history didn't support the claim, the quality of his pasta dishes certainly did.

'Here we are.' Morris appeared in the dining room, carrying a colossal cast-iron skillet. 'Here it comes.'

From the way his shoulders were shaking, it was evident that he was struggling with the weight of the pan. Hope grabbed a trivet from the buffet and hurriedly placed it on the dining table for him.

'Watch out now. It's hot. Sizzling hot.' Depositing the skillet on the trivet with a clunk, Morris breathed a sigh of relief at not having dropped their dinner en route.

Hope and Gram sighed, too, grateful that the chef didn't appear to have injured his back further in the process. Then they both leaned toward the pan, eager to see its contents.

'Tonight we have' – Morris spread his arms in front of the dish with a gesture of dramatic presentation – 'seafood risotto!'

'It looks and smells fantastic,' Hope complimented him, without exaggeration. The creamy, saffron-colored risotto was visually appealing, and the combination of the ocean's bounty had a deliciously spicy, smoky aroma. 'Shrimp, scallops, mussels. And I see you put in calamari. Summer loves calamari.'

Morris nodded. 'I did it with the hope that she might change her mind at the last minute and come tonight. That's also why I made the cheddar biscuits. I know how fond your sister is of a cheesy biscuit.'

Gram reached toward him and gave his hand a squeeze. 'That was so thoughtful of you, dear. Thank you.'

Two dots of red appeared on Morris's cheeks. 'Well, Summer is having a tough time of it right now, and even though I'm not able to do much to make it easier for her, I try to help in the little ways that I can.'

'Your little ways are wonderful.' Gram squeezed his hand again. 'And I appreciate them – and you – greatly.'

The red dots expanded to crimson circles. Morris shuffled his feet and gazed affectionately at Gram. She gazed back at him with tenderness. Looking between them, Hope couldn't help but smile. Forget moony-eyed teenagers. They couldn't hold a candle to Morris Henshaw and Olivia Bailey. And if Dylan really was trying to cause a rift between the pair, then he was going to have to do a lot more than find a pattern in who had handed Marilyn and Roberta their last food and drink.

Giving the two a moment of privacy, Hope headed toward the kitchen to retrieve the aforementioned cheddar biscuits. She found them already out of the oven and waiting in a doily-lined basket on the black granite countertop. Although Hope didn't get the same level of solace from comfort foods as her sister, she did have to admit that there was something inherently soothing about warm, cheesy biscuits.

'Maybe I could wrap up a few of the biscuits to bring back for Summer,' Hope suggested, as she returned with deliberate slowness to the dining room.

'Is Summer staying at the brownstone tonight?' Gram asked.

She nodded. 'When I left to come here, she was upstairs in her old room, trying to rest. I told her that I would go with her to the house tomorrow. I don't want her to be there alone – in case Gary pops in – and I figured that while Summer picks up some clothes and other essentials, I can make sure to get her checkbook and any important papers that she might need down the road. I don't trust what Gary will do with them if she leaves them behind.'

'So you think that they're headed for a divorce?' Morris questioned. 'They won't try to talk it through?'

'Talk it through?' Gram frowned at him. 'This isn't a little lovers' tiff. Gary didn't forget their anniversary or stay out too late drinking with his mates. The man is a liar and a cheat. That doesn't go away with a few sharp words, followed by a box of candy or a bouquet of roses.'

'Once a liar, always a liar. Once a cheat, always a cheat,' Hope said.

'I can't argue with you on that.' Morris moved to the dining chair next to Gram, sitting down slowly and awkwardly due to the back brace. 'But I hate to see any marriage end. Maybe there is still a way for them to work it out. Perhaps there has been some confusion about what exactly Gary did.'

'Trust me, there hasn't been any confusion,' Hope replied. 'I witnessed the lying and the cheating with my own eyes.'

It was Morris's turn to frown, and with it, he promptly converted from relationship therapist to legal consultant. 'Then it's a good thing that you're going with her to the house tomorrow. The sooner, the better. Collect all the documents that you can – don't forget about bank statements and copies of insurance policies – and pack up any item of value. Summer should get everything that she's entitled to. What about a separation agreement? Has she talked to a lawyer yet?'

'Oh, no. She only just found out the truth. She isn't remotely ready to—'

Morris didn't let her finish. 'I'll make some calls in the morning and ask around, see who has a reputation for handling these types of matters successfully. It's important to get an early jump on the situation and hire the best attorney in the area before Gary does.'

Hope cast an apprehensive glance at Gram. Although she was pretty sure that the marriage neither could nor should be salvaged, she was also pretty sure that Summer wasn't at the point where she could reasonably discuss its dissolution, especially not all the nitty-gritty particulars with a divorce attorney. Hope had been generous when she described Summer as resting upstairs in her room. More accurately, Summer had been alternately weeping, swearing, and sucking on a bottle of gin while pacing from one corner to another like a caged animal at the zoo. Hope had been reluctant to leave her, but Summer had been adamant that she go to Morris's as planned. And Hope knew from her own loss and grief only a few months earlier that there were moments when you dearly needed sisterly support and moments when you wanted to wallow in your misery alone.

Comprehending Hope's look, Gram said to Morris, 'I think that we might be getting a bit ahead of ourselves, dear. It will take Summer some time to process her thoughts and feelings before she can—'

'Time is the enemy,' Morris interjected emphatically, shaking his head. 'Speed is our friend. The marital assets must be safe-guarded. Gary can't be given the opportunity to sell off the cars or clean out the savings account.'

'Well, yes, that's true,' Gram acknowledged.

Morris turned to Hope. 'And is this woman who he's been involved with still in the picture?'

'I assume so. I have no reason to think that she's made a sudden exit.'

'Then we also have no reason to think that she won't convince Gary to pile up charges on his credit card for her benefit or take cash advances that will wondrously find their way into her purse.'

Hope glanced at Gram again, this time with some surprise. There had been no question that Morris was an intelligent person, but up until now his smarts had always seemed to be more of the scholarly sort. Hope had never heard him so canny and cunning before. He sounded downright calculating, at least in regard to Gary and Misty's potential financial finagling. And he was correct. Although Hope's knowledge of Mystique Monique was limited, the woman was certainly staying in a fancy, expensive hotel and booking services at a fancy, expensive spa. She may have made the reservations using her own credit card, but that didn't mean she was actually paying the bill. Gary could be the one ultimately writing the check – to Summer's considerable detriment.

'You see the problem, don't you?' Morris continued. 'I'm sure that Dylan will agree, too. He's been no stranger to these things in California. Physicians at the hospital marrying their nurses and assistants, and all the ugly breakups that ensue.'

Hope raised an eyebrow with interest. Had Dylan gone through a nasty divorce? It wasn't clear from the way that Morris had phrased it. But if so, then that could prejudice Dylan against any woman in a relationship with his father, namely Gram. Hope was about to prod Morris for more information on the subject when the doorbell rang. It was a deep bass gong.

'Perfect timing!' Morris exclaimed.

Gram's brow furrowed. So did Hope's. She hadn't thought that Summer would change her mind and come to dinner at the last minute, not with her face stained and swollen from so many tears, and especially not after drinking so heavily.

'I'll get it,' Hope said, heading toward the foyer.

Two more gongs sounded in rapid succession, followed by a sharp knock on the woodwork. It had to be the gin talking, because Summer wasn't normally so impatient.

'Jeez, take it easy,' Hope began, pulling open the heavy oak front door. 'You know that Morris and Gram can't move so quickly—'

Her rebuke broke off in surprise when she saw that it wasn't her sister waiting outside, eager for entry. It was Dylan Henshaw.

The man was dressed as stylishly as always, with perfectly cut trousers and a crisp shirt. He glanced at the same elegant wristwatch that Hope had noticed during their first encounter, and this time she couldn't help thinking – with a sigh – that its costly price tag was probably about equal to what Summer's legal bills would amount to with the ace attorney that Morris was planning on finding for her. Such an expense was fine for the evident wealth of the Henshaws; it was going to be a problem for the less-flush Baileys, however.

'Am I late? I thought dinner was scheduled for seven. But it appears' – Dylan gestured toward the basket of cheddar biscuits that was still in Hope's hands – 'you've started without me.'

It took her a moment to respond. Dylan had been invited to dinner? That explained the fourth place setting at the table. She had thought that it was meant for Summer in case her sister had a sudden change of heart, but apparently it was intended for Dylan instead. And unless Dylan was hiding it well, he didn't seem to be nearly as startled to see her standing at his father's door as she was to see him, which meant that he was much better informed about the plan for the evening than she was.

'We–we haven't begun eating yet,' Hope answered at last. 'You're right on time, actually. Your dad just revealed his grand culinary creation.'

'His grand culinary creation?' It was Dylan's turn to show surprise. 'My dad is the one cooking dinner?'

She nodded. 'He does every Saturday night. It's become a tradition of sorts. He'll never tell us the menu in advance. And we're all banned from the kitchen while he's preparing the mystery meal, so we can only speculate based on the various smells wafting through the house. Summer's guesses are usually the most accurate; I think it's her nose for herbs. But Gram's conjectures are the most fun. She comes up with the craziest possibilities.' Hope chuckled, remembering the time when Gram had been absolutely convinced that dinner was going to involve roasted veal sweetbreads. The dish in question had turned out to be a scrumptious (and organ-meat-free) eggplant parmigiana.

Rather than share her laugh, Dylan's expression grew increasingly somber, and all of his abundant confidence and conceit seemed to fade away. He looked suddenly young and vulnerable, like a forlorn child. A child who had lost his mother far too early in life and grown up without a father. It made Hope regret her words from a minute earlier. Dylan hadn't known that his dad cooked so well – or even possibly that he cooked at all – and she had called their dinners together *a tradition*, one that Dylan was not a part of. She hadn't meant to sound exclusionary, but she could understand how he might interpret it that way.

'The problem with mystery meals,' she went on lightly, trying to shift the subject as best as she could, 'is that you can never be sure what wine to bring for the occasion. But it looks like you smartly came prepared for all potentialities with a beautiful bottle of claret.'

Hope motioned toward the bottle of wine that Dylan was holding. Her view was partly obscured by his fingers, but she could see that it was an old label, the kind that connoisseurs stored in a cellar for a decade or two before withdrawing with great ceremony on the eve of a special event.

As though he had forgotten that it was there, Dylan glanced down at the bottle in his hand. When he looked back up at Hope, his expression had changed again. The fleeting vulnerability was gone, and the ego had returned with full force.

'Of course I had to bring my own beverage,' Dylan said. 'I can't trust what you and Olivia might give me.'

TEN

As he stood on the threshold of his father's house, Dylan's frosty tone matched the frostiness of his eyes. Hope's eyes weren't any warmer. She made no further attempt at polite niceties. Instead, she turned silently on her heel and marched back to the dining room. Tossing the basket of biscuits on the table, she sat down in her usual chair and shot Gram an irritated look. Had Gram known that Dylan was coming to dinner? If so, some advance warning would have been appreciated.

'Is it Dylan?' Morris asked her eagerly. 'I thought I heard his voice.'

There was no need for Hope to answer, because the man at issue stepped into the room a moment later. His cold gaze hit Hope first, but as it traveled across the table toward Morris and Gram, it melted into cordiality. Friendly greetings followed, as did gratitude on both sides. Dylan said that he greatly appreciated the invitation to dinner. Morris replied that he and Olivia were so pleased that Dylan could be with them. Dylan in turn responded that the pleasure was all his, because he got to enjoy their delightful company and a wonderful home-cooked meal instead of eating alone in the hotel restaurant.

It took Hope some effort not to roll her eyes. If he ever got tired of medicine, Dylan could always pursue a career on the stage. He sure was putting on a heck of a performance. The question was: why? She didn't doubt that he was truly happy to spend time with his father; even so, he was laying it on awfully thick. And she found it hard to believe that Dylan was ever forced to eat alone on a Saturday evening. With his good looks, good profession, and – based on his looks and profession – good bank account, getting a date in any city would be a snap for him. Maybe now that Gary's situation had turned unpleasantly messy on the home front, Mystique Monique might be in the market for a new and less complicated beau. Dylan could be just the ticket for her.

The idea of Misty jumping from Gary to Dylan brought a mischievous smile to Hope's face. Dylan must have noticed, because he returned the mischievous look and, with exaggerated chivalry, presented the bottle of claret to Gram. He called it a hostess gift, then immediately added that he didn't want to cause Gram any difficulty or inconvenience in rising from her seat; he would open the wine and serve it himself.

To what extent Gram fell for Dylan's purported gallantry was impossible to tell. Morris was so busy oohing and aahing in response to his son that Gram couldn't squeeze in a syllable. *How kind of Dylan*, Morris proclaimed. *How thoughtful, too. What excellent manners he possessed. And what excellent taste in wine. It looked to be a fine vintage. Had Dylan ever been to Bordeaux? A month-long trip through the region with his grandparents? How splendid! Did he think that the bottle needed to be decanted?*

Hope paid little attention to the exchange. She had never been to France, let alone on an extended journey through the country's famed vineyards. And at that moment, she had no interest in learning the tips and tricks of proper decanting. Instead, she was thinking about how much of a troublemaker Dylan Henshaw was. He seemed to enjoy making preposterous claims. First he had accused her and Summer of trying to kill Betsy Hughes with lemon balm. Then he had accused her and Gram of being involved in the recent deaths. The man's penchant for pointing fingers made her want to point the finger straight back at him. Perhaps Dylan knew that he had put Mrs Hughes on more medications than her body could tolerate. Perhaps Dylan was involved in Marilyn and Roberta's deaths.

As to Mrs Hughes, the stomach matter was already resolved, because Summer had supplied her with a new tincture to replace the one that Dylan had taken away. As to Marilyn and Roberta, although Hope wouldn't have minded hurling an accusation in return, she could think of no plausible way to link Dylan with the two women. He hadn't known either of them and wasn't with either of them when they died. Dylan had been at the boutique – with Hope, in fact – at the time Roberta became ill at the community center. When Marilyn collapsed in the spa, Dylan had been upstairs in the hotel.

If Gram was right about there being a pattern, then it seemed only logical that any person involved in the deaths should have been at *both* deaths. But maybe it just looked like a pattern, and in reality, the deaths were unrelated. Maybe whatever connection Gram was searching for in the back of her mind, it was simply the coincidence of two women who had known her and each other for many years dying unexpectedly in the same week. Except it was more than the same week. Marilyn and Roberta's deaths were within a day of each other, in what appeared – at least from the outward signs – to be a rather similar manner. How similar were they, actually?

'When,' Hope asked abruptly, 'will there be a definitive determination as to the causes of death?'

Morris gave a little start in his chair. He had moved from French vineyards to Scottish distilleries, and her question interrupted his lyrical narrative on the Highlands. Gram also looked at Hope in surprise – and relief. Morris's speeches, particularly those involving the subjects of ecology, geography, or history, could get somewhat long-winded. Meanwhile, the risotto was cooling and hardening.

For his part, Dylan didn't appear at all taken aback by Hope's inquiry. He continued uncorking the bottle of claret on the buffet as he responded, 'The initial blood work should be completed in a few days. Unless something strange shows up, in which case more tests will be needed.'

'Are you anticipating anything unusual?' Morris asked him.

Dylan shook his head. 'No. I told the detective that I expect a straightforward answer. Or I should say,' he amended, 'that I expect the lab results to be straightforward. I believe the final answer will be considerably more complicated.'

'More complicated?' Gram leaned forward with interest. 'How so?'

Turning from the buffet with the now-open bottle prominently in his hand, Dylan gave Hope a sideways glance. She had no difficulty understanding his meaning. He was reminding her again that she and Gram had been the source of the two women's last food and drink. Hope glowered at him.

Clearing his throat with what sounded like a hint of a laugh,

Dylan carried the bottle to the table. 'May I?' he said to Gram, suavely offering to pour the wine for her.

'Yes, please,' she replied, still leaning forward, waiting for his explanation as to the prospective complication.

Dylan filled Gram's glass, then without asking whether Hope also wanted wine, he began to fill her glass, as well. Her glower intensified. Dylan cleared his throat once more and turned back to Gram.

'I'm simplifying to a degree, of course,' he told her, 'but in most cases, an allergic response is relatively easy to determine. The associated test comes back either positive or negative.'

'And do you think that the results will show the same allergen?' Gram asked him. 'For both Marilyn and Roberta?'

'How could it be the same allergen?' Morris interjected. 'What are the odds of that happening? If Marilyn and Roberta had both become ill in the same place, then I would say that it's a good possibility. There could be a hidden trigger at the spot, such as a nest of hornets unnoticed by the maintenance staff or some inadvertent kitchen contamination from the caterers. But two women, in two different locations, on two different days, succumbing to the same allergen? The chances are too remote to be plausible.'

'That's the real issue, isn't it?' Dylan said, now filling his father's glass and his own. 'And that's where the answer becomes more complicated. Same allergen or not, how much coincidence in two deaths is too much? At what point do we need to look elsewhere?'

'Look elsewhere?' Morris frowned. 'Do you mean exposure elsewhere, or something other than an allergen?'

Having doled out the claret, Dylan set the bottle down on the table and seated himself in the empty chair next to Hope. Unlike Gram, who was still leaning toward him attentively, Hope leaned away from him.

'I think what Dylan means,' Gram said to Morris, 'is that the specific allergen doesn't matter nearly as much as how Marilyn and Roberta came into contact with it.'

'Yes!' Dylan nodded. 'That's it exactly.'

There was approval in his tone, and more than approval in his expression. Dylan was visibly impressed with Gram. If –

based on her age, or her cane, or her generally peaceable disposition – he had assumed that she was doddering and feeble, he now knew better. Olivia Bailey was smart, savvy, and perceptive, perhaps a bit more than his father.

Morris's frown deepened. 'I'm not sure that I agree with you. How can the identification of the responsible allergen – or in all probability, as I stated a minute ago, two discrete allergens – not be of primary importance? If we don't know what the allergens are, then we can't remove them. And if we don't remove them, then other people in the same locations may unwittingly fall victim in the same manner.'

'That's true, dear,' Gram responded gently. 'In theory, you're absolutely correct. Except you're assuming – being the kind, God-fearing man you are – that what Marilyn and Roberta encountered was either natural or inadvertent, like the hornets or the kitchen contamination you mentioned. Only what if it wasn't? What if there wasn't anything natural or inadvertent about it?'

'Not natural or inadvertent?' Morris echoed in confusion. 'But that would mean . . . That would make it . . .'

Gram reached over and patted his hand. 'I'm afraid so, dear. That would make it intentional. That would make it murder. Two murders, to be precise. As I said before, it feels like a pattern to me.'

Morris stared at her. Taking his wine, he gulped down half the glass. Then he turned his bulging gaze to his son.

'She's right,' Dylan told him. 'The pattern is clear. For me, the primary question isn't *if*, but *how*.'

'How someone managed to do it?' Gram said. 'Oh, that isn't difficult. A basic sleight of hand would work well enough. Shall I show you?'

Before Dylan could reply, there was a befuddled stammer from Morris. 'I . . . This . . . It's all very . . .'

'Yes, dear,' Gram responded in the same gentle manner that she had a minute earlier. 'At first blush, it may seem a little overwhelming. But on further reflection, you'll find that it's really quite simple.'

She reached over and patted Morris's hand again. Shifting somewhat closer to him, she then patted his shoulder. It was a friendly, reassuring, unobtrusive gesture. No one would have paid any attention to it. No one would have noticed that if there had been something concealed in Olivia Bailey's palm – a potential allergen or lethal toxin – she could have easily deposited it on Morris Henshaw's dinner plate or in his wine glass along the way.

'That was nicely done, Gram,' Hope complimented her. 'I doubt even Detective Phillips would have spotted it.'

Gram smiled. 'You see?' she said to Dylan. 'It's not difficult in the least.'

It was Dylan's turn to stare at her, although he didn't appear nearly as shocked as his father.

'No great skill or talent is required,' Gram went on. 'Anyone who has ever had a hobby employing their hands can do it. A knitter, a potter, a pianist. All it takes is a bit of deft movement.'

Dylan raised an eyebrow. 'I think it takes more than a bit of deft movement.'

'Well, some practice would probably help,' Gram admitted. 'Soften the rough edges, so to speak. Make it less sharp and sudden, thereby reducing the likelihood of getting caught. But in any event, specialized training isn't necessary – just a light touch. Take Hope, for example. She shuffles and deals cards so smoothly, so effortlessly, she could probably sprinkle poison better than a professional assassin.'

'Gram!' Hope exclaimed, and she immediately looked at Dylan to see how much fuel the remark – as well as the demonstration with Morris – would add to his already accusatory fire.

Both of Dylan's eyebrows were now raised, but to Hope's relief, there was more amusement than indictment in his expression. He didn't appear as though he was about to pick up the phone and report her and Gram to Detective Phillips. Instead, Dylan picked up the bottle of claret and refilled his father's glass, which Morris had emptied with a second stupefied gulp at the mention of poison.

'Remind me to never get on the wrong side of a Bailey,' Dylan said, lifting his own glass in Hope's direction before taking a more modest drink.

'The Baileys are as sweet as honey,' she informed him.

'From the front, maybe. From the back, you've got a wicked stinger.'

'Only if you deserve it.'

Dylan took another drink, slowly, studying her over the rim of his glass. Unflinching, Hope met his penetrating gaze. His eyes were no longer the pale blue of an ice-crusted lake. They had thawed, deepening into the turquoise of a tropical lagoon. Beneath the man's cool, composed exterior lay smoldering coals. She could see them, burning just below the surface. It was a warning to her to be careful. She didn't know what Dylan was like from the back.

There was a noise from Morris, a gurgle mixed with a few incoherent syllables. He was clearly struggling with the course of their conversation. Gram sagely moved to the more innocuous subject of the dinner before them.

'I'm sorry to say, dear, that your lovely seafood risotto seems to have turned somewhat rubbery from the delay. Should we try reheating it? Or maybe just a salad tonight, with a biscuit or two alongside? A lighter meal is always easier to digest this late in the evening, and we can reheat tomorrow instead. Hope, would you be so kind—'

'Yes, of course.'

Hope rose from her chair, salad bowl in hand. The leafy greens weren't looking the crispest anymore, either. With the passage of time, the raspberry vinaigrette had changed from an attractive pink tint to a muddy raisin brown. Knowing that Morris liked greens, Hope gave him a hearty portion. After serving Gram, she came to Dylan. Imitating his conduct with the wine, Hope didn't bother asking whether or not he also wanted salad. Instead, she unceremoniously plopped a pile on his plate. Dylan gave her a tetchy glance and might have responded with an equally tetchy word, but his father spoke first.

'I've been thinking,' Morris began. Having promptly tucked into his salad, he appeared considerably rejuvenated by the comforting crunch of cucumber and radish. 'You're going to Summer's house tomorrow – is that right, Hope?'

'That's the plan,' she answered.

Morris nodded. 'Well, I've been thinking about it, and I don't think that you should go alone.'

'She isn't going alone,' Gram reminded him. 'It will be her and Summer together – Hope explained that earlier – in case Gary shows up and decides to cause trouble.'

'It's not Gary that I'm concerned about,' Morris replied. 'If anything, Gary should be concerned about *them*.'

'You've got that right,' Dylan muttered. 'Hell hath no fury.'

Gram stabbed a recalcitrant grape tomato with her fork. Hope's lips twitched with a smile.

'I'm concerned about all of these . . .' Morris hesitated a moment. 'These peculiar things that are going on.'

'Peculiar things?' Gram asked, popping the tomato into her mouth.

'I am referring to what happened to Marilyn and Roberta, of course,' he said. 'If you and Dylan are correct, and it really was intentional – if it really is some sort of a pattern – well, then it's not safe. We don't know who might be next. We don't want the girls to become targets. They shouldn't go wandering about unaccompanied. It could be dangerous.'

'Good lord, Dad.' Dylan rolled his eyes. 'Hope and her sister are grown, independent women, not little girls in need of nannies and protection.'

Hope and Gram exchanged a look of amusement across the table.

'I'm astonished at you, Dylan. Truly, I am.' Morris shook his head sternly. 'Caring for and worrying about a person doesn't stop simply because they're no longer wearing rompers. I hope that all your highfalutin schooling and professional success hasn't turned you cold and made you forget the importance of helping others.'

This time Hope and Gram exchanged a look of surprise. Never before had Morris displayed even a modicum of disapproval toward his son. It must have surprised Dylan, too, because he was temporarily silent.

'Thank you, Morris,' Hope said. 'I really appreciate you thinking of Summer and me, but I don't see how we would become targets.'

'I have little doubt that the two ladies presently lying in the medical examiner's office assumed the exact same thing,' he responded briskly.

'You do have a point there, dear,' Gram agreed. 'And it's a point that has been bothering me for a while now. Why them? Why would somebody want to harm Marilyn and Roberta? Neither was a saint, certainly. But then none of us is. We've all committed our share of sins, one way or another, through poor choices and foolish deeds. Only I can't imagine what Marilyn and Roberta could have possibly done that was so egregious as to make somebody want to kill them. It doesn't make any sense to me.'

'It may never make any sense,' Morris told her, 'because maybe there's no sense in it. Maybe Marilyn and Roberta did nothing wrong. It could be like one of these biscuits.' He took a cheddar biscuit from the basket. 'I didn't pick *this* biscuit for a specific reason. It was just *there*. The same might apply to Marilyn and Roberta. They were simply in the wrong place at the wrong time. Two random selections, as horrible as it sounds.'

'But if it was random, then there wouldn't be the pattern,' Hope countered. 'The deaths wouldn't be so close in time or so similar in manner.'

'And the cards,' Dylan added, still somewhat subdued. 'There are also those Tarot cards.'

'Yes, the cards. The cards are troubling,' Gram mused. She turned to Hope. 'I think that Morris is right. You and Summer need to be careful where you go and what you do.'

'Oh, Gram—'

She clucked her tongue. 'Before you protest and declare me a silly old goat, consider a moment: the same card was found in both Roberta's handbag and Marilyn's pocket. How could that be due to mere chance?'

'It's highly unlikely,' Hope concurred. 'You won't get an argument from me on that. But whatever the purpose of the cards, whatever the reason for them being there, they don't have anything to do with me, or Summer, or even necessarily the boutique. As I told Detective Phillips, the cards could have been purchased anywhere. There's no special connection to us.'

'But there is a connection of some sort,' Gram said. 'With Marilyn and Roberta. I'm sure of it. If only I could remember . . .' She gave an exasperated sigh.

'Don't fret. It will come to you eventually.' It was Morris's turn to pat her hand. 'Probably when you least expect it. But in the interim, connection or not, it would make me feel much better if Hope and Summer didn't—'

Before he could finish, Dylan interjected, 'They won't go to the house alone tomorrow. I'll go with them.'

Hope's head snapped toward him. 'What? No, I don't—'

'What an excellent idea!' Morris exclaimed.

'Excellent,' Gram echoed, nodding cheerfully.

'I couldn't be more pleased.' Morris beamed at his son. 'You've set our minds at ease, Dylan. Hasn't he, Olivia?'

Gram nodded some more.

With the matter settled to their apparent satisfaction, Morris and Gram passed the biscuit basket around, returned to their salads, and began a lively discussion – mostly between themselves – about the varying quality of the produce they had seen at the farmers' market that morning.

'About tomorrow,' Hope said to Dylan in a low tone. 'You really don't need to come with us. It isn't necessary.'

'But I can't back out now,' he replied, calmly sipping his claret. 'I've made a commitment.'

She frowned at him, uncertain whether he was actually concerned about her and Summer's safety or – more likely – he was simply trying to get back into his father's good graces. A trace of a smile tugged at Dylan's lips. It was a smug smile, and it answered her question. He wasn't worried about her well-being or even Morris's favorable opinion. He was just being a pain in the neck.

ELEVEN

Summer was not pleased. She scowled at Dylan's car as it pulled up to the curb in front of the boutique. 'What is *he* doing here?'

'Don't blame me,' Hope said. 'It wasn't my idea.'

'But I thought that we were going to the house now.'

'We are going to the house now. Except Morris and Gram don't want us to go alone.'

'Why on earth not?' Summer retorted indignantly. 'It's my house, too. Not just Gary's. I have every right to be there and take my things!'

'Of course you do. It has nothing to do with Gary. They're worried about . . .'

Hope didn't finish. There was little point in a lengthy explanation. Summer was barely listening. She was too busy clutching her head in her hands.

'Oh, my head,' she moaned. 'My aching, aching head.'

'You poor dear. It's the price you pay for drinking that bottle of gin, I'm afraid.'

'I hate gin. Gin is the devil.'

'As I recall,' Hope remarked with a slight grin, 'you once said the exact same thing about tequila.'

'Tequila is also the devil.'

The grin grew. 'And then there was that time with the vodka . . .'

In spite of her suffering, Summer burst out laughing. 'The vodka was Megan's fault! She had that tour group from Poland staying at the hotel, and they were stuck inside all weekend because of the heavy rains. At Megan's insistence, I—' The memory and the laughter were cut short by another moan. 'Oh, merciful heaven. Make it stop. No noise. No laughter. My head can't take it. It feels like a herd of elephants is stomping on my skull.'

'Here,' Dylan said. 'Try these.'

Turning in surprise, Hope found him out of his car and standing on the sidewalk next to them. In Dylan's hands were a coffee cup, a bakery box, and a small paper bag.

'Try these,' he repeated, holding the items out to Summer. 'They should help.'

Summer squinted at them – and him – dubiously.

'Double shot of espresso. Double order of cheese Danish. Double bottle of aspirin,' he told her.

The squint dissolved into a look of gratitude. Summer took the proffered gifts and immediately swallowed two aspirin with a large swig of coffee. 'You're an angel,' she sighed to Dylan.

He responded with an amused snort. 'I don't think anyone has ever called me that before. Better than being called the devil with the liquor, I suppose.'

'No more mention of liquor,' Summer protested, grimacing and gesturing toward her queasy stomach.

'Fair enough,' he said.

Queasy stomach notwithstanding, Summer wasted no time opening the bakery box and digging into its contents. 'Cheese Danish are one of my favorites. How did you know?' she asked him.

'I didn't. It was a semi-educated guess. Last night at dinner somebody mentioned that you like cheesy foods, so I figured that it probably extended to breakfast, too.'

Summer's mouth was too full to do anything other than nod enthusiastically.

Dylan turned to Hope. 'There's an extra Danish in the box for you.'

'Thank you, but I'll pass.'

'Not a fan of cheese or not a fan of breakfast?'

Hope was tempted to reply that she couldn't be won over with baked treats quite as easily as her sister, but instead she answered simply, 'I'm not hungry.'

Dylan gave her a scrutinizing look. In the early-morning sunshine, his eyes were so light that they were almost translucent. 'The pastries haven't been poisoned, if that's what you're worried about.'

Summer choked. 'Huh? What?'

'Don't listen to him,' Hope said. 'The Danish is fine.'

Summer stared at the remnant of pastry in her hand.

'The Danish is fine,' Hope reiterated. 'He's only joking.' She frowned at Dylan. 'Although considering the circumstances, it isn't a very funny joke.'

He shrugged. 'Better to laugh than to cry.'

'Amen to that,' Summer agreed, finishing off her first Danish and promptly plowing into her second. 'I'm done crying over Gary.'

Hope was not done frowning at Dylan.

'You can stop glowering at me like that,' he said. 'I'm not poison, either.'

'Hmm,' Hope remarked skeptically.

The therapeutic combination of caffeine, sugar, and pain-killers must have started to take effect, because in a cheerful tone between bites of cheese filling, Summer said to Dylan, 'You shouldn't take it personally when Hope doesn't eat. It isn't you or the selection of food. She almost never eats anymore.'

Hope's frown shifted to her sister. 'That's really not helpful, Summer.'

'But it's true,' she countered. 'He might as well be told.'

'Hmm,' Hope commented again, no less skeptical than before.

'Since he doesn't appear to be leaving Asheville any time soon . . .' For confirmation, Summer turned to Dylan. 'You're planning on staying around here for a while longer, aren't you?'

'I am,' he answered.

She turned back to Hope. 'So there's no point in holding grudges or keeping secrets. We should try to get along as best as we can.'

As she said it, Summer licked the last of the pastry crumbs from her fingers. Hope couldn't help being amused at how quickly her sister had changed her tune. One minute she was scowling at Dylan in his car, and the next minute – after enjoying his *angelic* provisions – she was declaring the importance of their all being chummy. Apparently, the incident with Betsy Hughes's tincture was temporarily forgotten in light of the tasty cheese Danish.

'I believe, my dear Summer,' Hope drawled, 'that you might be a little too easily influenced by espresso and baked goods.'

'I believe you're right, my dear Hope,' Summer acknowledged. 'In my defense, however, during the whole course of our marriage, Gary never once brought me a box of fresh pastries – and I was sleeping with him.'

That made Hope laugh. 'Then you really are too easily bribed.'

'And you have become far too cynical and guarded for your own good. It's understandable, of course,' Summer added hastily, apologetically, 'with . . . with what happened in . . . in February.'

The sentence ended awkwardly, and an even more awkward silence followed. Her laughter gone, Hope's eyes were on the sidewalk. Summer fiddled with the lid of her coffee cup. Dylan looked back and forth between the two, waiting for some explanation. None came.

'What happened in February?' he asked after a minute.

This time Summer didn't risk her sister's ire by volunteering any additional information. Instead, she gave Hope a smacking kiss on the cheek and, in an evident effort to change the subject, headed toward Dylan's car.

'No worries,' she called over her shoulder to Dylan. 'My stomach is feeling much better now. Your upholstery should be safe from any motion sickness mishaps.'

'I'm glad to hear it,' he replied. 'Although, to be honest, I wasn't too concerned. It's a rental.'

Summer opened the back passenger-side door of the car, and as she slid on to the glossy, full-grain leather, whistled in admiration. 'Fancy rental. Must cost a pretty penny.'

'It does.' Dylan opened the front passenger-side door for Hope, who climbed in without meeting his gaze. 'I've been thinking of switching to a lease instead.'

'Then you must be planning on staying around here for a considerable while longer,' Summer said, referencing their earlier exchange. 'If that's the case, and you intend on treating more of your dad's patients, it would be lovely if you didn't overprescribe them quite so many medications. As much as I enjoy seeing my clients, I greatly prefer to see them healthy and happy, not sicker *after* a visit to the doctor than before.'

Hope struggled to repress a grin. Apparently, the goodwill purchased by a pair of cheese Danish had a short lifespan.

'If your supposed clients were so healthy and happy,' Dylan responded tersely, 'they wouldn't need to visit a doctor in the first place.'

Summer's mouth opened to argue, but either she couldn't think of a sufficiently snappy rejoinder or the after-effects of the gin had succeeded in outmuscling the influx of sugar and caffeine, because a moment later her head flopped back on the leather, and her eyes closed.

Without further ado – or conversation – Dylan settled himself into the driver's seat and started the engine. As they pulled away from the curb, Hope pondered briefly whether she should offer to provide directions, but then she saw that Summer's address was already programmed into the car's navigation system – courtesy of Morris, in all likelihood.

Summer and Gary's house was located in one of the newer suburbs. It wasn't an especially long or complicated drive from downtown Asheville. During the weekday rush hours, there were the inevitable slowdowns caused by too many vehicles squeezing into too few lanes, but on Sunday morning, the traffic was light.

At length, Dylan broke the silence in the car. 'So are you going to tell me about February?'

'No,' Hope snapped.

The sharpness of her reply startled her almost as much as it did him. She hadn't intended to be so curt, but it was not a topic that she was eager to discuss, especially not with Dylan, while Summer was sleeping in the back seat, on the way to shifty Gary's.

Her reticence was of little deterrence apparently, because Dylan continued, 'It isn't some sort of a diet, is it?'

'No,' she answered again, this time with annoyance.

'Good. I don't like women who are constantly dieting.'

'What a coincidence. I don't like men who are constantly judging.'

'It's not a judgment,' Dylan said. 'It's the simple truth. There isn't much pleasure in being with a person on a perpetual diet. You want to try out a great new restaurant that has an acclaimed chef, and instead of enjoying all the menu has to offer, you're sitting with someone who will only indulge so far as to squeeze half a lemon over a single stalk of asparagus.'

Hope wondered if *someone* was meant generally or referred to a specific ex from his past. 'I thought doctors were supposed to encourage people to eat a healthful diet focused on fruits and veggies.'

'Healthful, yes. Fad or starvation, no. Malnourishment isn't sexy.'

'So the best way into your bed is through a bottle of multivitamins?'

'You want to find out?'

He purred the words, the proposition unmistakable. Perhaps she should have been offended, but Hope found herself smiling instead.

'You are a smooth operator, Dylan Henshaw. I have to give you credit where credit is due. Sunday morning, not a drop of alcohol or a scented candle in sight, and you still managed to make that sound remarkably sensual. You must have every unattached female – and probably a good number of the married ones, too – wrapped around your little finger at that hospital of yours in California.'

'I'm not interested in them,' he responded in the same purring tone. 'How am I doing with you?'

Hope's pulse quickened, and she felt her face flush. It lasted only for a moment, but it was long enough to surprise – and disconcert – her. The man really was smooth. Too smooth for comfort. She didn't know whether he could see the pink in her cheeks, but she was saved from having to worry that her voice would quaver and betray her by the navigation system, which fortuitously announced that they were arriving at their destination on the left.

Handling the car with the same degree of confidence as he had handled the conversation, Dylan pulled into Summer's driveway.

'Why are we stopping?' Summer asked, yawning and stretching in the back seat. 'What's going on?'

'Rise and shine,' Dylan told her. 'We're here.'

'Here?' Summer looked out of the car window and saw her house in front of them. 'Wow. That was fast.'

Hope wasted no time in opening the car door and climbing out, eager for a breath of fresh air. Dylan followed suit.

'It's nice enough,' he remarked, taking a sip of his own coffee as he stood on the driveway and admired the house's façade. 'Well designed, and attractive color on the brick. But if I'm being honest, it's too cookie-cutter subdivision for my taste. I like older houses with history and character.'

'In my experience, *history* and *character* equal never-ending leaks, drafts, and expensive repairs,' Hope said.

'You mean your brownstone, I presume? That's exactly the kind of place I'm talking about. It's a great old building. Got real substance to it. I didn't have a chance to view much of the interior that one time I was inside . . .'

Probably because you were too busy accusing Summer and me of trying to kill little old ladies, Hope thought wryly.

'But from what I did see, it appeared to have some outstanding architectural details. The woodwork looked exceptional.'

'Exceptional and rotting,' she replied. 'You don't get hundred-year-old woodwork that's not rotting somewhere.'

'Are all three floors livable?' Dylan asked her.

Hope nodded. 'The third floor can get awfully hot in summer, though, so it isn't the best choice for bedrooms and sleeping. We use it mostly for storage these days, and that has the added benefit of letting us avoid going all the way to the attic.'

'You don't like the attic? Too many ghosts up there giving you trouble?'

Her nose twitched. He clearly said it in jest and had no idea how right he actually was. 'The rickety stairs have also been a problem. Gram slipped on them last year and came close to breaking her good hip. Your dad was so upset about it that he wanted her to shut off the attic permanently, which she refused to do.'

'Why?'

'The ghosts, of course. They wouldn't like to be sealed in.'

'But can't they just wander through the walls or slip through floorboards?'

'Some can, and some can't,' she answered. 'It depends on the ghost.'

A crease had formed in Dylan's brow. The natural assumption was that she was joking as well, but Hope could tell that he wasn't entirely sure. Her nose twitched again.

'Gary had been promising to get one of his construction buddies to look at the stairs and see what could be done without commencing a major remodeling project,' she said, 'but I think it's a safe bet that won't be happening now. Speaking of which, where is Summer? Did she go into the house?'

Turning to look for her, they found Summer where they had left her: still in the back seat of Dylan's car.

'Are you coming?' Hope called to her.

Summer shook her head.

Hope walked back to the car and opened Summer's door. 'It's time to get moving, sleepyhead. You can nap later.'

She shook her head again, anxiety visible in her hazel eyes.

'If you're worried that he's here, he's not,' Dylan told her. 'Not unless he's gotten rid of his car. I can see through the window that the garage is empty.'

'It's not Gary,' Summer said. 'It's them.'

'Them?'

The hazel eyes moved from side to side, in the direction of one neighboring house and then the other. Hope followed her sister's gaze.

'Whoa! I see what you mean,' Hope said. 'They are lurking.'

'Who is?' Dylan asked.

'The neighbors. Take a look; just don't make it too obvious.'

As though he was inspecting the tires or checking for nicks in the paint, Dylan circled once around his car, surreptitiously surveying the surrounding houses. In every direction a neighbor had suddenly emerged to engage in some ostensibly necessary activity. To the right a man retrieved the newspaper from his front lawn. To the left a woman watered the pansies in her window box. Across the street a couple adjusted the furniture on their front porch. Next door a woman brushed off her stoop. They all moved at tortoise speed, with one extraordinarily slow step after another, while at the same time keeping their gazes fixed on Summer's house and the current occupants of the driveway. Not one neighbor smiled, or waved, or called out a greeting. They just lurked and stared.

'Damn, that's creepy,' Dylan said. 'It's like one of those black-and-white sci-fi films from the 1950s. Pod people or invaders from Mars.'

Hope grinned. She turned to Summer. 'So what if they're watching? Let them goggle and gossip.'

'But they'll speculate as to who left whom and why. They'll post all sorts of stuff about it. I'm sure they will!'

'Since when do you care about that?' Hope rejoined. 'I heard you and Gram just the other day wishing a pox on anybody who had ever shared a photo of their pet dressed in a costume.'

Dylan chuckled. 'I take it, then, that the Baileys aren't great fans of social media?'

Hope shrugged. 'It's fine. It has its purpose, more or less. But when you grow up in a mystic shop like we did, you learn pretty fast that the spirit world doesn't put much stock in the internet.'

'I'll keep that in mind – and keep my Halloween baby animal snapshots to myself.'

It was Hope's turn to chuckle. 'Thank you. That would be much appreciated.'

'Come on,' Dylan said encouragingly to Summer. 'Ignore the creepy pod people. Your marriage isn't any of their business, and if they get too obnoxious, tell them that. I know you can. You told me to mind my own business really well the first time we met.'

That was enough to make even Summer crack a smile – and finally summon the courage to climb out of the car. No sooner had her feet touched the concrete than a shout came from across the street.

'Yoo-hoo! Hope! Summer!'

TWELVE

'Yoo-hoo! Hope! Summer!'

Turning toward the voice, they found Rosemarie Potter – along with pug Percy – standing on the opposite sidewalk, waving at them excitedly.

'Yoo-hoo!' Rosemarie called again, with Percy adding a salutatory bark.

Summer groaned. 'Oh, no. Not Rosemarie. I can't handle her divorce stories. I just can't. Not today.'

'Run,' Hope said.

'Huh?'

'You can't hide in the car, and we can't drive off now that she's seen us. The only other option is the house,' Hope explained. 'Run, and I'll hold her at bay.'

The groan became a sigh of relief. With a grateful glance at her sister, Summer spun on her heel and raced up the driveway, hastily disappearing between her house and the detached garage.

Her escape didn't come a moment too soon. By the time Hope looked back around, Rosemarie had already crossed the street, jogging as fast as her strappy gold sandals would allow. She arrived at Dylan's car huffing and puffing. Percy, who didn't appear any more accustomed to strenuous activity than his owner, was panting and wheezing, as well.

'I . . . I didn't' – Rosemarie gasped for air – 'I didn't expect to . . . to . . . see you here, Hope.'

Rosemarie was wearing one of her usual billowy flowered dresses. Today's pattern was scarlet hibiscus. It was a bold choice, particularly together with her blazing scarlet hair. In the bright sunshine, the combination was bordering on blinding.

'What a . . . what a lovely surprise,' Rosemarie continued. 'Isn't it, Percy?'

Percy agreed with a little woof, wiggling his rump enthusiastically.

'Sorry, sweetheart.' Hope shook her head at him. 'We aren't at the boutique, so I don't have any of your cookies.'

He may not have understood the words, but he certainly comprehended the end result: no treat. With a sulky snort, Percy plopped himself down on the driveway.

'Don't be an old grouch,' Rosemarie chided him, having at last caught her breath. 'It's much too nice a day. Such a beautiful morning,' she said to Hope. 'Perfect for a stroll. Fresh air and exercise. We want to keep fit and look our best, don't we, Percy?'

Percy glanced up, still saw nothing resembling food, and snorted a second time.

'It's always a thrill to discover who's out and about at this hour,' Rosemarie went on. 'One never knows what new and interesting people one might meet.'

'Such as a handsome, single man who also happens to be taking a Sunday-morning stroll in search of fresh air and exercise?' Hope remarked with a smile.

'If the fates should be so kind,' Rosemarie answered cheerfully. 'I can't meet someone worthwhile sitting on my sofa in my pajamas. I've got to get out there. And I *know* that I'll meet him sooner or later – you told me so.' She held up her palm to remind Hope of the reading that she had most recently given her.

'You can predict when people are going to meet?' Dylan said.

Hope looked at him. Up until that point, Dylan had been leaning against the side of his car, quietly observing the proceedings. There was no discernible laughter in his voice, but there was a distinctly amused glimmer in his eye.

'Of course she can,' Rosemarie responded, nodding earnestly. 'If it's there, Hope can read it. In your hand and in the cards.'

'Rosemarie—' Hope started to object.

'Except she's not reading the Tarot these days,' Rosemarie amended.

'Why is that?' Dylan inquired.

'Well, because of February and—'

'Rosemarie!' Hope exclaimed.

Scarlet spots matching her hair and dress appeared in

Rosemarie's cheeks. 'Oh, gosh. I've overstepped, haven't I? Me and my big mouth. My first husband always said that I reminded him of a largemouth bass. He always reminded me of a dyspeptic hippopotamus, so I guess that makes us sort of even. My second husband was more like a walrus. He had whiskers and a long, curling mustache. You remember him, don't you, Hope? He came to the boutique with me a couple of times.'

Not waiting for Hope's reply, Rosemarie prattled on, 'I've decided that I don't like such hairy men. I hope that my next husband will be bald. A buzz cut would be OK, too. At a minimum, he must be clean-shaven. Like you,' she said to Dylan.

Dylan smiled at her.

His smile evidently had the same effect on Rosemarie as his chiseled jaw did when they were last together at the boutique, because she gave a girlish giggle, and her entire face turned scarlet.

'Oh, gosh. I–I suppose a super-short cut isn't necessary, after all,' Rosemarie told him. 'Your hair isn't really short, but it's *very* nice.'

Dylan's smile grew. 'Thank you.'

Hope could see that he was holding back heavy laughter, but Rosemarie didn't seem to notice or mind; she just giggled and flushed some more. Hope started to laugh herself at how easily Rosemarie had fallen under Dylan's spell, but then she realized that it offered her an opportunity to make a quick exit.

'Well, the two of you seem to have plenty to talk about—' Hope began.

'Don't tell me that you're jealous?' Dylan interjected.

She raised an eyebrow at him. 'I want to check on Summer and make sure that she's not—'

This time Rosemarie cut her off. 'Yes, where is Summer? Wasn't she here just a minute ago? I could have sworn that I saw her from across the street.' She leaned down and searched around, as though Summer might be camouflaged between the clumps of iris or concealed behind the birdbath.

'Summer went inside. The neighbors were getting a little too . . .' Hope hesitated, trying to find the right word and not insult Rosemarie in the process.

Straightening back up, Rosemarie looked at the surrounding houses – and found all of their owners still standing outside, staring back at her. 'How rude!' she declared indignantly.

'Annoying, aren't they?' Hope agreed.

'I have little patience for such nosy nellies. They're like pushy seagulls at the beach, just waiting for your potato-chip crumbs and leftover hot-dog buns.' Rushing forward several paces, Rosemarie waved her arms and clapped her hands at the onlookers. 'Shoo! Shoo!'

No longer able to contain himself, Dylan burst out laughing. Hope grinned. Rosemarie looked like an irascible seagull herself, squawking and flapping its wings.

'Shoo now!' Rosemarie waved her arms and clapped some more. 'Get, get!'

Having shown no emotion before, the neighbors now seemed to universally cringe, although it was difficult to say whether they were more embarrassed for themselves or for Rosemarie. In any case, one by one they turned, and in the same extraordinarily slow manner in which they had emerged, they all went back to their homes.

Rosemarie gave an exultant nod. 'That's the only way to get rid of pesky folks. Same as squashing ants at a picnic.'

Dylan laughed harder.

'Nicely done,' Hope complimented Rosemarie. 'They will still be staring, but at least now they'll have to do it from indoors, through the windows.'

'And they won't be able to listen to our conversation – or at least not quite so easily,' Rosemarie said. 'Which reminds me, while we're on the subject, Percy and I overheard something interesting yesterday. Didn't we, Percy?'

Percy, who had raised his head at all the noise and commotion, offered a congenial grunt before returning to his snooze on the sun-warmed driveway.

'It was a lovely afternoon,' Rosemarie told Hope. 'Percy and I went to the park for a Saturday stroll . . .'

Hope was tempted to ask teasingly whether the Saturday-afternoon stroll had been any more fruitful in regard to meeting a prospective third husband than the Sunday-morning stroll, but she restrained herself.

'Percy and I were in the corner by the big fountain, and who do you think we saw there?'

Having no clue, Hope shook her head.

'Sylvia Norquist!' Rosemarie declared. 'And you'll never guess who she was talking about . . .'

'Probably Kirsten Willport and her divine skin,' Dylan remarked drolly.

Hope looked at him with a mixture of surprise and amusement. 'You have a good memory.'

'I tend to remember what people say while standing over a dead body,' he replied.

Rosemarie's eyes stretched wide. 'A dead body?'

'You were telling us about Sylvia?' Hope said, deflecting as quickly as she could. Although Marilyn and Roberta's deaths were certainly no secret, Hope had little interest in commencing a discussion of all the morbid details with Rosemarie in the middle of Summer's driveway. As much as she liked Rosemarie, it was also no secret that Rosemarie had loose lips. Hope wasn't eager to have half the city learn that Gram had been present at one death and she had very nearly been present at the other.

'Well, um . . .' Rosemarie hesitated, either wanting to return to the subject of the dead body or momentarily forgetting her story regarding Sylvia Norquist.

'You saw Sylvia in the park?' Hope prompted her.

'Yes! Percy and I were heading toward the fountain, and Sylvia was on one of the benches along the path. There was a man sitting next to her.'

'A man?' Hope asked, somewhat absently. Her gaze and thoughts had drifted to Summer's house as she wondered how her sister was holding up.

'That's part of what makes it so interesting,' Rosemarie answered excitedly. 'He wasn't Sylvia's type at all.'

'Oh?'

'You know how much care Sylvia puts into her appearance. She's always trim and tidy with her sweater sets and pearls. And this man was the exact opposite. Shaggy hair, flabby belly, sloppy shirt and shorts.'

'Oh?' Hope said again, still only half listening. 'Maybe the two weren't together. Maybe they were just sharing a bench.'

'But they were talking,' Rosemarie countered, 'about Olivia!'

That immediately drew Hope's full attention. 'They were talking about Gram? What about Gram?'

Taking a step toward her, Rosemarie lowered her voice slightly, as though the matter was hush-hush. 'Sylvia said that if anybody had the paper, it would be Olivia.'

'Paper? What paper?'

Rosemarie shrugged.

'Not a newspaper, right?' Dylan asked her. 'You mean some sort of a document?'

Rosemarie shrugged again. 'I don't know. All I heard was *paper.*'

Dylan gave her a skeptical look. 'You didn't hear anything else?'

'No. That was it. Well,' Rosemarie amended after a moment, 'there was some mention of the boutique, but that's to be expected. We're all always going to Hope and Summer's boutique.'

'Not Sylvia,' Hope remarked, more to herself than to the others. Sylvia rarely came to the boutique. Hope couldn't remember the last time she had been there. When Gram and Sylvia saw each other, it was usually at some place like the community center, not the boutique. But even with the mention of the boutique, Hope didn't find Rosemarie's report especially interesting. She didn't know who the man on the bench was or what paper Sylvia might be referring to. It could be anything from a lost bingo card to an updated menu for the next spaghetti supper. At this point, Hope had bigger concerns.

'I really should check on Summer,' she said, 'so if you'll excuse me . . .'

Not waiting for a response, Hope turned and walked swiftly up the driveway. Just before she reached the garage, she glanced back to see whether Rosemarie and Dylan were following her. To her relief, they weren't. It was hard enough already for Summer to be at the house, collecting bits of her life and marriage, without also having to force a brave face in front of other people. Thankfully, though, Rosemarie and Dylan remained on the sidewalk. Rosemarie had moved closer to Dylan and was touching his arm while talking rapidly. Hope couldn't hear what she was saying, but knowing Rosemarie, it was a tale of epic proportions, probably in relation to one of her ex-husbands. *Poor Dylan*, Hope thought. If he didn't come up with his own excuse for a departure soon, he was going to get stuck listening to Rosemarie for a long time.

Passing between the house and the garage, Hope emerged into Summer and Gary's rectangular, fenced backyard. Even if she hadn't known about their relationship troubles, one look at the garden would have told her that Summer wasn't happy. Just as she lovingly tended the boutique's flowers and herbs, Summer usually took great care with her own plantings at home. But not this year. There had been no spring cleaning of the beds. Dead annuals were matted down with decaying leaves. A few feisty perennials were trying to sprout from beneath last fall's faded foliage, with little success. It was a sad sight, as though the couple's withered borders were somehow a metaphor for their withered marriage.

The screen door on the back porch was ajar. Assuming that was where she would find Summer, Hope headed inside. The interior of the house was dim and dusky. Brilliant bands of sunlight were streaming through the windows, but the rays couldn't seem to pierce the shadows. A gloom had settled down, spreading over the rooms like a melancholy blanket. The contrast was so stark that it stopped Hope in her tracks. In the past, Summer's house had always been such a bright, cheerful place, filled with so much joy and laughter, so many hopes and dreams – and now, suddenly, they were all gone.

'Hello? Summer?' Hope said.

There was no answer.

'Summer?' she called again, louder this time. 'It's just me. I'm alone. Rosemarie and Dylan stayed in the yard, so it's safe to come out.'

Still no answer. Hope listened for the sound of footsteps upstairs or the telltale creak of a closet door, but there was nothing. Only silence in the gloom.

'You're starting to worry me, Summer. Please make a noise and let me know that you're all right.'

At last, a sniffle came in reply. It sounded close by.

'Are you down here? In the kitchen?'

Another sniffle. Hope hurried to the kitchen. It was empty. Maybe the living room? Turning the corner, she found her sister in the foyer.

'There you are!' Hope exclaimed with relief. 'What are you doing on the floor?'

Summer was sitting on the braided entry rug, next to the closed front door. The door had a brass mail slot, and she was surrounded by a pile of catalogs, envelopes, and assorted advertising flyers. Apparently, Gary hadn't been home to collect the mail for the last several days. In Summer's hand was a promotional postcard.

'Did a store send a good coupon?' Hope asked, trying to lighten the dour mood. 'We could go shopping later, if you want.'

For a long moment, Summer didn't respond. She just stared at the postcard, as though studying its terms in fine print. Finally, she turned it toward her sister, and Hope saw that she was wrong. It wasn't a postcard at all. It was a Tarot card, the same as Marilyn and Roberta's. A third Fool.

THIRTEEN

'If the neighbors thought it was interesting before, now they'll really have something to get excited about,' Hope observed drolly. She was standing by the window in Summer's kitchen, watching the two uniformed police officers as they circled around the outside of the house, searching the perimeter for anything suspicious.

Summer, who was sitting on one of the bar stools at the kitchen island, sank her face into her hands. 'Oh, lord, the neighbors. I forgot all about them.'

'The neighbors?' Detective Phillips looked up from the stack of Summer and Gary's mail that he had been thumbing through, checking that there were no other items of concern in the pile. 'Have you previously had trouble with them? A disagreement or grudge, perhaps? Some incident that might have escalated . . .?'

'No, no. There hasn't been anything like that,' Summer answered. 'The neighbors are harmless.'

The detective's brow furrowed. 'Then what's the problem?'

'There is one part of the neighbors that's dangerous,' Hope explained. 'Their tongues.'

He nodded, understanding now. 'And a bunch of cops pulling up to the door and wandering about are going to set those tongues wagging?'

'Mercilessly,' Hope said.

Her face still in her hands, Summer grumbled, 'It's already bad because of Gary.'

The furrow in the detective's brow resurfaced. 'Has your husband been causing difficulties? Has he had run-ins with the neighbors?'

The tips of Summer's ears turned pink.

'Difficulties, yes. But not with the neighbors,' Hope told him. She added in a discreet tone, 'Summer and her husband have separated.'

Summer's ears promptly went crimson. Detective Phillips's cheeks had a slightly rosy hue, too. His reaction to the news brought a smile to Hope's lips. *Thank goodness for small favors*, she thought. If she and Summer were going to have repeated dealings with the police, then it couldn't hurt that the detective in charge of the matter had some warm feelings toward her sister.

There was a brief pause, then Detective Phillips seemed to recollect himself. 'Well, there isn't anything to worry about in here,' he determined, setting the mail down on the counter.

'That's one relief, at least,' Hope said.

'A relief,' Summer agreed, 'but embarrassing. Terribly embarrassing. I overreacted. I saw the Tarot card with the mail, and I jumped to the most dreadful conclusions: *I was next. I was about to die. The same thing was going to happen to me that happened to Marilyn and Roberta.* It was silly. Ridiculously silly. I realize that now, of course. And I'm mortified. I frightened Hope. I wasted police time and resources—'

As she spoke, Summer lifted her head. Her peachy skin was flushed. Her eyes were soft and her lashes damp. She looked exceedingly pretty and vulnerable and in need of protection. Detective Phillips didn't disappoint.

'You didn't overreact in the slightest,' he told her, moving from the counter to the island. 'And you didn't waste police time. You were absolutely right to call me. In fact, you would have been wrong *not* to call me. This is a serious matter. There is nothing whatsoever for you to feel silly about.'

He concluded by putting a sturdy, comforting hand on Summer's arm, like a watchful shepherd guarding a defenseless little lamb. Hope's smile grew. Although her appearance at that moment suggested otherwise, there was nothing helpless or feeble about Summer. Olivia Bailey had not raised her granddaughters to fear howling wolves.

'You're very kind to say so, Detective,' Summer began, 'but—'

'Nate,' he corrected her. 'I asked you before to call me Nate.'

'You're very kind to say so, *Nate*,' Summer amended, 'but it doesn't make me feel any less foolish.' She laughed lightly. 'Maybe the card applies to me, after all. Maybe I am the Fool.'

'Now you really are being silly,' Hope said.

'I was a fool to ever trust Gary,' Summer rejoined.

'That may be true, but you know perfectly well that the Fool in the Tarot isn't an actual fool.'

'I do know. But fool or not' – Summer sighed – 'I can't help cringing at how gullible I was to believe so many of Gary's lies – and for so long.'

Hope sighed with her in sympathy. She also noted that Nate's hand remained on Summer's arm.

'The Fool isn't a fool?' Nate said, perplexed. 'How can that be?'

'Don't you remember what Hope told you at the boutique?' There was a touch of impatience in Summer's voice. 'The cards are representational, not literal.'

'I remember, but it's titled . . .' He held up the card at issue, now protected in a clear plastic evidence bag. '*The Fool.*'

'Do you also remember some of the other cards belonging to the Major Arcana that I showed you?' Hope asked him, more patiently than her sister. She was used to the many questions and confusion that the cryptic nature of the Tarot engendered. Summer's herbs were much easier to explain.

'Yes. The Devil. And the Lovers,' Nate added with enthusiasm.

Hope swallowed a chuckle. There was nothing cryptic about the direction of his thoughts. 'Those are two excellent examples of how the title and the picture on the card can belie its true meaning,' she said. 'The Devil doesn't mean that an evil horned guy with talons is coming to get you. And the Lovers doesn't mean—'

'Sex,' Summer finished for her. 'The Lovers doesn't mean sex.'

'Well, it can include sex,' Hope clarified, 'but usually in a broader context, not a specific, one-off event.'

'That's good to know,' Dylan said.

They all jumped at the unexpected interruption. None of them had noticed Dylan enter the house, and from the casual way that he was leaning against the frame of the screen door leading to the back porch, it appeared that he had been inside for some time.

'Stealthy,' Summer observed.

Dylan looked at her. 'From your tone, I'm not sure whether I should take that as a compliment.'

'It depends,' she answered.

'On?'

'On whether you came in quietly like a cat or crept in like a rat.'

'I am sure that being compared to vermin isn't a compliment,' Dylan said.

'Then don't creep,' Summer told him. 'Hope and I aren't fond of surprises.'

'I'm learning that,' he replied.

If he was offended by Summer's remarks, he didn't show it. Perhaps he was also learning that Summer's mood could be somewhat unpredictable. Dylan turned toward Hope.

'Going back to what you were saying before, if the Lovers card shows up during a reading in the afternoon,' he asked her, 'I shouldn't assume I'll get lucky that evening?'

Hope raised an amused eyebrow. 'It depends,' she answered, echoing her sister from a minute earlier.

'On?'

'On who you're trying to get lucky with.'

Dylan grinned. 'Is that so?'

'Of course,' she said. 'The Lovers are always intertwined. You have to look at the rest of the cards in the reading. Just as no man is an island, no card in the Tarot stands alone. But I think that you're asking the wrong question.'

'Am I? Then what's the right question?'

It was Hope's turn to smile. 'If you get lucky in the evening, will you regret it the next morning?'

'Or will the woman?' Summer interjected wistfully.

'Never,' Dylan said.

It wasn't clear whose regret he was referring to, but for Hope's part, as she met Dylan's compelling blue eyes, there was a moment when she thought that she probably wouldn't regret it the next morning, either.

'True love never regrets,' Summer went on, even more wistfully than before. Suddenly, she burst out laughing. 'Listen to me. I'm starting to sound like Rosemarie when she gets sappy. All fairytales and romantic notions.'

Hope laughed with her sister, glad to have a pretext for breaking her gaze from Dylan. She had little doubt that those eyes had compelled more than a few women into his arms – and bed. 'Speaking of Rosemarie,' she said, glancing around generally, even though her question was directed at Dylan, 'where is she? She can't still be standing on the driveway?'

'She went home,' Dylan answered.

'Did she? How fortunate. Rosemarie can be difficult to get rid of. She's so . . . so . . .' Summer searched for the right word.

'So concerned with our well-being?' Hope suggested.

Summer laughed again. 'That's a polite way of putting it. I was thinking more along the lines of *overly inquisitive*, particularly when there's the possibility of a good story coming out of it.'

'Rosemarie was curious about what was happening, especially when the detective arrived' – Dylan gestured toward Nate – 'and she wanted to come inside with me, but the dog wouldn't let her.'

'He wouldn't?'

'Nope. She woke him up from his nap, after which he apparently decided that it was his lunchtime, and that meant he had no intention of going into anyone's house other than his own.' Dylan chuckled. 'Cantankerous little chap. I like him.'

'Remind me to give Percy an extra cookie when he and Rosemarie come to the boutique next week,' Hope said to Summer. 'In gratitude.'

She nodded and turned toward Dylan. 'You should be grateful to Percy, too. Otherwise, you might have been trapped with Rosemarie for ages. Some of her stories – usually the marriage and divorce ones – can drag on interminably.'

'Actually,' he replied, 'the particular story that she was telling me was rather interesting. Except it wasn't about *her* Prince Charming.'

Summer groaned. 'So on top of the nosy neighbors, I've got super-chatty Rosemarie narrating my history with Gary in the front yard.'

Dylan didn't respond. Instead of looking at Summer as she spoke, he was looking intently at Hope. At first, Hope didn't understand why. Then a slow, unpleasant realization spread over her. The Prince Charming that he was referring to wasn't Gary. Rosemarie hadn't been discussing Summer's love life in the front yard. She had been discussing *Hope*'s love life. And it wasn't hard for Hope to guess which story Rosemarie had been sharing.

Her throat tightened, and the air caught in her lungs. How much had Rosemarie told him? Plenty, presumably. Maybe not every last painful detail, but they had certainly been together on the driveway long enough for Rosemarie to have given Dylan a sufficiently detailed account of the events in February.

Although she could feel Dylan continue to look at her, Hope didn't meet his gaze. Her eyes were on the door to the porch. She needed to leave, to get out of the house and find a way to breathe. She couldn't deal with February. Avoidance had kept her afloat these past few months, and she didn't want to sink now.

Either Nate was also hoping to avoid further discussion of some subject – namely, Summer's husband – or he remembered why he was at her house to begin with, because he abruptly changed the topic.

'Returning to the more pertinent matter at hand,' he said, holding up the evidence bag, 'if the Fool isn't a fool, then what is he?'

Hope had never been so happy or relieved to have a conversation about the Tarot. 'Freedom,' she answered unevenly.

'Freedom?' Nate asked her.

'Yes. At its most fundamental level' – Hope's voice steadied – 'the Fool represents freedom. Freedom from all the constraints and burdens of daily life. No concern over food, or shelter, or money, or health. In that way, the Fool is free from the Minor Arcana. But he is also set apart from the rest of the Major Arcana. You'll notice' – she motioned toward the evidence bag – 'that the numeral at the top of the Fool is zero. The remaining cards in the Major Arcana are numbered one through twenty-one.'

Nate took a closer look at the card. 'Zero. Does that mean the beginning of something, or the end?'

'The beginning,' she said. 'A blank slate, with full potential. It's a new opportunity, a choice to be made, a change in direction – and the freedom, the ability, to take that next step.'

'If you have the courage to take it,' Summer chimed in.

'If you have the courage to step off a cliff, plunge to the bottom of a ravine, and shatter every bone in your body,' Dylan commented dryly.

Summer shook her head in reproach. 'You should trust more and doubt less.'

Although Dylan looked ready to offer a snappy rejoinder, Hope spoke first.

'Stepping off the cliff is precisely the point,' she told him. 'It's a leap of faith, a journey into the unknown. But the Fool isn't worried. There is no fear. He is at peace with whatever befalls him. Because the future isn't set. *That* is the secret of the card.'

Dylan's jaw twitched, but he was silent.

'The Tarot is pretty complicated,' Nate mused, still studying the card.

Hope and Summer exchanged a smile. 'Human existence is pretty complicated,' Hope replied.

'But it doesn't make any sense,' Nate countered.

'What doesn't?' Summer asked him.

'Setting aside this most recent card for a moment and focusing only on the first two cards, why choose the Fool? Why put a card representing freedom and new beginnings in the pocket and purse of your victims? Roberta King and Marilyn Smoltz are dead. Death is an end, not a beginning. There are no opportunities, or choices, or changes in direction – not earthly ones, at least. I suppose it could be argued that death is freedom from all the burdens in our lives, but isn't that taking it too far and becoming overly semantic?'

'Indeed.' Hope nodded in agreement. 'We could parse and debate the esoteric symbolism of the Tarot all day long, but it's like sliding down the rabbit hole. There is no *absolutely* correct interpretation of any card, let alone the Fool. I can give you a general meaning, but how a card appears as part of a reading, in response to a specific question, can change everything.'

'Not to mention if the card comes up reversed,' Summer pointed out.

Hope nodded again. 'That's an issue, too.'

Nate frowned. 'How can a card be reversed?'

'When it lands with the top pointing down, which then alters its meaning,' Summer said.

The frown deepened.

'A reversed card,' Hope explained, 'doesn't necessarily mean the opposite – or at least not the direct opposite – of one that's right side up, but in most cases, it's considerably more negative than positive. An upside-down Fool, for example, can indicate hesitation and indecision, missteps and misdirection.'

'Damn. This really is complicated,' Nate muttered.

'Too complicated,' Hope said. 'Which is why I'm inclined to believe that we're overanalyzing it. I don't think that whoever killed Marilyn and Roberta, and – assuming it's the same person – put the card in Summer's mail, is trying to convey quite so much. I could be wrong, of course. The cards could be intended to have multiple layers of complex meaning that we're supposed to unravel and interpret, like some sort of convoluted Tarot puzzle. But I doubt it. I'd wager that the solution is much simpler.'

'But you can't think that the cards were left for no reason at all?' Summer protested. 'They must have *some* meaning.'

'Certainly. And in my opinion, you were on the right track earlier.'

'I was?'

'Yes – when you took the card literally.'

Summer's hazel eyes widened. 'I see what you mean. We're assuming too much. The murderer might not know anything about the Tarot.'

'Well, they probably know a little,' Hope returned, 'because otherwise they wouldn't have used the cards in the first place. But they most likely looked at some silly book or website and got a faulty notion of the Tarot into their head—'

'Like when people create their own love potions and voodoo dolls,' Summer exclaimed, 'without having the slightest clue what they're doing!'

'Exactly!'

Both Dylan and Nate were staring at them, but Hope and Summer took no notice.

'OK, so the simplest – albeit wrong – interpretation of the Fool is that someone's foolish, right?' Summer said. 'Which means the murderer believes that Marilyn and Roberta were foolish somehow, and that I'm foolish, too, presumably.'

'That was my initial thought also,' Hope agreed, 'but then another possibility occurred to me. What if we've made a second wrong assumption? What if the card wasn't meant for you? It wasn't addressed. It was just pushed through the mail slot. Maybe the card was actually intended for Gary. Maybe it means that Gary is the foolish one.'

'A fool and his money are soon parted in a divorce,' Dylan remarked wryly.

Summer grinned. 'Too bad Gary doesn't have any money to be parted from—' She let out a horrified gasp. 'Good God! What if Gary is dead?'

FOURTEEN

The idea that there might have been a third murder, that Gary might be lying dead somewhere, took them all with such surprise that there was a long moment of stunned silence. Then they burst into action. Summer began racing through the house, frantically searching one room after another. Nate shouted to the police officers outside to inspect the garage and the garden shed. And Hope dashed down the steps to check the basement. The only one who didn't move was Dylan, who calmly and astutely reminded them – when he finally managed to get their collective attention – that the previous two Tarot cards had been found *with* the victims, therefore making it unlikely that Gary had suffered the same grievous fate as Marilyn and Roberta.

Summer's relief was short-lived. She promptly switched from panicking about finding her husband's murdered body to panicking that they wouldn't be able to keep him from being murdered. This time Hope and Nate remained calm alongside Dylan. Nate told Summer that there was no reason for her to worry. The police would contact Gary, alert him to the situation, and take all necessary steps to ensure his safety. Furthermore, just because the Tarot card might have been intended for him, it didn't automatically mean that he was the next target. As Dylan had pointed out, this situation was considerably different from that of Marilyn and Roberta, indicating a different possible plan and outcome.

It was a well-reasoned and well-intentioned speech from the detective, no doubt meant to reassure Summer. For her part, Summer listened politely, nodded once or twice, and mumbled some words of assent, but Hope could see that her sister was not the least bit comforted or convinced. The moment Nate turned away to begin making phone calls and update the officers outside, Summer moved quickly next to Hope.

'Amethyst, don't you think?' she said in a low tone.

'That's my best guess, too,' Hope agreed.

'It seems the most likely place Gary would be, considering that . . .'

Summer didn't finish the sentence. She didn't need to. Hope knew what she was thinking, because she was thinking the same thing: considering that it was Sunday morning, after Saturday night, another weekend spent in the arms of Mystique Monique.

Dylan – who had been listening with a keen ear – remarked critically, 'You're not thinking of going to the hotel to warn him?'

'Of course I am!' Summer responded, aghast. 'Just because I'm furious with Gary, and I won't believe a word that comes out of his lying mouth ever again, and I wouldn't mind getting some payback for how he's treated me and our marriage, it doesn't mean that I want to see him *dead*.'

'I wasn't suggesting that you should let him get hauled away in a body bag,' Dylan returned sharply. 'My concern is with your level of exposure in such a public place. Don't forget that we're only guessing the card was intended for Gary. It could just as easily have been intended for you.'

Forced to acknowledge the truth of what he said, Summer had no rebuttal.

'You will also be sending a message to your dear husband that you may not want to send,' Dylan told her.

Summer's brow furrowed. 'I will?'

'There's a good chance. If he doesn't know about what happened to Marilyn and Roberta, and if he doesn't know about their Tarot cards, then he won't understand your anxiety, and he might interpret it as an attempt at reconciliation.'

'That's not likely,' she argued. 'After what he did to me, Gary couldn't honestly think I would just forgive and forget.'

Dylan responded with a sardonic smile. 'Vanity will make men – and women – believe all sorts of things.'

'Gary has never been known for his humility,' Summer admitted. She chuckled ruefully. 'Instead of the Fool, someone should have given him a card depicting vanity.'

'Is there a Tarot card for vanity?' Dylan asked.

'I don't know, but I assume there must be. Vanity is a part of pride, and pride is one of the seven deadly sins, after all.'

They turned expectantly toward Hope, awaiting a definitive answer. They didn't get one. Hope was frowning at a shriveled orange in the fruit bowl.

'Hello?' Summer nudged her with her elbow to get her attention. 'Hope?'

She glanced up from the bowl. 'Huh?'

'Have you heard a word we've said?'

'Sorry. I was just . . . I was just thinking . . .' Hope paused absently.

'About Gary?' Summer prompted her.

'No.' She frowned again. 'I wasn't thinking about him. I was thinking about something you said earlier, before all the panic about Gary. You said the murderer believes that Marilyn and Roberta were foolish somehow.'

Summer nodded. 'And that I'm foolish, too – or Gary is – or whoever the card was intended for.'

'Ignoring you and Gary for the moment, my question is: how? How exactly were Marilyn and Roberta foolish?'

'I don't know. Does it matter?'

'Well, yes,' Hope said. 'It goes to possible motive. If we can figure out what Marilyn and Roberta did that was supposedly foolish, it could tell us – or at least give us a hint – who would have wanted to kill them.'

'That's a great idea!' Summer exclaimed, now nodding vigor-ously. 'And then we might also have a better idea what the third card means.'

Hope nodded back at her.

Dylan didn't share their enthusiasm. 'Don't get too excited yet. It's a nice theory, but you're making one really big assump-tion that could turn out to be wrong.'

'How so?' Hope asked him.

'You're assuming that there was some specific incident of foolishness on the part of Marilyn and Roberta. Instead, it could have been their general folly or foolhardiness that the murderer objected to.'

'Nonsense,' Summer retorted. 'People don't kill other people just because they think they're a bit silly or stupid. *Everybody* is silly or stupid sometimes, and we're not all going around murdering each other because of it.'

'Dylan is correct,' Nate said, having concluded his latest phone call and joining the conversation. 'At this point, we can't be sure whether it was a specific or general antipathy that motivated the killings.'

'General antipathy resulting in two murders? I don't buy it,' Summer scoffed, folding her arms across her chest. 'It isn't rational.'

'Trust me,' Nate replied, 'criminals – and murderers in particular – aren't always the most rational.'

Although Summer couldn't dispute his professional expertise, her arms remained folded, indicating that she wasn't persuaded. Hope wasn't persuaded, either. She responded with greater diplomacy, however.

'I have no doubt that you're right,' she said to Nate. 'You have much more knowledge on the subject than we do. But I don't think that there can be any harm in us trying to find out if there was a foolish episode in Marilyn and Roberta's pasts that could have angered or upset someone to an extreme degree. Anything we learn could help us more clearly understand the third card.'

'Certainly, it could help,' Nate agreed. 'But how do you propose to find out something like that? Foolish episodes tend to fade with the passage of time. I thought you didn't know either of the victims very well.'

'I didn't know them very well,' Hope acknowledged. 'Neither did Summer. But we do know someone who can remember nearly every foible ever committed in her vast circle of acquaintances.'

Summer started nodding vigorously once more as she realized who her sister was talking about. 'If anybody knows, it will be her!'

Nate looked between them in confusion. 'Who?'

'Gram,' they answered in unison.

The drive to the hotel bore little resemblance to the one earlier that morning to Summer's house. For starters, instead of nursing a hangover and sleeping in the back seat of Dylan's car, Summer was alert and animated, so much so that she talked in a steady stream of questions the entire way. They mostly revolved around Gary. Would he be at Amethyst? Was it safe for him to remain there? Could they rely on the police to protect him? If a warning from her might be misinterpreted as an attempt at reconciliation – as Dylan had suggested – perhaps Hope should warn him instead? Or maybe Megan could do it?

Summer didn't wait for answers. She just continued with her rambling train of thought. Hope commented only once, reminding her sister that Megan didn't work on Sundays. Otherwise, she was happy not to interrupt the ceaseless chatter. Now that the immediate alarm at the appearance of the third Fool had passed, Dylan could return to the subject of February and all that Rosemarie had told him on Summer's driveway. Hope knew that he wanted to talk about it. She could see it in the pitying way that he kept looking at her, as if she were a pathetic puppy that had gotten caught in a cold rain and was standing outside, shivering and bedraggled. It irritated her. She didn't need Dylan's pity. She wasn't whimpering at him to open the door. On the contrary, she preferred for the door to remain firmly shut.

To Hope's relief, Dylan found no opportunity to broach the subject. Summer was simply too loquacious with her ever-expanding list of worries. It wasn't until she began fretting that the police might accuse *her* of being the murderer if Gary became the next victim that Dylan finally interjected – by laughing.

'I don't know about murder, but no one can ever accuse you of not having an active imagination,' he chortled.

'It's not my imagination,' Summer rejoined indignantly. 'It's a legitimate concern. When something happens to a husband, the police always look at the wife first.'

'That may be true, but I highly doubt Detective Phillips is going to arrest you.'

'He very well could,' she countered. 'If Gary were murdered, it might be viewed as an act of revenge. My husband cheated on me, so I decided to kill him. The police could allege that I copied the previous two murders to make Gary's look like it was perpetrated by the same person. They could even contend that I put the Tarot card through my own mail slot in an attempt to throw off suspicion.'

Dylan laughed harder. 'And I would contend that you've been watching too many crime dramas.'

'I watch hardly any crime dramas,' Summer snapped.

'While we're on the subject of law enforcement,' Dylan continued in amusement, 'you may want to consider talking a little less about your husband when you're in the company of the detective.'

'So you do think that he would suspect me if something happened to Gary!'

'No, I think that you would have a better chance of Nate asking you on a date if he didn't have to hear about your husband all the time.'

That made Hope laugh. 'He has a point,' she told her sister.

For the first time since they had left her house, Summer paused to consider. 'You think that Nate might ask me on a date?'

'Well, a date might be a bit premature,' Hope conceded, 'especially since we don't know much about his personal situation, but it has been pretty obvious to me – and Megan – and Dylan also, apparently – that Nate is attracted to you.'

Summer blushed. 'Really?'

'Really.'

There was another pause as Summer leaned back in her seat, her cheeks pink and looking rather pleased.

'It's not too late to change your mind,' Dylan said to Hope after a minute. 'We're almost at the hotel, but I can take you to the boutique instead.'

She checked her watch. 'No, let's stick with the hotel. We're cutting it close time-wise, but Gram and Morris usually linger over brunch. Amethyst has an excellent Sunday brunch. Have you tried it?'

He brushed the question aside. 'If you want to talk to Olivia, you should do it somewhere less public. My concern is the same as it was before, and Nate agrees with me. You shouldn't go to the hotel. It's too exposed.'

'But I'm at the hotel all the time for client appointments and to see Megan. It isn't new or unusual for me to be there.'

Dylan shot her an impatient look. 'You're not taking this seriously enough. That third card means something, and you're gambling that it's connected to Gary rather than you and your sister.'

Hope frowned. 'I'm taking this plenty seriously. It's why I'm going to talk to Gram about Marilyn and Roberta. In my opinion, you're being paranoid.'

'And in my opinion,' he replied, pulling the car into Amethyst's cobblestone drive, 'you're being just as foolish as the Tarot card predicted.'

A tetchy response bubbled on Hope's tongue, but Summer – who had been too busy with her own deliberations to pay attention to theirs – spoke before she could.

'I've thought about it,' Summer said, opening the door of the car when it had come to a stop in front of the hotel, 'and you're right. There's no sense in running after Gary. The police will warn him. He'll probably listen to them better anyway.'

'A wise decision,' Dylan commended her. He added under his breath, 'At least one of you takes my advice.'

Hope glared at him. Following her sister, she opened the car door to climb out. Just as she was about to step on to the cobblestone, Dylan reached over and grabbed her arm.

'Wait.'

She turned back with annoyance. 'What?'

His grip remained firm, but his voice softened. 'Don't go in there, Hope. Don't be so reckless as to risk another murder.'

Her annoyance faded with the warmth of his tone. 'I appreciate your concern, but there's really no need to worry. I'll be cautious.' She offered a conciliatory smile. 'I'm pretty good at taking care of myself.'

Dylan didn't return the smile. 'Are you sure of that? Because from what I've heard, you're not so good at taking care of others. Haven't you had enough death?'

Hope looked at him hard. There was no longer any pity in his gaze. There was no warmth or concern, either. Dylan's expression was cold and contemptuous, making his meaning amply clear. He wasn't talking about Marilyn and Roberta, or even Summer and Gram. He was talking about February.

The blood drained from Hope's face. It was replaced by wrath. She yanked her arm free, jumped out of the car, and slammed the door behind her.

'Hope—' Dylan began through the open window.

Whatever he had to say, she didn't listen.

FIFTEEN

Megan met them just inside Amethyst's sparkling glass entrance, grinning waggishly. 'Was that Dylan I saw dropping you off? On a Sunday morning, no less. Getting kind of cozy, eh?'

Still fuming, Hope bristled at the inference. 'There is nothing *cozy* about Dylan Henshaw.'

'He is somewhat aloof,' Megan agreed. 'But that could be considered advantageous.'

'In what way?'

She winked. 'Icy men make fiery lovers.'

'That's great,' Hope replied dryly, 'if you enjoy hypothermia followed by third-degree burns.'

Megan burst out laughing.

Summer, who had been glancing around the hotel lobby apprehensively, gave a sigh of relief. 'Good news. There's no sign of Gary.' She glanced around again. 'What happened to Dylan? Is he parking the car?'

'He left,' Hope told her, and before Summer could ask why, she turned back to Megan. 'So what brings you here today? I thought you didn't work on Sundays.'

'I'm not *scheduled* to work on Sundays,' Megan said, 'but evidently that doesn't apply when wedding planners are involved.'

Hope groaned. 'A bridezilla?'

'Yup. Not aggressive, but inanely indecisive. The woman can't make up her mind about anything. The flowers, the color scheme, even the candles. First roses, then lilies, now tulips. Blossom pink, then carriage green, now spring coral—'

'What is spring coral?' Summer asked.

'An extremely unflattering shade of orange. Imagine cantaloupe mixed with tomato.'

'Blech.' Summer wrinkled her nose. 'Hey, I've got an idea. If the bride has such bad taste, maybe she'd like some Beach

Breeze candles. Hope and I have a whole box available at the boutique. We'd sell 'em to her cheap.'

Hope chuckled. 'I doubt that we'll be able to convince even the tackiest bride that rotting fish is the newest trend in scented candles.'

'That's probably true,' Summer conceded. 'If I get married again, forget the big wedding and fancy reception. I'm going to have the good sense to elope.'

'That's jumping ahead a bit, isn't it?' her sister responded teasingly. 'The divorce issue aside, Nate hasn't even asked you out yet.'

The hue of Summer's face was remarkably close to spring coral.

Megan's waggish grin resurfaced. 'Goodbye, shifty Gary. Hello, Detective Phillips!'

'Any interest the detective might have in me,' Summer said in a plaintive tone, 'will vanish the instant he discovers my fingerprints on the Tarot card.'

Hope rolled her eyes. 'You're beginning to sound just as paranoid as Dylan. Why do you keep assuming the police are going to accuse you of something? Did you kill Marilyn and Roberta?'

'Of course not!'

'Then don't fret about the fingerprints. Nate knows that you and I both touched the third Fool before we realized what the card might mean and that it could be evidence. He expects the lab to find our prints on it. He's hoping that the murderer's prints will be there, too, although he said it's unlikely considering that the first two Fools were completely clean, without so much as a smudge.'

'Hold on. There's been a third Fool?' Megan asked in confusion. 'Does that mean there's also been a third murder?'

'Not that we're aware of, thankfully,' Hope told her. 'But Summer found a Tarot card with the mail at her house this morning, so she's worried that Gary might be the next intended target.'

Megan shrugged with indifference. 'It's nothing more than he deserves.'

'Megan!' Summer protested.

She shrugged again. 'I'm sorry if it seems callous, but after how that man has behaved, I wouldn't care if a piano fell on his head.'

'Oh, but, Megan—'

As Summer's voice rose in remonstrance, several people in the lobby turned to look at them. For the first time since they had entered the hotel, Hope noticed how busy the place was, how many guests and visitors and employees were bustling about the purple sofas and black marble tables, and it occurred to her – much to her chagrin – that maybe Dylan wasn't being paranoid, after all. On the contrary, maybe he was correct. Not about her being reckless by going to the hotel, but about how public and exposed it was, especially in the lobby. Anyone could see them. They had been speaking quietly for the most part; even so, if somebody was trying to listen in, it wouldn't be difficult to catch snippets of their conversation.

'We shouldn't discuss this here,' Hope said, interrupting her sister. 'It's too open. We don't know who might be watching.'

'At Amethyst,' Megan replied, with a significant look, 'you can be assured that someone is *always* watching.'

Hope nodded. 'We're here to find Gram. She and Morris came for brunch. Have you seen them?'

'Yes, when they first came in, but that was a while ago. They're probably gone by now. You might get lucky, though, if they lingered over coffee.'

Megan led the way toward the restaurant. Unlike the lobby with its cold, gleaming design, the hotel's main dining room was decorated in a warm, muted Mediterranean style, with wooden beams and yellow stucco walls that were accented by colorful ceramic tiles. As Hope had expected, they found that brunch was nearly concluded. The hostess stand was unoccupied, as were almost all of the dining tables. The kitchen staff had begun to clear the various serving stations.

'It smells so good,' Summer said, gazing longingly at the stainless-steel trays and platters that were being carried away, many still full of food. 'I'm famished.'

'That's the one benefit of being forced to work on a Sunday,' Megan told her, also eyeing the trays with interest. 'There are always piles of leftovers from brunch. But we better hurry, because the good stuff moves fast once it hits the back room.'

Summer spun toward Hope. 'We can talk to Gram later. Let's eat now!'

Hope hesitated. 'What about bridezilla?' she asked Megan.

'Bridezilla has an entourage with her. She won't even notice that I'm gone. And when I reappear, I'll bring one of the remnant dessert trays with me. Then instead of flowers and color schemes, she can struggle to decide between a cheesecake bite and a brownie bite.'

'Yum, cheesecake.' Summer rubbed her hands together excitedly. 'Come on. No dawdling. We don't want to miss out.'

With her sister practically drooling on the restaurant floor at the prospect of her favorite dessert, Hope was about to agree – until she saw Morris. He was sitting alone at a table on the opposite side of the dining room, along a sunny wall of windows. As Megan had conjectured, he was lingering over a cup of coffee.

'There's Morris,' Hope said, pointing at him. 'But I don't see Gram . . .'

Summer made a dejected little noise, like a deflating helium balloon.

Hope laughed. 'Go, eat, enjoy. I'll check on Morris and find out where Gram is.'

She brightened. 'Are you sure? Don't you want anything?'

In truth, Hope wasn't hungry, but she knew that such a response would only make her sister anxious, so instead she answered, 'OK. Bring me a croissant, or a muffin, or something else easy to carry.'

Without further ado, Megan and Summer dashed after the departing platters of food. Based on the lack of waitstaff remaining in the dining area, it looked as though they were going to have stiff competition in the back room. Hope watched them disappear, then she headed toward Morris. Aside from a coffee cup the color of a robin's egg and a matching saucer, his table was empty, covered by a white linen tablecloth that was wrinkled and spotted from a heavy morning's use.

'Hi, Morris,' she greeted him. 'How's the coffee today?'

Morris jumped in surprise, nearly knocking the cup out of its saucer.

'I'm sorry if I startled you,' Hope apologized. 'I thought you saw me.'

He seemed to have been looking at her as she had approached the table, but now that Hope was closer, she realized that Morris had been dozing with his eyes open. Either Amethyst's coffee was unduly weak, or the man had had a poor night's sleep. She guessed that it was the latter, because with the bright light reflecting on his face from the windows, his skin appeared sallow and deeply creased.

'Forgive me for saying so, Morris, but you look tired.'

'That's because I am tired, Hope. Exhausted, really.' He shifted clumsily in his chair, wincing with pain.

'Your back's bothering you?'

Morris nodded. 'It's bad. So bad that it's been keeping me up half the night. Which in turn makes the pain worse, and then I sleep even less. It's a vicious cycle.'

Hope nodded back at him sympathetically.

'Dylan recommended a pair of new pain medications for me to try, but I told him that I didn't want any more drugs. I'm already uneasy with some of the dosages that I've been taking. Dylan says my concerns are unfounded. Nevertheless, I don't feel comfortable with such high levels of—' Morris cut himself off abruptly and glanced around the dining room. 'Is Dylan here with you? That's proof of how tired I am. I didn't recall until just now that you and he were planning on going with Summer to her house this morning. How did that turn out?'

'Well, um . . .' Hope hesitated, debating how much information to give him. Considering the circumstances, she thought that maybe it would be better to talk to Gram first.

Morris seemed to forget his own question, because instead of waiting for her answer, he motioned toward the empty chairs at the table. 'Apparently, I also can't recall my manners. Won't you have a seat? Would you like a cup of coffee, or some tea, perhaps?'

'No, I'm fine, thanks.' She remained standing. 'I wanted to have a quick chat with Gram. Is she—'

'Speaking of tea,' Morris continued distractedly, 'Olivia suggested that I talk to you and Summer about getting one of the boutique's teas. One that might improve my sleep?'

'Certainly,' Hope said. 'Summer makes her own blend. It's primarily linden and lavender blossoms, with a few other herbal additions . . .' Morris looked at her with such eagerness – almost desperation – that she felt compelled to add, 'I don't want you to have unrealistic expectations. The tea isn't an analgesic, so it can't offer much in the way of pain relief. But it will provide some help with sleep, inflammation, and general relaxation.'

'I understand. I'll take any help I can get.'

'Then I'll let Summer know that you need a batch, and unless she's missing one of the ingredients, it shouldn't take her long to put it together. We'll do our best to get it to you before tonight, with instructions on how to brew it properly, so you can make yourself a cup whenever you need to. How does that sound?'

Morris grasped her hand and squeezed it. 'I'm exceedingly grateful, Hope. Exceedingly grateful.'

He appeared so relieved that it brought a lump to Hope's throat. 'You're very welcome. Summer and I are always happy to—'

Dropping her hand and his voice, Morris glanced around the dining room once more. 'Only . . . please don't tell Dylan.'

'About the ongoing pain?'

'No, the tea. Please don't tell Dylan about the tea. I don't want another long argument with him regarding the course of my treatment. He's a skeptic and tends to discount natural remedies.'

Hope suppressed a laugh. That was a bit of an understatement. Considering that Dylan had accused her and Summer of trying to kill Betsy Hughes with lemon balm, heaven only knows how he would react if he learned that they were giving linden and lavender to his father. 'My lips are sealed,' she promised Morris. 'Your tea is your business.'

The discussion of tea must have made Morris thirsty, because he reached for his coffee cup. As she watched him pick it up, it occurred to Hope that there should have been a second cup and saucer on the table.

'Where is Gram?' she asked him.

Morris gave a weighty exhalation. 'Your grandmother abandoned me, I'm afraid.'

Hope smiled. 'You mean she went to the ladies' room?'

'No. She told me to go away and not come back.'

'Huh?'

Taking a drink, Morris's mouth curled with displeasure at the tepid beverage. 'I'm supposed to close my eyes and cover my ears, so I don't see or hear anything.'

'I don't understand,' Hope said.

'Olivia is over there.' Morris gestured across the room.

Turning to where he had indicated, she spotted Gram tucked in the far back corner of the restaurant, sitting at a small, shadowy table away from the windows and the lobby entrance. To Hope's further surprise, she saw that Gram wasn't alone. There were two people seated at the table with her, their backs toward Hope. With the shadows and the distance, she couldn't make out who they were.

'Why is Gram huddled in the corner?' she asked Morris. 'And who is that with her?'

'Olivia has her secrets,' he said, 'and she has no intention of sharing them with me.'

Hope frowned at him in confusion. Morris drained the remainder of his cup and frowned back at her. She waited for him to offer some additional information or explanation, but he didn't. That confused her even more, because although Morris was rarely garrulous, he also wasn't usually cagey. Perhaps it was simply fatigue.

'Well, I'll go over and say hi to Gram . . .' she began.

Morris's chin sagged, and his eyelids drooped. Hope turned quietly and started to walk away, figuring that it was best to let him sleep if he could.

'She won't share them with you, either,' Morris murmured after her.

SIXTEEN

Hope had no idea what secrets Morris was referring to, and her initial inclination was to disregard his remarks as weary, incoherent ramblings. She had more pressing concerns on her mind, namely whether Gram knew anything about Marilyn and Roberta's pasts that could help explain why the murderer would consider the two women foolish. But as Hope headed toward the back corner of the restaurant, she began to wonder if she had been too quick to discount Morris's comments. Gram looked directly at her as she approached the table, and her expression was not welcoming. She offered no smile, no cheerful greeting, no friendly recognition whatsoever. Unlike Morris, Gram was wide awake and fully alert, and her gaze was so stern that Hope's pace reflexively slowed. She couldn't remember the last time that Gram had given her such a disapproving stare. Even when she had misbehaved as a child, Gram had always been more of a hugger than a scolder.

Gram shook her head slightly, and Hope stopped walking. Something wasn't right. Did Gram really have secrets that she was concealing from Morris – and from her, too? Not sure whether she should continue forward or withdraw instead, Hope wavered. The decision was made for her a moment later when one of the people at the table with Gram turned around in her chair. It was Sylvia Norquist.

There was nothing startling about Sylvia being at the restaurant. On the contrary, it was exactly the sort of place that Hope expected to find her. Sylvia Norquist was a social butterfly, continually flitting from one group and activity to the next. It was why she attended the bingo and spaghetti supper at the community center and why she could tell Marilyn Smoltz about Kirsten Willport's divine skin courtesy of the French green clay at the hotel spa. Sylvia liked to see and be seen, and she participated in almost everything. Amethyst's Sunday brunch was the perfect opportunity for her to learn what matters of local interest had occurred during the previous week and what was on the calendar for the coming week.

Sylvia's choice of table, however, surprised Hope. The dark corner of the dining room, far away from all the windows and the lobby entrance, where nobody could notice her and she couldn't notice them in return, was out of character for the woman. It couldn't be because she was embarrassed by her appearance that day. Sylvia – who was around the same age as Gram, maybe a year or two younger – was as neat and collected as always, revealing neither a strand of gray in her jet-black hair nor a blemish in her burgundy lipstick. She wore a cherry-red sweater set and double strand of cultured pearls with pleated gingham trousers. The only indication that she might not have been as composed internally as her polished façade otherwise suggested was her hands. They were clenched together so tightly in her lap that the skin on her knuckles was translucent white.

'Hmm. Hope,' Sylvia said.

It wasn't much of a salutation. Sylvia looked even less pleased to see her arrive at their table than Gram did. Although Hope didn't know what exactly had transpired with Morris, she could now understand from the chilly reception she received why he would think they wanted him to go away and not come back.

Hope mustered a small smile. 'Hi, Gram. Hello, Sylvia. Hello . . .'

Her voice faded as she turned toward the third person at the table, a man seated next to Sylvia. Hope didn't recognize him, but he seemed strangely familiar somehow. He was in his early to mid-forties, dressed in a rumpled navy shirt and shorts, with a bald spot on the crown of his head surrounded by a scraggly brown bird's nest.

There was a heavy pause. Both Gram and Sylvia frowned. The man sucked on his teeth. Hope had the distinct impression that she was supposed to turn around and walk away, closing her eyes and covering her ears as she went, so that she didn't see or hear anything, just as Morris had said.

'Hmm,' Sylvia remarked again.

The man grunted as though he agreed with an unspoken sentiment.

Hope looked at him. He seemed out of place at the table

with Sylvia and Gram, who were both trim and tidy, while he appeared to have just stumbled from his bed. And then suddenly Hope realized why he felt familiar to her. At Summer's house that morning, Rosemarie had mentioned seeing Sylvia on a bench in the park with a man who wasn't Sylvia's type. Rosemarie had said he was the opposite of Sylvia, with shaggy hair, a flabby belly, and a sloppy shirt and shorts. That description matched this man perfectly.

As the uncomfortable silence lengthened, Hope was tempted to retreat and return to Morris, but at the same time, she was worried about Gram. It wasn't that Gram appeared to be in danger or under duress. Quite the reverse. Gram looked calm, composed, and more or less in control of the situation. Except Hope was concerned about what exactly that situation was. For starters, Gram had never before given her – or Morris, either, as far as Hope was aware – the cold shoulder as she was doing now. And second, Hope remembered what else Rosemarie had said about Sylvia and the man sitting next to her. Rosemarie had overheard them talking about Gram, about some paper they assumed she had. Hope hadn't given it much thought at the time, but considering how oddly they were behaving, it seemed suddenly relevant.

Hope turned toward Sylvia. 'Have you found that paper you were interested in?'

Sylvia didn't immediately respond, but from the way that her already clenched hands tightened further – the skin on her knuckles looked ready to split – Hope could see that she had hit a nerve.

'How did you hear about it?' the man demanded from Hope. Not waiting for her answer, he growled at Sylvia, 'Did you tell her?' Then he barked at Gram, 'I thought you said nobody else knew.'

'Silence, Gerald!'

Sylvia's command was so sharp and forceful, like a professional trainer handling a security dog, that Hope took a startled step backward.

Gerald began to protest, but Sylvia shot him a blistering look, and his mouth closed with a whimper. Based on his abashed expression, if the man had been a canine, he would have tucked his tail between his legs and scurried to the security of his crate.

Instead, he folded his arms across his chest and slouched petu-
lantly in his chair.

Another awkward silence followed, although this one was
short-lived.

'What are you doing here, Hope?' Gram said, after a
protracted sigh. 'I thought that you and Summer were going to
her house this morning.'

Gram's voice was tense but not unkind. She didn't seem
angry that Hope was there; she seemed uneasy.

'We did go to her house,' Hope replied. 'But then Summer
. . . Summer found . . .'

Hope hesitated. She had intended to tell Gram about the Tarot
card in Summer's mail, but she wasn't sure whether she should
also tell Sylvia and Gerald. So far, only a handful of people
knew about the third Fool: her and Summer, Dylan and Megan,
Nate and the police. Hope was beginning to think that maybe
it would be better to keep the number small. Perhaps it could
even work to their advantage. Someone might slip up and reveal
themselves to be the murderer simply by knowing that there
had been a third card. It was a long shot, but Hope figured that
if Gram was keeping secrets, then she could, too, at least from
Sylvia and Gerald; after all, she had no idea if she could trust
them.

'What did Summer find?' Gram prompted her after a
moment.

'Summer found it stressful,' Hope said. It was the truth, albeit
a rather truncated version. 'She started to get anxious, so we
left.'

'That's too bad. I hope she's feeling better now.'

Although Gram's tone was sympathetic, it was also somewhat
stilted, an indication to Hope that Gram knew she wasn't telling
the whole story. Gram didn't pursue the matter, however, and
Hope wondered if she should take that as a sign Gram didn't
trust Sylvia and Gerald, either.

'Where is your sister now?' Sylvia inquired, her narrow gaze
surveying the nearly empty dining room.

'Tracking down lunch,' Hope answered vaguely.

Gram surveyed the room also. Her expression grew increasingly pensive when she saw Morris sitting along the wall of

windows. Whatever secrets she had, she didn't appear happy to be keeping them from him.

'Well, Sylvia,' Gram said, after another protracted sigh, 'I believe the time has come to tell her.'

Sylvia's gaze narrowed further. 'I don't think that's a good idea.'

'I think it is,' Gram rejoined quietly but firmly.

'If you want my opinion—' Gerald began.

Sylvia pursed her burgundy lips at him, and Gerald didn't conclude his opinion.

'Clearly, she already knows something about it,' Gram continued. She cast a quizzical glance at Hope, perplexed as to where she had gotten her information.

'And whose fault is that?' Gerald muttered.

'One more word from you—' Sylvia hissed.

Gerald harrumphed and slouched lower in his chair.

Sylvia turned her narrow gaze on Hope. 'I'm curious who told you about the paper.'

Hope didn't respond. She had no intention of squealing on Rosemarie, the more so because she was grateful to her. Without Rosemarie eavesdropping in the park with Percy, she wouldn't have known that there was any paper at issue. Considering how agitated Gerald had become at the mere mention of it, and how reticent Sylvia and Gram were on the subject, Hope was inclined to think that Dylan's initial guess was correct. The paper was some sort of a document. A secretive one, apparently.

'I want to know who told you,' Sylvia pressed her impatiently.

'And I want to know why you're making it so cloak-and-dagger,' Hope countered. 'I assume that's why you're huddled here in the corner, hiding and whispering among the shadows.'

'We're not hiding and whispering,' Gram said.

'Morris certainly thinks you are,' Hope replied. 'Granted, he's only half lucid from his back pain and lack of sleep, but he was talking about you abandoning him in favor of your secrets.'

'Oh, good heavens.' Gram clucked her tongue with exasperation. 'I haven't abandoned him. I simply encouraged him to rest while I took care of some business. I was trying not to burden him with all of this. I was trying not to burden you or your sister with it, either,' she added.

'We promised not to tell anyone about it,' Sylvia reminded her.

'We did indeed,' Gram agreed. 'But *you*, evidently, haven't abided by that promise.' She motioned toward Gerald.

Sylvia sniffled and shifted in her chair. 'Yes, well, that promise was made a long time ago. And, well, he is my son.'

Hope's eyes widened in surprise. Gerald was Sylvia's son? That explained why he submitted so docilely to her high-handedness.

'Considering everything that's happened over the past week,' Sylvia went on, 'Gerald is entitled to know.'

'By the same logic,' Gram responded, 'Hope – as my granddaughter – is also entitled to know.'

Sylvia sniffled and shifted again. 'But what assurances do I have that she isn't the one who killed Marilyn and Roberta?'

Hope's eyes stretched wider. Sylvia was accusing her of being the murderer? She started to laugh.

'I do not find it humorous,' Sylvia snapped.

'You should,' Hope returned, still laughing,' because what you said is absolutely absurd.'

'It's not absurd in the least,' Sylvia retorted indignantly. 'You were at the community center; I saw you there. And you were at the spa; Gerald watched you leave the hotel lobby and go down the stairs. You were in both locations. You can't dispute that.'

'I have no need to dispute it. The police know where I was and when.'

'Good.' Sylvia gave her an imperious nod. 'Then you can be held to account, if appropriate. The way I see it, whoever is responsible for both deaths must have been in both locations.'

Hope didn't dispute that, either. In fact, she had thought the same thing herself. The problem was that lots of people had been at the community center around the time of Roberta's death, and lots of people had been in the hotel and spa around the time of Marilyn's death, so making a comprehensive list and crossing off the possible suspects one by one until a single name remained, thereby revealing the guilty party, was nigh impossible. Ironically, however, by pointing the finger at Hope, Sylvia had unwittingly implicated herself and her son.

'You do realize,' Hope said to her, 'that you just admitted that you and Gerald were in both locations also? By the same logic,' she echoed Gram from a minute earlier, 'the two of you could have killed Marilyn and Roberta.'

'That's–that's outrageous!' Sylvia sputtered.

'Outrageous!' Gerald exclaimed, the crown of his head reddening.

Hope shrugged in reply, which only seemed to infuriate the pair further.

'How dare you accuse me!' Sylvia's face contorted with rage. 'How dare you accuse my son!'

The top of Gerald's head became nearly as burgundy as his mother's lips. 'How dare you!' he shouted.

'You have no proof,' Sylvia continued in a fury, waving her hands about wildly. 'No proof whatsoever!'

'Oh, good heavens.' Gram clucked her tongue as she had before. 'Calm down, Sylvia. You'll give yourself palpitations, and we'll have to call an ambulance for your heart. No one is claiming to have proof against you. No one is blaming you – or Gerald – for anything.'

Hope raised an eyebrow. Blame or not, proof or not, Sylvia and Gerald's reaction was so inordinately defensive that it made her wonder whether they might actually be guilty of something.

Sylvia seemed placated by Gram's words. Her face relaxed, and her hands returned to her lap, clutched together once again with white knuckles. As though realizing that her response might have been a bit too vigorous, she said, 'You shouldn't think me unreasonable. I don't want to appear hysterical. But it grieves me tremendously that there could be even the slightest suspicion that Gerald and I had any connection to our dear, dear friends Marilyn and Roberta being poisoned.'

'Of course there's no suspicion that you and Gerald had any connection—' Gram began.

Cutting her off abruptly, Hope turned toward Sylvia. 'How do you know that Marilyn and Roberta were poisoned?'

SEVENTEEN

With the grace of a gasping trout, Sylvia's mouth opened, then closed, and opened again. Gerald's burgundy head became beaded with sweat. Hope watched them in silence – and waited. Was it an admission of guilt? An inadvertent slip of the tongue? Could there be an innocent explanation?

Gram's patience was short. 'Hope asked you a question, Sylvia. How do you know that Marilyn and Roberta were poisoned?'

'I . . . well, um . . .' Sylvia gulped and gasped some more.

Gerald squirmed in his seat, rivulets of water trickling down to his temples.

Sylvia coughed and tried again. 'I–I think . . .'

'You think that you heard it from the police,' Gerald supplied, his voice cracking. 'The police told you how it happened.'

'Yes. Yes, that's it.' Sylvia nodded vigorously. 'I heard it from the police. The police told me how it happened.'

Hope looked at Gram. Did she believe Sylvia? Gram's brow was furrowed. There was a hint of perspiration there, too, although nothing compared with Gerald's.

'The police told you how it happened?' Gram questioned. She turned to Hope. 'Have the police told *you* how it happened?'

'No. In fact,' Hope said, 'I saw Nate – Detective Phillips – this morning, and he didn't mention anything about the blood work having been completed or the lab results coming in. Neither did Dylan.'

'I didn't mean' – Sylvia cleared her throat – 'that someone in authority contacted me personally regarding lab tests, or blood results, or whatever. I was referring to what the police said—'

'Also the news,' Gerald proffered.

'Right. Yes. What the police and the news,' Sylvia amended, 'said about the deaths. Public information, official statements, et cetera.'

There was a pause. Gram's brow remained furrowed. Gerald

reached for a napkin and blotted his head. Sylvia brushed some imaginary crumbs from her trousers.

'Not to mention,' Sylvia added after a moment, her tone growing in confidence, 'that it's obvious.'

'What is?' Gram asked her.

'That Marilyn and Roberta were poisoned, of course! I didn't see Marilyn. I only heard second-hand reports about her. But I witnessed everything with Roberta – or nearly everything. The way that she grabbed her stomach and thrashed around on the ground, plus all that swelling and those hives. And it was during dinner. There must have been something on her plate or in her cup. She must have been poisoned. It's obvious.'

Was it obvious? Hope mused to herself. Perhaps it was. From the beginning Dylan and Morris had talked about anaphylaxis and allergens, not poison, but they were both doctors. If she hadn't had the benefit of the Henshaw medical expertise, Hope had to admit that considering the manner of the two deaths, as well as the seeming connection with food and drink, she might have thought that Marilyn and Roberta had been poisoned, too.

'It's obvious,' Sylvia insisted, when no one else spoke.

'Obvious,' Gerald agreed.

'Besides,' Sylvia continued officiously, 'we had no more reason to kill Marilyn and Roberta than you did.'

Hope squinted at her. 'Huh?'

'Don't pretend that you don't understand me. If you know about the paper – which you made clear that you do just a few minutes ago – then you also know that Gerald and I don't stand to gain any more from the deaths than you and Olivia.'

'Gain from the deaths?' Hope echoed in confusion. 'What are you talking about?'

Sylvia responded by straightening her pearls.

Hope turned to Gram. 'Do you have any idea what she's talking about?'

Gram winced. It was only slightly, but enough for Hope to know that she understood exactly what Sylvia was talking about.

Hope threw up her hands in frustration. 'Will you please explain to me what is going on? Is this one of the secrets that Morris was worried about?'

'It isn't a secret,' Gram replied, also in a tone of frustration.

'Or at least it was never meant to be one. Yes, we promised not to tell anybody about it, but—'

'That sounds like a secret,' Hope said.

'Well, it could be interpreted that way,' Gram admitted, 'but honestly, that wasn't our intention. It was simply meant to be a private arrangement among friends.'

'That's true.' Sylvia nodded. 'A private arrangement among friends.'

'And it would have gone on being a private arrangement,' Gram continued. 'It could have remained small and quiet, of no interest to anyone but ourselves, except now—'

'Except now,' Gerald cut her off brusquely, 'two of those friends have been murdered, and what was supposed to be small and quiet has turned into a damn big deal. I can't speak for you, but I don't plan on sitting around, twiddling my thumbs, waiting to become the third victim.'

Hope's mind went immediately to the Tarot card that Summer had found. Did Gerald know about the third Fool? 'You think there will be a third victim?' she asked him.

'Why wouldn't there be a third victim?' he countered. 'Why would the murderer stop at two when the rest of us are still alive and kicking?'

Sylvia gave him a disapproving tsk-tsk.

Gerald shot her an agitated look. 'You can pretend that it doesn't apply to you, Mother, but it does. If somebody is going after everyone who was a part of it, then they're going after you, too. You aren't magically excluded. You're not immune because you imagine yourself to be fancier, or smarter, or just plain better than your friends.'

'Gerald!' Sylvia exclaimed, aghast. 'I do not imagine myself to be better than my friends.'

He grunted dubiously.

'Gerald!' Sylvia cried again, this time ending on a sharp note, once more commanding silence from her son.

With another grunt, Gerald slumped back in his chair.

Hope was thoughtful. It didn't sound as though Gerald knew about the third Fool. Not unless his reference to Sylvia imagining herself to be smarter than her friends meant that he considered them – or his mother – to be fools.

'I don't see why there should be a third victim,' Sylvia declared after a moment. 'I don't see what purpose it would serve.'

'But you can see what purpose the first two murders served?' Hope said.

There was an amused snort from Gerald, which was promptly squelched by a glare from his mother. The glare then turned to Hope.

'Of course I can't see their purpose,' Sylvia rejoined crossly. 'I'm not a mind reader. I can't climb into people's heads and—'

'Hope makes a good point, Sylvia,' Gram interjected. 'If we don't know why Marilyn and Roberta were targeted – what purpose their murders served, at least in theory – we can't know whether anyone else will be targeted.'

Sylvia harrumphed.

'Gerald also makes a good point,' Gram went on. 'If somebody is going after everyone who was a part of it, then we must assume that we're all targets. No exceptions or exclusions. Everyone connected to the tontine.'

'The what?' Hope asked.

'Have you not been paying attention?' Sylvia snapped. 'The tontine. The paper. The document. The thing that we've been discussing for the last hour. The sole reason we're here.'

That answered one of Hope's questions. The paper was indeed a document. But what was a tontine? She turned to Gram quizzically.

'Do you remember how I thought there was a pattern?' Gram said. 'A connection between the deaths?'

Hope nodded.

Gram nodded back at her. 'I knew there was something – something beyond Marilyn and Roberta simply knowing each other – but I couldn't put my finger on it. It probably would have come to me eventually, as Morris said. Thankfully, it came to Gerald sooner. He put it together and told Sylvia, and then she told me. And they're right. I'm sure of it.' This time she nodded at Sylvia. 'The connection is the tontine. It must be. It's the only thing that makes sense.'

'Certainly, it's the tontine,' Sylvia argued. 'What else could it be?'

'I don't know,' Hope said. 'Because I don't know what a tontine is.'

Sylvia looked at her askance, as though she didn't believe her ignorance.

'A tontine is a bet,' Gerald told her. 'A bet on death.'

'It isn't a bet,' Gram corrected him.

'Really?' he retorted. 'A bunch of people all put in money, and the last one standing gets the entire pot. If that's not betting on death, what would you call it?'

'I would call it a group life insurance policy, of sorts.'

As he had with his mother a minute earlier, Gerald responded to Gram with a dubious grunt.

'A group life insurance policy,' Gram repeated, although she didn't sound entirely convinced herself. 'In a tontine,' she said to Hope, 'each subscriber contributes an equal share at the outset, and every year each subscriber receives a small payment.'

'Like an annuity?' Hope asked.

'An annuity combined with a lottery,' Gerald replied. 'Except instead of praying for the winning numbers, the subscribers are praying to outlive one another.'

Hope frowned, not understanding.

'When a subscriber dies,' Gerald explained, 'their annual payment is divided among the remaining subscribers. When there is only one subscriber left, the tontine is dissolved, and that final survivor gets everything – all the money.'

'But what about the beneficiaries of the other subscribers?' Hope said.

'There are no beneficiaries, at least not in the traditional sense. No one outside the group inherits. A share can't be handed down through a will or trust like a condominium or brokerage account. A tontine is exclusive to the original participants. It's based on their lifespans only.'

Hope's frown deepened. 'I've never heard of such a thing.'

'That's probably because it isn't legal,' Gerald said.

'Our arrangement is perfectly legal!' Sylvia protested.

Gerald merely shrugged.

It was Gram's turn to frown. 'A lawyer wrote up the paper for us. He didn't say anything about it not being legal.'

'Maybe you're right.' Gerald shrugged again. 'Maybe it was

legal in North Carolina then. Maybe it still is. But tontines have been banned in lots of places.'

'They have?' Sylvia questioned. 'How do you know?'

'When you first told me about it, I was like her' – he motioned toward Hope – 'and had never heard of a tontine. So I did some research and found that they've been around for centuries, in various forms, across the globe. Tontines have been used by governments and companies, royalty and average citizens, to raise capital for everything from war and conquest to pension funds and building projects. High or low, big or small, they're all schemes. Morbid schemes, in my opinion, plenty of which also turned out to be giant scams. That's why many countries have made them illegal.'

Hope looked at Gram in surprise. 'How on earth did you ever come up with such an idea?'

'Rebecca Huber,' Gram said.

'Rebecca Huber,' Sylvia echoed.

'She read about it in a book.'

'It seemed like fun,' Sylvia said.

Hope raised an eyebrow.

'Obviously, it doesn't seem like fun now,' Sylvia amended.

'That tends to happen when two members of your tontine die under suspicious circumstances,' Gerald muttered.

Sylvia's nostrils flared with indignation, but Gram spoke before she could.

'In our defense, it was a long time ago. Almost thirty-five years. Before you or your sister were even born,' she said to Hope. 'Your mom was away at college. When Rebecca mentioned it to us, we thought it sounded interesting. It wasn't a huge sum of money. And we were all around the same age, give or take a few years. I was the oldest. Rebecca was the youngest.'

The name wasn't familiar to Hope. 'Have I met Rebecca?'

Gram shook her head. 'No. She was diagnosed with cancer shortly after we organized the tontine. She died within a year.'

'How awful,' Hope said.

'I wish you could have known her. Rebecca was such a kind person. Always willing to go out of her way to help someone. And she never—'

'Yes, yes. That's all nice and good,' Sylvia interrupted Gram.

'But the most important point is that because Rebecca is already dead, she can't be the one who killed Marilyn and Roberta.'

Gram gave her a look of reproof.

'Scold me if you like,' Sylvia returned defiantly, 'but it's the truth. It doesn't matter what sort of person Rebecca was back then: thin or fat, short or tall, smart or dumb. We need to worry about *now*. The present, not the past—'

Struck by Sylvia's choice of words, it was Hope's turn to interrupt. 'Was Rebecca smart or dumb?'

The question startled Sylvia into momentary silence.

'Based on what's happened to Marilyn and Roberta, the past appears to be much more important – at least to the murderer – than you imagine,' Hope said. 'Was Rebecca considered intelligent or foolish?'

Gram reflected a minute. 'I see what you mean. You're thinking about the cards, aren't you? From that perspective, Rebecca was definitely intelligent. She was a partner in a successful accounting firm. I doubt that anyone – then or now – would have considered her foolish.'

'Did she have any children or other close relations . . .' Hope began. 'Forget that. You said inheritance and beneficiaries don't matter in a tontine.'

'They don't matter,' Gerald confirmed. 'As my mother pointed out earlier, I don't stand to gain any more from the deaths than you do.'

'Yes, but the remaining members stand to gain plenty – potentially,' Hope reminded him. 'Who else was part of the tontine?'

'There were six of us,' Gram said. 'Sylvia and me. Marilyn and Roberta. Rebecca and Kirsten Willport.'

'No one else? You're sure?'

'Of course she's sure!' Sylvia exclaimed, regaining her voice. 'We were all in the lawyer's office together. We know who else signed the paper.'

'Where is the paper now?' Hope asked. 'Still with the lawyer?'

'No. He retired some years ago. Moved to Wyoming, if I recall correctly.'

'Too bad you can't also recall what you did with the paper,' Sylvia sniped at Gram. 'You never should have gotten it. You should have given it to me.'

'You didn't want it *then*,' Gram retorted. 'No one did. And one of us had to take it. When he closed his business, the lawyer returned all the documents he was holding to the clients.'

Sylvia grumbled.

'So you don't know where the paper is now?' Hope pressed Gram. 'Because it would be good for us to read it. There could be something in there – something in the fine print, so to speak – that could help explain what's going on.'

'I don't remember there being any fine print,' Gram mused. 'It was just a simple little agreement.'

'What seemed simple thirty-five years ago might not be so simple anymore,' Hope said. 'Which is why we really need to take a look at it. Do you have any idea where you put it?'

'Certainly. It's at the brownstone. There's no question about that.'

Sylvia turned to Gerald with a triumphant air. 'You see? I told you it was at the boutique.'

'Not the boutique,' Gram corrected her. 'The attic.'

Hope groaned. 'Oh, no.'

Gram responded with an apologetic smile. 'I'm afraid so.'

'But there are a hundred unmarked boxes in the attic. Please tell me that you have some clue which one it might be in.'

Another apologetic smile. 'I'm afraid not.'

Hope sighed, knowing that she was going to be the one who would have to search through all those boxes. And she was going to have to do it with the possible opposition of the attic's inhabitants, although she certainly couldn't say that in front of Sylvia and Gerald.

'I hope this isn't just an excuse,' Gerald remarked in agitation. 'Some concocted pretext because you don't want us to see the paper.'

'Are you suggesting that I might have an ulterior motive?' Gram chuckled. 'Don't be a fool.'

Hope didn't laugh with her.

EIGHTEEN

Some six hours later, as the sun was beginning to dip below the edge of the city, Hope sank down wearily on one of the rattan settees on the back patio of the brownstone. A glass of wine in one hand, she propped her feet up on a corner of the box that contained the new raised bed for the garden. Given the dismal state of Summer's marriage, there was absolutely no chance that Gary was going to use his illustrious carpentry skills to assemble the bed for them now. She wondered if Nate was at all handy. Perhaps Summer could sweet-talk him into doing a bit of construction work.

'Hope?'

She jumped at the unexpected voice and, to her surprise, found Dylan standing at the edge of the garden, just outside the wrought-iron fence that separated the rear of the property from the alleyway. He appeared almost otherworldly, illuminated in the orange glow of the horizon.

'I knocked on the door of the boutique,' he said, 'but no one answered.'

'We're appointment-only on Sundays.'

There was a brief pause, then he tried again.

'I could see that there were lights on further inside, so I thought you might be home. Am I intruding?'

Another pause. Hope hadn't forgotten his appalling remarks from earlier that day, but after spending the afternoon lifting, lugging, and combing through stacks of cobweb-covered boxes in the attic, she no longer had the energy to be angry.

'The gate is unlocked.'

She didn't need to tell him twice. Dylan immediately lifted the latch and entered the garden. He found a winding path of flagstones, surrounded by giant pots, towering trellises, and half a dozen beds of varying sizes. Every inch of soil was crowded with herbs and edibles and ornamentals, all flush with fresh spring growth.

'This is a really nice space you have back here,' he said.

'Thank you,' Hope responded politely. 'We all work on it, Gram included. It's wonderfully cool on summer evenings when the rest of Asheville is baking like a convection oven.'

'I can imagine. Your own private oasis in the middle of the proverbial concrete desert.'

As Dylan navigated his way through the labyrinth of greenery, Hope debated with herself. Should she invite him to sit down? Offer him a glass of wine? She had little desire to pick a fight. And she didn't want to cause any further tensions between Morris and Gram. Gram was presently at Morris's house attempting to heal the current rift by explaining the secret of the tontine to him.

'What did you plant today?' Dylan asked her, when he reached the patio.

'Nothing. Why?'

'Well, for starters, you look like you've been digging.'

'Do I?' Glancing down, Hope saw the streaks of dirt on her arms and shirt. 'I wasn't expecting any visitors this evening, so I didn't bother to tidy up.' She picked a dust bunny off her shoulder and tucked some stray strands of hair behind one ear. Realizing that there were probably smudges of dust and dirt on her face, too, she remarked ruefully, 'I must look lovely right now.'

'I can't imagine you ever not looking lovely.'

The compliment surprised her. It might have been baloney, but it was still flattering, and any remaining grudge on Hope's part was temporarily pushed aside.

'Take a seat, if you like.' She gestured toward the neighboring settee. 'There's an open bottle of wine – along with a few other options – on the potting stand by the patio door.'

Dylan turned toward the stand, saw the extensive collection of liquor bottles and mismatched glasses, and laughed. 'Those are more than a few options. And that's the first time I've seen a potting stand used as a bar.'

'It was Summer's idea. She says there's no point having a patio if you don't stock it properly.'

Laughing some more, Dylan took a quick survey of the bottles. He selected a bonded bourbon and poured a generous serving into a chunky square glass.

'Cheers,' he said, settling himself on the neighboring settee.
'Cheers.'

They sat without speaking for some time, sipping their drinks
and watching the sun sink slowly out of view. A hummingbird
flitted to the crimson feeder for a last drop of nectar. A chip-
munk scurried over the flagstones toward its protective burrow.

When he had emptied his glass, Dylan rose for a refill.
'Another for me. More wine for you?'

Hope nodded.

'So if you weren't planting back here this afternoon,' he said,
refreshing their respective beverages, 'were you helping out at
some archeological dig?'

She smiled. 'You're not that far off, actually. Except instead
of hunting for prehistoric bones and pottery shards, I was
searching for ancient documents.'

'In the garden?' Dylan remarked incredulously.

'In the attic – hence the dust and dirt. It tends to accumulate
up there. As I told you before, we try to avoid going into the
attic when possible.'

'Because of the rickety stairs and the ghosts, right? Did either
give you much trouble today?'

'No. The stairs were fine. But the ghosts will be restless
tonight. I disturbed their space – and their peace, such as it is.'

The last time she had discussed the attic's inhabitants with
him, a befuddled crease had formed in Dylan's brow. This time
he placidly took a sip of bourbon.

'Did you find what you were looking for?' he asked, returning
to his seat and handing Hope a full wine glass.

'Unfortunately not. The place is jammed with a mountain of
boxes, bins, crates, and containers. Almost none of it is labeled
or organized in any practical way. There is everything from old
rocking chairs and housewares to tattered toys and sporting
equipment. Speaking of which, would you believe I found a
pair of antique snowshoes? They look as though they've been
strung with natural rawhide. It's beautifully done, almost like
artwork.'

'Native American?'

'That's my best guess. I have no clue how they got into the
attic. But in any event, there is way too much stuff up there,

which makes locating one small specific thing – in this case, a piece of paper – frustratingly difficult.'

Now a crease did form in Dylan's brow. 'Do you mean the paper that Rosemarie mentioned this morning? The one that Sylvia Norquist was talking about in the park with some mystery man?'

Hope's eyes widened. 'You really have an impressive memory.'

'At times.' Dylan shrugged. 'But it can be both a blessing and a curse.'

She looked at him questioningly. Although his face was shadowed by the approaching dusk, she could see that his expression was grave.

'Remembering too much isn't always good,' he said. 'I'm sure you understand.'

There was such somberness in his tone that Hope knew instantly he was referring to February, and she looked hastily away, grateful for the concealing shadows.

Dylan hesitated a moment, took a large draft of bourbon, and then cleared his throat. 'I owe you an apology, Hope. I shouldn't have said what I did this morning. It was unfair and unkind.'

She didn't respond. She couldn't. She was too startled by his contrition – and also by her ready willingness to forgive him. It might have been partly because of how tired she was from her efforts in the attic, but Hope knew that it was mostly due to her overall fatigue. She was exhausted from thinking about what had happened in February for so many subsequent weeks and months. Exhausted from turning the events over in her mind a hundred, a thousand, a million times. Dylan was right. Too good a memory was indeed a curse.

After another large draft, Dylan said, 'I shouldn't have listened to Rosemarie on the driveway at your sister's house. It's not her story to tell.'

With some effort, Hope found her voice. 'No, it's not Rosemarie's story. But it's also not a secret. Secrets don't help anyone.'

She thought about Gram's secret. Morris would have been much happier knowing about the tontine from the beginning. And the police should have been told promptly, as well. Nate wasn't going to be pleased when he learned that they had kept potentially relevant information about Marilyn and Roberta's deaths from him.

'Secrets don't help anyone,' Hope repeated to herself. Then she took a deep breath and said aloud, 'His name was Tom – Tom Ellis – and he was a paramedic. We had been engaged since Thanksgiving. Our wedding was planned for September.'

After a shaky drink of wine, she continued, 'We had several bad storms in this area during the past winter. The worst one was in February. It was solid ice. Trees and power lines were down everywhere. Most of the city and half of the state were without electricity for over a week.

'Tom worked almost non-stop for three days. So many people were injured. There were collapsed roofs, chimney fires, broken bones, frostbite. And on the fourth night, it happened. He had been called to the scene of a car accident. It turned out to be only a minor crash. Just a fender bender on a slippery road. But it was pitch-black outside.' Hope swallowed hard. 'As Tom was checking on one of the passengers, a driver in the oncoming traffic was distracted by a phone call and hit them full force. Tom died on impact.'

There was silence.

'I'm sorry for your loss,' Dylan said.

Hope breathed a sigh of relief. She was relieved to have the story out in the open. And she was relieved by Dylan's limited response.

'Thank you,' she said, 'for not making a speech. I can't bear to have one more person tell me how grateful I should be that it was a quick death and Tom didn't suffer. Of course I'm grateful he didn't suffer! But after the fiftieth person hugs you and tells you it's all somehow a blessing in disguise, you really want to scream.'

Dylan nodded. 'I can relate. Even after so many years, whenever anyone finds out that my mom died due to complications from childbirth, they insist on discussing it. It's never a simple word or two in sympathy. It's always a grand oration, usually with a good deal of religious sentiment. I know they mean well, but I wish they would step back and realize how difficult it is for me to hear over and over again.'

Hope nodded back at him in commiseration, then she leaned her head against the settee and looked up at the twilight sky. There were only a few streaks of indigo left along the horizon. The first pale stars were beginning to appear.

'Could I ask you something?' Dylan said after a moment.

'Go ahead.'

'Rosemarie said that you stopped working with the Tarot because of the accident. I'm curious why.'

Hope's eyes remained on the sky. 'The simple answer is that I blamed the Tarot for what happened. In truth, though, the cards weren't to blame. The cards are never to blame. The fault lies with the reader – and the reader was me. I was so busy with trivialities that I didn't pay attention to the bigger picture. I didn't see the forest for the trees, as the saying goes.'

'But is it really possible to see the forest? To see something of actual consequence?' Dylan replied, his voice heavy with skepticism. 'I understand that looking at the cards – like reading palms or tea leaves – can make the people who come to your boutique feel better about their lives. You offer them a sense of control and reassurance in a spinning, rocky world. But you can't honestly think there's more to it than that. You can't truly believe the Tarot is able to show anything of genuine import.'

Under other circumstances, Hope might have been offended. Or she might have laughed at Dylan's naiveté. But not tonight. Gazing up at the heavens, Hope felt more at peace than she had in a long time. Perhaps it was from talking about Tom. Or the extra glass of wine she'd had. Or listening to the evening lullaby of the red-breasted robin perched on the garden gate. Regardless of the reason, Hope's response was mild.

'Ask a question,' she told Dylan, 'and the cards will answer. We each choose how to interpret that answer, how much significance to give it.'

'What if I don't ask a question?' he rejoined.

'Then you won't get an answer.'

'But what kind of answers could I possibly expect from a bunch of plastic-coated pieces of paper!'

Although Hope couldn't fully see his face, it was clear from Dylan's tone that he did not share her feeling of peace. It occurred to her that while talking about Tom had been comforting to her, talking about his mom might have had the opposite effect on Dylan. A little light and a slightly lighter topic seemed a wise choice.

'It's gotten awfully dark,' Hope said, rising from her settee. 'I'll get some candles.'

Along with the liquor bottles and drinking glasses, there was also an assortment of candles on the potting stand. Hope collected several and set them in a haphazard row on the resin coffee table in front of the settees. It took her a moment to find the box of fireplace matches that had been tucked behind a flowerpot. Striking one of the long matches, she succeeded in lighting all the candles before the flame reached her fingers.

'That's better.' She blew out the match and dropped it into her empty wine glass.

'Much better,' Dylan agreed. 'Now I won't trip and fall in my quest for the bourbon bottle.'

Hope smiled, pleased that his mood had brightened. 'While we're on the subject of quests' – she handed him the bottle before returning to her seat – 'Summer is currently on a mission – in her bedroom, on the internet – to learn everything she can about chandlery.'

'Chandlery?'

'Candle making. We've had such bad luck with our candle orders for the boutique lately that Summer thinks we should try making them ourselves.'

Dylan refilled his glass. 'Back in college, I had a girlfriend who made her own candles.'

'And?' Hope said.

'And we broke up.'

'No, I mean, how were the candles?'

He shrugged. 'They weren't much better than the relationship. All the candles tilted. And they made popping and crackling noises whenever we burned them. I think she said it was from air bubbles that had gotten into the wax. One time she scalded her arm so bad while melting the wax that I had to take her to the emergency room.'

'Yikes.' Hope frowned. 'That doesn't sound promising. Maybe we won't try making candles ourselves, after all.'

'If you do, I'm sure that you'll be better at it than she was.

She was never the sharpest knife in the drawer. From everything I've seen, you're smart and competent. You run your own business. That's impressive.'

It was the second compliment that Dylan had paid her that evening, and it surprised Hope as much as the first. While deliberating how to respond, a flickering candle caught her attention. She looked over at it and saw wax streaming down the side of a leaning pillar.

'Speaking of tilting candles,' she said, getting up and hurriedly putting a coaster under the pillar. The top of the table was already scratched and marred from many years of patio use; even so, a puddle of hot wax wasn't beneficial.

Dylan raised his glass in salute. 'Crisis averted.'

Hope laughed. 'Let's cross our fingers that it's the biggest crisis we have this coming week. Because we really don't want a repeat of last—'

She didn't finish the sentence. Dylan was suddenly on his feet, standing next to her. In one swift movement, he had his arms around her, and his lips were on hers.

NINETEEN

ope's first instinct was to protest, but the reflex faded as quickly as it had arisen, drowned by waves of warmth. Dylan's body was warm, and his mouth was warm, and his tongue had the fiery taste of bourbon. She pressed against him, wanting more. His arms tightened around her, and his kisses deepened. A rush of energy raced along her spine. Dylan's hands were in her hair, his long fingers caressing the back of her neck. His mouth moved along her jaw and down to the hollow of her throat. Hope's head spun, lost in sensations of pleasure. It felt good. Almost painfully good. She hadn't been held – she hadn't been kissed – in what seemed like such a long time. Since February, since Tom. And then Hope stiffened, abruptly remembering where she was and who she was with.

Dylan's kisses stopped at her sudden restraint, but his arms didn't release her.

'How's that for a crisis?' he said, smiling at her.

The question and the smile came leisurely. If he was at all shaken or unsettled by what had just happened between them, he didn't show it. Dylan appeared thoroughly at ease, one of his hands lingering in her hair. For her part, Hope's heart was pounding furiously in her chest. Her legs were so wobbly beneath her that she was glad of Dylan's support.

'We–we shouldn't . . .' she began unevenly.

'Shouldn't we?' he returned.

Hope looked at him. Reflected in the candlelight, Dylan's eyes were a glittering midnight blue. She couldn't read them. Whatever he was thinking – or feeling – it was hidden from her view.

'We–we hardly know each other,' she reminded him. 'And there's Gram and your dad to consider. And Tom . . .'

The last words were a whisper. A guilty, confused whisper. Hope knew what Megan would have told her, because Megan had told her it before: *As much as she had loved him, Tom was gone. She needed to move forward. She couldn't live in the past.* And in theory, Hope knew that it was true. But no amount of truth could stop the wretched feeling that she had just betrayed the man she had lost.

'That's quite a list of reasons,' Dylan said.

He didn't dispute any of them, nor did he give any indication of being troubled by them. Hope would have pressed her point, except she was having difficulty concentrating with Dylan so close to her. It was as though his touch had a hypnotic quality. She could think clearly for a moment – about Tom, or Megan, or Morris and Gram – until Dylan's fingertips glided over her skin. Then all reasonable thought evaporated, and she was left with an overwhelming desire to have his lips on hers again.

As though reading her mind, Dylan ran his hand slowly down her cheek, lingering at the curve of her mouth. He was no longer smiling. His gaze was dark and intense, drawing her toward him. Hope could feel herself relenting, forgetting every objection, wanting almost desperately to take what he offered.

'Hope . . .' Dylan's voice was husky, imploring.

She didn't speak, not trusting her tongue. She didn't trust the rest of her body, either, and with supreme effort, she extricated herself from his arms and took a step backward.

'Hope—'

He was interrupted by a loud shout, followed by a series of thumps. For a moment, neither one of them reacted, each still focused on the other.

'If I'm not mistaken,' Dylan said at last, clearing his throat, 'that sounded like somebody falling down a set of stairs.'

'Summer!' Hope cried in alarm.

Without a second of further delay, she whirled around and dashed toward the patio door. Throwing it open, Hope sprinted inside. Was Summer all right? A person could be seriously injured from a fall down the stairs. Morris continually worried about Gram slipping and breaking a hip, or even worse. Hope raced through the kitchen, past the library, and along the hallway. Turning the corner toward the main staircase, she expected to find Summer lying on the floor, battered and bruised, but to Hope's immense relief, the foot of the stairs was bare.

'Hope!' Summer came tearing around the corner from the opposite direction. 'I heard that noise and thought something terrible had happened. Thank goodness you're OK!'

'You're OK, too!' Hope exclaimed, gratefully reciprocating her sister's bear hug.

'She's fine. You're fine. We're all fine,' Dylan said, amusement in his tone.

Both Hope and Summer looked at him in surprise. Hope hadn't noticed that he had followed her into the brownstone, and Summer hadn't expected to see him at all.

'Well, hello,' Summer greeted Dylan. 'I wasn't aware that we had company this evening.'

'Hope and I were outside on the patio, enjoying the night air.'

On the face of it, that seemed like a simple response, but there was something about the way that Dylan emphasized the second part of the sentence that gave it a sensual undertone.

Summer raised a curious eyebrow. 'On the patio? How interesting . . . Wait a minute—' She cut herself off abruptly. 'If you two were outside, and I was in my room, then where did that noise come from?'

In unison, they all turned toward the staircase. It was empty and quiet. There was no visible sign of a disturbance.

Hope was perplexed. 'I was sure that somebody shouted.'

'Me, too,' Summer concurred. 'And there were those thumps.'

'It couldn't have been Gram. She's at Morris's.'

'What's your basement like?' Dylan asked. 'Could something have fallen off a shelf or the wall, and it echoed as it hit the ground?'

'No. We don't have a basement,' Hope told him, 'only a dirt crawl space. It's hard to access, so we don't hang or store anything down . . .' The sentence trailed away as she realized that Dylan had the right idea but the wrong location. 'Uh-oh.'

'Uh-oh?'

Hope gave her sister a meaningful look. There was a short pause, then Summer drew a sharp breath, understanding.

'I was up there all afternoon,' Hope said. 'I moved a lot of stuff around.'

Summer nodded. 'And in the process, there was a lot of

disturbance. Did you accidentally put something too close to the door? Something that – with a little nudge – could have tumbled down the steps?'

'Definitely not. I was very careful when I left, as I always am. Nothing sitting on the windowsills. No teetering towers in the middle of the room. And the doorway and stairs were completely clear.'

'Are you talking about the attic?' Dylan said.

'Of course we're talking about the attic!' Summer responded impatiently. She turned back to Hope. 'Maybe it was more than a nudge. That hasn't happened in a while, but if you were digging around in something that somebody didn't like . . .'

'And they were sharing their unhappiness . . .' Hope was thoughtful. 'Except that doesn't explain the shout. We never get any shouts.'

'Plenty of other sounds, but no shouts,' Summer agreed.

'Which means there must be more going on.'

'Probably nothing good.'

They frowned at each other, both knowing what had to be done and neither one wanting to do it.

'Well' – Hope heaved a sigh – 'I'd better bite the bullet and take a look. Before it becomes a fire, flood, insect infestation, or other calamity.'

Summer was apologetic. 'I'm sorry that it has to be you. But I can't go up there. You know what happened the last time.'

Hope shuddered. 'That was bad.'

'What was bad?' Dylan demanded. 'One of you can go up to the attic, but the other one can't? Why?'

There was a mixture of confusion and frustration in his voice. Hope didn't blame him for being exasperated. She and Summer were engaged in a conversation that he wasn't a part of and didn't understand. The problem was that if she tried to explain it to him, he probably still wouldn't understand – and considering his previous skeptical remarks about the mystical world, in all likelihood he wouldn't believe her. Hope didn't mind, and she knew that Summer didn't mind, either. In their line of work, they dealt with plenty of cynics. But she didn't want Dylan to take the issue up with Morris, thereby causing difficulties for Gram. It seemed to her that the best solution for everyone involved was to encourage an exit now, before Dylan saw or heard anything even more inexplicable.

'Thank you for coming over,' Hope said to him politely.

She took several deliberate steps away from the staircase. Summer caught her sister's hint immediately. All the Baileys had been obliged on occasion over the years to hurry guests out of the brownstone. It was not a new phenomenon.

'It was nice to see you,' Summer added with matching courteousness, also turning away from the staircase.

'Feel free to drop by any time.' Hope motioned in the direction of the boutique. 'No appointment necessary.'

Summer began to move toward the front door. 'We'll show you out.'

'Seriously?' Dylan's tone was sharp. And he didn't budge an inch. 'You're seriously trying to get rid of me?'

Hope and Summer exchanged a glance.

'It's getting late.' Summer pointed at the hall clock. 'Don't you have patients to see in the morning?'

'I do have patients,' Dylan acknowledged, 'but I certainly wouldn't consider this to be late.'

'It's late enough,' Hope remarked. 'It's after dark.'

'At least it's not after midnight,' Summer said to her sister. She gave a weary little smile. 'Thank heaven for small favors.'

Dylan was not amused. 'You aren't honestly suggesting that you have a curfew?'

Hope looked at him, and after a brief hesitation, she shrugged, more to herself than to Dylan. 'It's an attic curfew. We avoid the witching hour if at all possible.'

'Hope!' Summer exclaimed, not expecting the admission.

'I know, I know.' She nodded. 'The smartest thing would be for us not to tell him anything about it. Once we do, he'll no doubt think we're a few apples short of a bushel. But he probably already thinks that.' Hope shrugged again. 'In any event, Dylan has no intention of leaving. You can see it from the way that he's set his jaw—'

'Damn right I have no intention of leaving!' Dylan snapped. 'What sort of a man do you take me for? I heard that noise, too. If there's an intruder in here, I'm not going to wish you a good night and walk merrily out of the door while that person is roaming about the house!'

'Such chivalry,' Summer murmured drolly.

Dylan didn't appear to hear her. 'And what the hell is the *witching hour*?'

Hope and Summer exchanged another glance.

'How detailed an explanation would you like?' Hope asked him. Not waiting for his answer, she offered an abbreviated version. 'Generally speaking, spiritual activity fluctuates throughout the course of the day. In the case of our attic, the energy is stronger after sundown, especially from midnight to around four a.m. That time is commonly referred to as the witching hour, because in traditional folklore, witches, ghosts, demons, and other super-natural entities are considered to have more power then.'

As Hope had predicted, Dylan stared at her as though she were a few apples short of a bushel.

'He's going to recommend psychiatric treatment,' Summer muttered.

'Better that than being burned at the stake,' Hope replied under her breath. To Dylan, she said, 'I'm afraid the clock is ticking. I'm not eager to go up there, but I really need to check the attic. I would greatly prefer to have it done before midnight, so if you'll excuse me . . .'

Without more ado, she turned toward the staircase.

'I'll stay down here.' Summer chewed anxiously on her bottom lip. 'The farther away I am, the safer it will be for you.'

'It will probably turn out to be nothing.' Hope feigned more confidence than she felt. 'We haven't heard a peep since the original noise. Maybe it was just a bit of restlessness, and it's already calmed down.'

Summer chewed harder on her lip and gave her sister an encouraging squeeze of the hand as she passed by and started up the stairs.

'Wait . . .' Dylan called after her.

Hope glanced back.

'You're not going alone,' he said. 'I'm coming with you.'

'No,' Summer protested. She shook her head at him, then at Hope. 'That's not a good idea.'

'It's not a good idea,' Hope agreed.

Undeterred, Dylan headed toward the stairs.

'You really can't.' Summer moved in front of him to block his path. 'He really can't,' she said to Hope. 'You remember what happened to the electrician when he went up there? He had to take early retirement afterward.'

Dylan stepped around her. 'Your electrician, plumber, dentist, and veterinarian may all be afraid of spooks and specters. I am not.'

They weren't going to stop him. That was clear to Hope. Dylan's jaw was set the same way as when he had announced his intention of not leaving the brownstone. All they could do was warn him and hope for the best.

'All right,' Hope acceded. 'If you're determined to see the attic, then be my guest.' She turned back around and started up the stairs once more. 'But don't complain later on that we didn't explain the risks. We assume no liability for events beyond our control.'

Dylan chuckled. 'Nice disclaimer. You do realize that it's not legally binding?'

Despite the circumstances, his flippancy made Hope laugh. 'Go ahead. Try suing a ghost. I dare you.'

'Don't joke,' Summer admonished her. 'And don't let him go up the attic steps first, in case – well, you know.'

'In case what?' Dylan asked Hope, as they climbed the main staircase together.

'In case one of those spooks and specters that you're not afraid of decides they don't like you and hurls a pair of old snowshoes at your head.'

From out of the corner of her eye she saw him frown, but he didn't otherwise respond. When they reached the second-floor landing, Dylan's attention shifted to the architecture.

'Wow! This place is fantastic,' he said in admiration. 'The craftsmanship and attention to detail. Look at that woodwork! It's even more impressive than I thought it would be. How much do you know about the history of the house?'

'We know a portion of it,' she answered vaguely.

Dylan marveled at the design of the building, the preservation of the antique fixtures, and the imposing stained-glass window at the end of the hall.

'What direction does the window face?' he asked.

'East.'

'So early light would be the best. The glass must be stunning when it's fully illuminated.' Dylan turned to her, a smile tugging at his lips. 'I would greatly enjoy seeing it in the morning.'

The words might have been innocent, but the smile definitely wasn't.

'I bet you would,' Hope replied dryly.

'I remember you telling me' – Dylan moved a step closer to her – 'that the bedrooms are on the second floor. Am I correct in assuming that includes *your* bedroom?'

His smile was now a full-fledged grin.

'You're not getting a tour of my bedroom.'

'Why not?' He moved closer still. 'There's no time like the present.'

Although Dylan didn't touch her, the nearness of his body made Hope's pulse quicken.

'What happened to your grave concern about an intruder?' she said, trying to shift the conversation.

'There is no intruder. I don't know what that noise was before, but I've been listening carefully ever since we came inside, and it's been perfectly quiet. Unless they're better concealed than a mouse, no one is here. We're all alone.'

They were not all alone; Hope could guarantee him that, but she saw no benefit in contesting the matter, particularly because the longer they stood there together, the more she began to waver about the tour of her bedroom.

Dylan cupped her chin in his hand and lifted her face to him. Her skin tingled beneath his fingers. Her breath caught in her throat as she met his smoky gaze.

'I'm starting to believe in that witching hour of yours.' Dylan's voice was low, almost purring. 'You've certainly bewitched me.'

And with the skill of a snake charmer, he was in the process of bewitching her. Hope was on the verge of melting into his arms when – somewhere above her – there was a moan.

She pulled away, keenly alert. 'Did you hear that?'

'Hear what?'

'That sound. Listen.'

A clock chimed. A floorboard creaked. A pipe clanked.

'I don't hear anything out of the ordinary, only the usual noises that houses of this age and condition make.' Dylan tried to draw her back toward him, but it was too late. The spell was broken.

'I know what I heard.' Hope raised a wary eye toward the ceiling. 'And I know where it came from.'

Turning from the second floor, she continued swiftly up the main staircase. The third-floor hall was narrower and shorter than the one below.

'Watch your head,' she cautioned Dylan. 'There are a couple of low spots, and you're tall enough that you might hit . . .'

She didn't finish the sentence as she stepped on to the landing and switched on the hall light. All the doors on the third floor were closed, except for one. Halfway down the hall, on the right-hand side, the door leading up to the attic steps was ajar. There was a round, dark object on the floor protruding from the gap. Hope squinted at it, trying to identify it. She began to move forward for a closer look and halted abruptly in surprise. The object was a brown leather loafer – and it was attached to a foot.

TWENTY

D ylan saw it, too.

'Is that a foot . . .?' he began. 'And a leg – oh, hell!'

His medical training must have instinctively kicked in, because he immediately raced down the hall toward the owner of the loafer. For a moment, Hope was too startled to follow him. She had expected to find some sort of a disturbance in relation to the attic. Groans, sighs, and whimpers were all common. Banging doors and windows also. Items were occasionally thrown across the room or pushed down the attic steps. But not a person.

Hope drew a shaky breath. There actually was an intruder in the brownstone. That explained the shout and the series of thumps. But who was it? What were they doing there? And how badly were they injured?

'The good news,' Dylan reported, kneeling down and completing a cursory examination of the person, 'is that he's alive. Only minimally conscious but alive.'

As though to prove it, the man gave a low, pitiful moan, similar to the one that Hope had heard a minute earlier from the second floor.

'He's lucky,' Dylan continued. 'It looks like cuts and contusions mainly. One of his ankles isn't right, but my guess is that it's no more than a bad sprain. I can only ascertain so much from this position, and I'm hesitant to move him without assistance and proper equipment. I don't think there's any serious damage to the neck or spinal column, but I would rather not take the chance. He should go to the hospital where they can do all the necessary tests.'

Leaning over the landing, Hope called down to her sister, telling her that an unidentified man had fallen down the attic steps and needed an ambulance. After a few stunned seconds, Summer ran to the phone. Hope headed toward Dylan and the man.

'Normally, I would advise you to stay back,' Dylan said, as she approached them. 'He could be armed and dangerous. But I haven't found any weapons on him, and in his current condition, the only hazard that he poses is to himself.'

'I don't understand how he got inside,' Hope mused. 'We're good about keeping the doors and windows locked. And why is he all the way up here? The third floor of a house like this isn't usually the best place to find cash and other valuables, plus it increases the chance of getting caught.'

Having done what he could for the man, Dylan rose to his feet. 'I don't pretend to be an expert on burglars, but this guy doesn't appear to be a criminal mastermind. He doesn't have a mask – or even a hat – to conceal his face, and he's not wearing gloves. He looks, well, pretty ordinary, like some chap you'd see—'

'Like some chap you'd see sitting on a bench with Sylvia Norquist,' Hope finished for him.

Not comprehending the connection, Dylan frowned at her. She, in turn, frowned at the man lying on the floor in front of them. It was Gerald. He was dressed in the same navy shirt and shorts that she had seen him in earlier that day with Gram and Sylvia in the hotel dining room. His bird's-nest hair was even more scraggly than before, matted down on one side with a thick streak of dark red blood. There was a streak of blood on the crown of his head also, and several more on his arms, no doubt from abrasions sustained in his fall. A large purple welt was beginning to form above his left knee.

Gerald's eyelids flickered, and he moaned once more.

'Don't worry, Gerald.' Hope reached down and gave him a gentle pat on the shoulder. 'Help is on the way. They'll take you to the hospital, and the doctors there will set you right. The doctor here says that you'll be just fine. Probably a little sore for a while, though.'

'You know him?' Dylan asked in astonishment.

She nodded. 'I met him today – for the first time – at Amethyst's brunch. He's the mystery man from the park. The one that Rosemarie overheard talking about Gram and the equally mysterious piece of paper. This is Gerald, Sylvia Norquist's son.'

'What is he doing here?'

'Looking for the paper, I presume. At brunch, Gram told us that it was in the brownstone, in the attic. That was what I was searching for all afternoon, without success. Gerald must have been so anxious to get the paper that he crept into the house and tried to find it.'

Dylan's frown resurfaced. 'What is on this piece of paper? And if it's so important to everyone, why is it kept in the attic?'

No sooner were the words out of his mouth than the door at the top of the attic steps slammed shut with a thunderous bang. Both Hope and Dylan jumped at the sound, but only Dylan turned toward it.

'I've never seen an attic with multiple doors before,' he said, peering up the steps. 'One at the bottom of the stairs, and another at the top. Why are there two?'

'Privacy,' Hope told him.

'Privacy? Who would need privacy in an unfinished attic that's used primarily for storage?'

She was saved from having to elaborate by her sister.

'Hope?' Summer called from downstairs. 'Are you and Dylan all right?'

'We're fine,' she answered. 'No worries.'

'Thank goodness. I heard the door slam, and I wanted to make sure that you didn't get stuck in the attic or, worse yet, that Dylan got stuck in the attic . . .'

With a puzzled expression, Dylan peered up the stairs again.

'The ambulance should be here shortly,' Summer continued. 'I'm on the phone with Nate now, and he's heading over as quickly as possible, too.'

'Okey-dokey.' Hope couldn't help smiling at the cheerful way her sister announced the imminent arrival of the detective.

Dylan chuckled. 'Most people aren't quite that eager to have the police drop by.'

'Anybody who gets Summer's mind off Gary for even a short while is good in my book, police or not.'

'Speaking of Gary,' Dylan said, still studying the steps, 'I can see why you wanted him – or one of his construction buddies – to do something about these stairs. They are incredibly dangerous. The staircase is much too steep and narrow for its height, the overhanging ceiling appears to be buckling in several spots, and there's no handrail for support. I highly doubt whether it's insurable, and if modern safety codes are applied, the property in its current condition may not even be saleable.'

'Lucky, then, that we're not trying to sell it.'

Dylan shook his head at her in reproach. 'I've seen some horrendous staircase accidents over the years. My dad is right. Olivia should never go anywhere near these steps. Neither should you, for that matter. Or anybody else who values their health and appendages. I agree with my dad's recommendation that the attic be shut off permanently—'

He was interrupted by a low growl from behind the door at the top of the steps.

'Was that a dog?' Dylan was confounded. 'In the attic?'

Hope feigned a shrug. 'Let's change the subject. Before anyone gets too upset.'

'I'm not getting upset.'

'I wasn't referring to you . . .'

To Hope's relief, Gerald chose that moment to regain his senses. He coughed and spluttered as if he had just taken a tumble in an ocean wave and sucked up a gallon of sea water in the process.

'What! Huh!' His eyes flew open in alarm. 'What's going on?'

'Easy. Easy does it.' Dylan set his hands on Gerald's shoulders to keep him from rising. 'Don't get up. Stay where you are.'

'Don't get up? Why not?' Gerald coughed and spluttered some more. 'What's happened?'

'You've fallen down the stairs, picked up a couple of bumps and bruises along the way, and hit your head. That's why everything seems fuzzy and muddled right now. I have a few questions. Try to answer them to the best of your ability . . .'

Dylan began a series of medical tests. Hope presumed that their purpose was to check the severity of Gerald's head injury and also to confirm whether his motor skills were functioning properly. In any case, she was happy to have Gerald awake and to have Dylan focused on his patient's condition rather than that of the attic steps. Dylan was taking far too great an interest in the attic, and by the sound of it – considering the slamming door and the growl – the attic was taking far too great an interest in him.

Watching Dylan work, Hope was impressed by his composure and professionalism, particularly in view of the fact that Gerald was still technically an intruder in the house. She was also struck by how Dylan's inquiries gradually, adeptly became less like a doctor's and more like a detective's.

'Were you heading up the stairs when you fell?' he asked Gerald. 'Or had you already been in the attic and were heading back down?'

It was an excellent question. If Gerald had been in the attic, could he have found the paper when she couldn't? Hope looked at his hands. They were empty. There was also no paper protruding from his pockets. One pocket did have a bulge, but it was bulky and heavy, like a wallet or a phone.

'I think I was heading up . . .' Gerald paused to consider. 'Yes, I was heading up the stairs, and there was a door at the top. That's strange, isn't it?' He looked at the door next to him. 'A door at the bottom, and a second one at the top?'

'It is strange,' Dylan concurred, before encouraging Gerald to continue. 'Did you reach the door at the top?'

'Yes.' He paused and considered again. 'I remember standing there and asking myself: Now if I were an important document that somebody had decided to hide in the attic, where would I be?'

Dylan gave Hope a sideways glance. 'And what answer did you come up with?'

'I didn't. The door was open, but the attic was too dark to really see anything. I could only make out some shadows and the outline of a few boxes. I was trying to figure out where the light switch was when all of a sudden, out of the blue . . .' Gerald faltered, wincing at the memory.

Hope found herself wincing, too, wondering what he had encountered and how she was going to finesse an explanation.

'Out of the blue,' Gerald repeated, taking a gulping breath, 'or more accurately, out of the black, there were these red eyes. *Glowing* red eyes. And they were looking straight at me. At first I thought it must be a cat. Cats have those reflective eyes that shine in the night. But as the eyes started to move toward me, I saw that they were much too big for a housecat's – and much too tall. They were waist-high, at least. Then it growled. It was a terrible sound. Deep and rumbling, like a predator . . .'

Gerald shivered and looked apprehensively up the steps. It must have suddenly occurred to him that the purported predator was still in the attic – only a staircase and one closed door away – while he was lying helplessly on the floor below, because he blenched and with considerable effort, began to drag himself away from the stairs.

'Don't do that.' Dylan hurriedly stopped him from moving. 'You'll injure yourself further. You need to keep still and remain where you are.'

'I'm not remaining here!' Gerald protested. 'Not when *it's* up there!'

'There is nothing up there,' Dylan told him.

'Yes, there is! It was growling and salivating. I'm sure of it. And it was stalking me. First it circled around to the left, then it went around to the right, and all the while, it was getting closer and closer. It was hunting just like a predator in the jungle or the woods, except we were in the attic, and I was the prey!'

Dylan responded by once more stopping Gerald from rising.

'I am *not* staying here,' Gerald insisted. 'You can think that I'm crazy, but I know what I saw and heard.'

'I don't think that you're crazy,' Dylan replied calmly. 'I do think that you've suffered a significant head trauma, which can make the most rational person believe they've seen and heard all sorts of things that aren't actually there.'

'But I was so certain . . .' Gerald started to waver. 'I was positive that . . .'

'How about this for a compromise?' Dylan said. 'I will help you to sit – but not stand – up, so we can get you off the floor and out of the doorway. Having observed you for a while now, I don't think that should cause any problems from a medical perspective.'

Gerald didn't hesitate in accepting the offer. With Dylan's assistance, he moved slowly and carefully away from the stairs and into the hall. There were a few exclamations of pain and grimaces of discomfort along the way, but Gerald was too determined to quit. He gritted his teeth and struggled onward until he finally managed to get himself seated upright, leaning against the hall wall for support.

The moment that Gerald was clear of the steps, Hope closed the attic door, giving it an extra pull to make sure it was firmly shut. Dylan raised an eyebrow at her, but he didn't comment.

'Thank you,' Gerald said to Dylan, breathing heavily from his exertions. 'Odd as it may sound, I feel better now. The pain is worse in my leg and my head, but lying there on my back, utterly defenseless, was awful.'

'Perhaps you should have thought of that before you decided to enter someone's home uninvited,' Dylan remarked, his tone unsympathetic.

'My sentiment exactly,' Hope agreed. 'How did you get in here anyway?'

Gerald's brow furrowed, and he mumbled something.

'What was that?' Dylan folded his arms sternly across his chest. 'Speak up.'

'I, um . . .' Gerald stammered. 'I . . .'

Rather than complete the sentence, he reached into his pocket and withdrew the bulky object that Hope had noticed earlier. To her surprise, instead of a wallet or a phone, the bulge turned out to be a jangling keychain.

Dylan was surprised also. 'You have a key to the house?' he asked incredulously.

Gerald stammered some more.

Hope leaned forward to take a closer look at the keychain. There was something familiar about its triangular silver shape. And then suddenly she realized why. It was Gram's keychain – holding Gram's keys.

'Are those Gram's?' Hope exclaimed. Then a horrifying possibility struck her. 'Is Gram all right? What did you do to her?!'

'Me? Huh?' Gerald was flustered. 'I didn't do anything!'

'You must have done something,' Hope snapped. 'You have her keys! Where is she? How—'

'Wait a minute,' Dylan interjected. 'I thought that Olivia was with my dad tonight.'

'She is with your dad tonight. Or at least she was supposed to be.' Hope turned heatedly back to Gerald. 'You better not have hurt my grandmother – or Morris, either. Because if you did, I promise you that what you experienced in the attic this evening will be child's play in comparison.'

Gerald's face went deathly pale. 'I didn't hurt anybody. I swear! Certainly not your grandmother. And I barely know Morris.'

Dylan took a menacing step toward him. 'Then how did you get Olivia's keys?'

Gerald hesitated.

Ignoring his injuries, Dylan grabbed him by the collar of his shirt. 'If you don't tell us right now—'

'My mom,' Gerald bleated.

'Your mom?' Hope echoed. 'Why would Sylvia have Gram's keys?'

Again Gerald hesitated. Dylan's fingers curled into a fist.

Cringing in anticipation, Gerald answered hastily, 'My mom took the keys from your grandmother's purse after brunch, as we were all leaving the table. She did it so that we could get into the house – into the attic – for the paper.'

Hope stared at him.

Dylan began to question Gerald further, but he was interrupted by voices below. The ambulance had arrived. Summer could be heard letting in the paramedics and responding to their inquiries.

'I'll go downstairs and talk to them,' Dylan said to Hope.

She nodded. 'But you won't tell them . . . too much, will you?'

'The bare minimum. Only what they need to know in relation to his injuries.' Still holding Gerald by his collar, Dylan gave him a forbidding look. 'You slipped and fell down the stairs. It was a simple accident. You weren't paying enough attention. That's the official story. Got it?'

'Yes,' Gerald squeaked.

Dylan roughly released him. 'If you move one inch from that wall while I'm gone, there's going to be another accident. You understand me?'

This time Gerald couldn't even manage a squeak.

With quick steps, Dylan headed down the main staircase.

Hope waited until she heard him reach the ground floor and greet the paramedics. Then she turned toward Gerald, cautiously keeping her voice low.

'They'll be up here in just a minute or two,' she said, 'so you need to answer my questions fast. If you don't, I'll open both the attic doors – in which case, a minute or two will seem like an eternity.'

'Don't open them,' Gerald begged.

'Then you better start telling me the truth, because I don't believe your story. Not one word of it. The Sylvia Norquist I know would never steal keys from another woman's handbag or consider trespassing in someone's home.'

Gerald swallowed hard. Hope took it as a sign that she was on the right track.

'Your mom cares far too much for her reputation to risk being branded a thief among the sweater-set-and-pearl crowd.'

Either from a fear of the attic or a desire to protect his mother's good name, Gerald gave an anguished confession.

'It was me,' he admitted, his voice strangled. 'I was the one who took the keys from your grandmother's purse. But I had to do it! I had to get the paper!'

Hope was skeptical. 'And you thought that you could just wander up to the attic, the paper would magically fall into your lap, and you would be able to stroll out the front door with it, easy as pie?'

Gerald's pallid lips trembled.

She frowned at him. 'I still don't believe you. There's something missing from your story, and you have five seconds to tell me what it is.' She put a threatening hand on the lower attic door.

'You don't understand!' Gerald exclaimed, his neck and shoulders now trembling also. 'I didn't have an option. She didn't give me a choice. She made me do it!'

'Who did?'

There were footsteps on the main staircase, followed by voices. Dylan was headed back up, accompanied by the paramedics. Gerald must have heard them, too, because he reached toward Hope and desperately grabbed her arm.

'Tomorrow. At noon. In the spa.' His words tumbled out in

a frantic rush. 'You have to bring her the paper. If you don't, she'll—'

Gerald's whole body began to shake violently. Not sure if it was from too much stress and agitation or something more serious, Hope knelt down next to him.

'It's all right. You're all right,' she said, as soothingly as she could. 'Try to breathe. Try to relax. We'll get everything with the paper sorted out. Don't worry. It will be fine . . .'

'No, no!' Gerald cried. 'It won't be fine. Not unless you go to the spa and give her the paper. You *must*! Your grandmoth—'

Although his mouth continued to move, only garbled syllables emerged. Gerald's eyes rolled back in his head, and his hand tightened painfully around her wrist.

Struggling out of his grasp, Hope spun toward the staircase. 'Dylan, hurry! Something is wrong with Gerald! I think he's having a seizure.'

Dylan was next to her in an instant. The paramedics were only a step behind. Hope moved hastily out of their way, letting them do their jobs. She watched for a moment as they bustled about Gerald, then she turned and headed down the stairs to the nearest phone.

TWENTY-ONE

Hope breathed a tremendous sigh of relief when Gram answered her phone. She and Morris were safe and sound, curled up on Morris's sofa, having just finished a Sunday-evening bowl of popcorn and a nature documentary featuring the nesting habits of ospreys. Gram expressed surprise that Hope was calling at such a late hour. Although Hope had intended to tell her about Gerald and the stolen keys and his fall down the attic stairs in pursuit of the paper, when she heard Morris yawning in the background and murmuring something about heading off to bed, she changed her mind. There was no need to share all the trouble with them now. The news could wait until the morning. At least that way Morris and Gram stood a chance of getting a peaceful night's rest, which was more than Hope expected for herself. In the end, she simply told Gram that she had found her keyring. It turned out that Gram hadn't even known it was missing.

'Are they OK?' Summer asked anxiously when her sister entered the living room after concluding the call.

'Gram is fine. Morris is fine. They're snug as two bugs in a rug.' Hope restrained a smile as she said it. Although not curled up together, Summer and Nate looked quite snug themselves sitting on the same sofa.

'I can send a car over to check on them,' Nate offered.

'That's kind of you, but I don't think it's necessary,' Hope replied, settling herself in one of the yellow-paisley wing chairs across from the sofa. 'I was concerned mostly because Gerald – he's the man who fell down the stairs – had Gram's keys. That's how he got into the house.'

'It's Gerald Norquist up there?' Summer exclaimed in surprise.

Hope nodded. Immediately after the conversation with Gram, Sylvia, and Gerald in the hotel dining room, she had shared all the details with Summer, including regarding the tontine. 'He was trying to get into the attic.'

'And the attic decided against him, apparently,' Summer chuckled.

A crease formed in Nate's brow. 'So it wasn't an attempted burglary, after all? He isn't trespassing?'

'Oh, Gerald is definitely trespassing, and he was most certainly attempting to burgle us, but . . .' Hope hesitated, deliberating how much information to give the detective.

'But we would prefer to keep the matter private,' Summer finished for her. 'Gerald is the son of our grandmother's friend, and we don't want him to end up in court or jail when there hasn't been any actual harm done. Isn't that right, Hope?'

'No harm done,' Hope agreed, following her sister's lead.

Summer turned back to Nate. 'I'm sorry for dragging you out here so late in the evening – and on a Sunday, too. That's twice today I've called you in a state of panic, wasting your valuable time, when there's really been no need.'

'You haven't wasted my time tonight any more than you wasted it this morning,' Nate corrected her. 'I'm glad that you called me. I *want* you to call me—' He stopped abruptly, no doubt realizing that he sounded considerably more personal than professional.

'Thank you.' Summer gave him a winsome smile. 'You've made me feel much less guilty about it. Even so, I wish there was a way for me to make it up to you.'

'That isn't necessary. It's my job to handle these sorts of matters and ensure the safety of—' Nate stopped himself again, and this time he chose the personal. 'I wouldn't say no to a drink. Another evening, when I'm not here in an official capacity?'

A tinge of pink blossomed in Summer's cheeks. 'Another evening would be lovely.'

'I can highly recommend the bourbon on the patio,' Dylan said.

They collectively turned toward the hall, where Dylan had suddenly appeared. There was no sign of Gerald or the paramedics.

Hope rose from her chair. 'How is Gerald doing?'

'He's in shock,' Dylan told her. 'And it didn't help that we had to get him down so many stairs. Those narrow landings make it awfully tough to maneuver. But we did the best we could. They're loading him into the ambulance now.'

'Is he conscious?' Hope started to move toward the hall, in the direction of the front door. 'Can he talk?'

'No, on both counts. So if you're heading outside to speak to him, don't bother. He's been given a sedative. A strong one. He won't be able to respond to anything for at least the next twenty-four hours, and it might be substantially longer. I was wrong about his ankle. The damage is worse than I initially thought. An orthopedist will probably want to schedule him for surgery as soon as possible.'

Hope frowned. If she couldn't talk to Gerald, then he couldn't tell her who had made him take Gram's keys and who he was supposed to meet tomorrow in the spa. Perhaps he had told Dylan instead. 'Did Gerald say anything to you when you were treating him or bringing him downstairs?' she asked.

'You mean aside from him sobbing in pain and hallucinating that the attic was going to attack him?'

Her frown deepened. Could Gerald have been hallucinating about having to bring the paper to someone at the spa? She didn't think so. There was no question that Gerald had been suffering from his injuries, but he had seemed lucid enough. He had been perfectly clear about the time and location of the meeting.

Nate turned to Summer. 'I know you said a minute ago that you would prefer to keep the matter private, but I would strongly recommend against it. Whether the man is an acquaintance or not, it's important that a report be made, especially when the paramedics have been called to the scene and serious injuries have occurred.'

Hope and Summer exchanged a glance.

'We appreciate your advice,' Summer replied, leaning slightly toward Nate as though to emphasize the point. 'I understand why – under ordinary circumstances – a report would be best, but in this instance, Hope and I would rather have it stay quiet.'

'You would rather defend a lawsuit?' Dylan said.

They looked at him.

'If Gerald decides to sue you for his medical bills, physical and emotional distress, and whatever other bogus claims some ambulance chaser comes up with, you'll need a police report to prove that he entered the house without your knowledge or consent. Otherwise, you should get ready to write him a big, fat check.'

'Dylan is right,' Nate concurred. 'Filing a report today is the best way to protect yourselves tomorrow.'

Summer shook her head. 'I'm sure that Gerald wouldn't sue us.'

'You were probably also sure that your husband wouldn't have an affair,' Dylan remarked under his breath.

He was still in the hall, so only Hope heard him. She gave Dylan a sharp look, but she couldn't argue with him. Although it was gone now, Summer certainly used to have a blind spot in regard to Gary. As to Gerald, however, Hope was inclined to agree with her sister. It was unlikely that Gerald would sue them, partly because Sylvia wouldn't allow it for fear of her reputation being tarnished in the process and partly because of the attic. Regardless of how many sedatives he was given and surgeries he might have, Gerald was never going to forget the brownstone's attic.

Nate continued to press the need to file a report, while Summer continued mildly but firmly to resist. Dylan walked over to Hope, who was leaning against the wainscoting at the edge of the living room.

'Is she using the privacy excuse because she doesn't want to tell him what Gerald was looking for upstairs?' Dylan said in a low tone. 'You're going to have to tell the police eventually. You can't avoid it forever, not if that paper has any relation to the two deaths.'

Hope sighed, knowing that he was right. She wasn't eager to share Gram's secret, but it couldn't be helped. With Gerald's fall down the stairs, the time had come for full disclosure. Or at least substantial disclosure.

'As much as we might want to,' Hope said to her sister, interrupting her debate with Nate, 'we can't keep it quiet. Not anymore.'

Summer wrinkled her nose in displeasure.

Hope nodded. 'I feel the same way, but now that Morris knows, it's only a matter of time before Dylan hears about it.'

'What does my dad know?' Dylan demanded. There was undisguised irritation in his voice. 'Am I the only one who's being kept in the dark?'

'I haven't a clue, either,' Nate said, appearing equally annoyed.

'Your dad just found out tonight, from Gram,' Hope told Dylan. Then she turned to Nate. 'Gram should have come clean with you, as well. Immediately. The moment that she – and Sylvia – realized there was a connection.'

'In Gram's defense,' Summer interjected, 'there isn't any proof of a connection. It could simply be a coincidence.'

'That's true,' Hope agreed, not reminding her sister that she was the one who supposedly didn't believe in coincidences. 'But proof or not, there's no denying the facts. Two members of the group are dead, within a single day of each other, under highly suspicious circumstances. Gerald was the first to make the connection, and considering that he crept into the house and tried to search the attic, he's obviously pretty convinced of it.'

'What connection?' Dylan said, still sounding miffed.

'What group?' Nate added impatiently.

Expecting that a lengthy explanation would be required, Hope returned to the yellow-paisley wing chair across from Summer and Nate. Dylan seated himself in the matching chair next to hers.

'The connection between what happened to Marilyn and Roberta,' Hope said, answering both Dylan and Nate at the same time, 'and the tontine.'

She awaited a confused reaction. To her surprise, she didn't get one.

There was a brief pause, then Dylan chuckled. 'So Olivia is part of a tontine?'

'Together with Sylvia, Marilyn, and Roberta?' Nate said.

Summer, who – like Hope – had never heard of a tontine before that afternoon, frowned at them. 'You know what a tontine is?'

'I didn't graduate from the police academy yesterday,' Nate responded. 'I have been a detective for a good long while.'

'Oh, no, I didn't mean to imply . . .' Summer let the sentence trail away awkwardly.

'And you?' Hope asked Dylan.

'I'm familiar with tontines,' he told her, 'because I'm in one.'

'You're *what*?'

Dylan chuckled again. 'Am I correct in assuming – seeing as there's been two murders – that Olivia's tontine is based on the members' lifespans?'

Hope was too flabbergasted to do more than nod.

'From what I understand, that's the most common type,' Dylan said. 'My tontine is different. It's based on marital status.'

Nate grinned. 'I've heard of those, but I've never met anybody who's been part of one before. How did you get involved in that, if you don't mind me asking?'

'I don't mind in the least. It was during medical school. A bunch of us – all guys – spent a couple of days at a friend's beach house after exams. As you might guess, there was quite a bit of drinking and discussion of women . . .'

Nate grinned some more.

'By the end of the weekend, we had formed a tontine. The last bachelor standing wins.'

'Still ongoing?' Nate inquired.

'Still ongoing,' Dylan replied. 'Only a few of us remain in the running, though. There was some debate after the first divorce took place whether re-entry would be permitted, but the consensus was against. It was deemed a violation of the spirit of the contract.'

'Not to mention that allowing re-entry would worsen the other members' chances of winning.'

'Damn right. There's a fifty-year-old bottle of Scotch at stake. A single-malt Glenfiddich, distillery bottled.'

Nate gave an appreciative whistle. 'Very nice. You've got some fancy friends. Invite me to one of their parties, won't you?'

'So long as you realize that you can't join the tontine this late in the game.'

As Dylan and Nate shared a laugh, Hope and Summer looked at each other. For all their astonishment at the course of the conversation, they had learned something that neither one of them had been absolutely certain of previously. Dylan and Nate were both single.

Dylan turned to Hope. 'While we're on the subject of winning, what's at stake in Olivia's tontine?'

'Money, I believe. Gram said something about a small annuity every year. And Gerald mentioned a pot at the end.'

'Yes, but how big is the pot? How much money are we talking about?'

Hope shook her head. 'I don't know. I didn't ask.'

For a moment, Dylan appeared incredulous. Then he smiled. 'That's a refreshing change. You're probably the only woman I've ever met who wouldn't think to ask.'

'Then you've met some lousy women,' Summer snapped. 'Hope is worried about Gram – and the others. She doesn't care about a couple of bucks stashed in an envelope decades ago.'

Dylan's smile grew. 'There's no need to get defensive. I was giving your sister a compliment.'

'In all likelihood, it's considerably more than a couple of bucks stashed in an envelope,' Nate told Summer. 'Otherwise, I wouldn't be investigating two deaths. The desire for money is a powerful motivator.'

'But that's what I don't understand,' Hope said. 'The only people who can get the money are the original members of the tontine. I can't see one of the six killing the others, regardless of the sum involved.'

'There are just six members?' Nate asked her. 'Marilyn and Roberta. Olivia and Sylvia. And who else?'

'Kirsten Willport and Rebecca Huber.'

Nate leaned forward with interest. 'I haven't heard of Rebecca before.'

'She died – of natural causes – a year or two after the tontine was formed.'

'Which leaves three,' Dylan said. 'Olivia, Sylvia, and Kirsten.'

Nate nodded. 'All three were at the community center.'

Dylan nodded back at him. 'And all three are familiar with the spa.'

'Except none of the three could be the murderer,' Hope countered. 'That's my point as to the money. Neither Gram nor Sylvia nor Kirsten is interested in money.'

'*Everybody* is interested in money,' Nate said.

'Yes, of course,' Summer responded, a touch sharply. 'Money is a necessary evil in the world. No one is disputing that. What Hope means is that Gram and Sylvia and Kirsten aren't desperate for money. They can eat their fill each day, sleep in a safe place at night, and buy clothes to cover themselves.'

'Not to mention book plenty of beauty treatments at the spa to maintain their divine skin,' Dylan added wryly.

Hope was tempted to laugh – knowing that he was referring to Kirsten – but her sister was not amused.

'That isn't funny in the least,' Summer rebuked him. 'And frankly, I'm surprised at you, Dylan. Why are you so determined to make Gram look guilty? If you cared even slightly about your dad's happiness, you would be putting your efforts and arguments into defending Gram, not accusing her of murder!'

Dylan rolled his eyes. 'Don't be absurd. I'm not accusing Olivia of murder. I don't think that she killed anyone. I do, however, think that you – and your sister – are relying too heavily on the notion that dire financial straits are necessary to commit a heinous act for the purpose of winning the tontine. In my experience, some of the people with the most money are also the greediest and will do anything in their power to get their hands on more.'

'Exactly right,' Nate agreed. 'And conversely, it's easy to be fooled by the appearance of wealth. There are plenty of people who look like they're living in luxury, but it's just a façade. In actuality, they don't have two cents to their name. So I'm hesitant to place much importance on how rich or poor any member of the tontine might seem to be.'

'But that doesn't make sense,' Summer protested. 'Not in this case, at least. Not with the timing.'

'The timing?' Nate asked.

'If the murders aren't because somebody *needs* the money rather than simply *wants* the money, then why now? Why start killing members of the tontine nearly thirty-five years after it was formed? It isn't logical.'

'You make a good point,' Dylan said. He considered a moment. 'Perhaps there's something about the tontine and the money at stake that has recently changed. The pot has grown substantially larger, for instance, due to a sudden stock appreciation or bond maturity. We need to know how the assets are being held.'

'Gram should be able to tell us that. It's probably also part of the paperwork in the attic.' Summer turned to her sister. 'What do you think, Hope?'

Hope sighed. 'I think that I have to search the attic again, but considering the number of boxes and my lack of success this afternoon, the chance of finding anything quickly is pretty slim.'

'We can all help search,' Nate suggested. 'Four sets of hands and eyes work a lot faster than one.'

There was a pause.

'They're hesitating,' Dylan told Nate, 'because of the attic curfew. We're in the middle of the witching hour.'

Startled, Hope and Summer looked at him.

'Midnight to four a.m., didn't you say?' Not waiting for their reply, he continued to Nate, 'Apparently, the attic is off-limits during that time. Bad energy or something.'

Nate's mouth opened, but no words came out.

'That was my reaction, too,' Dylan said. 'But even outside of the witching hour, Summer won't go into the attic. For some mysterious reason, Hope is allowed up there, but her sister isn't.'

Hope rose from her chair. Summer rose from the sofa.

'And now,' Dylan concluded, his lips curling with a hint of a smile, 'we're about to be – ever so politely – kicked out of the house.'

TWENTY-TWO

The knob on the door turned, and a sliver of light crept across the bedroom floor.

'Hope?' Summer whispered.

Reluctantly, Hope's eyes opened a crack. She had gone to bed shortly after Dylan and Nate had left, but sleep had been elusive. Her mind wouldn't rest, jumping from one disjointed thought to the next. Who was Gerald supposed to meet at the spa? Where was the paper in the attic? Would Dylan win his tontine? Finally, she had managed to doze off, but it had been restless – and far too short.

Summer tried again. 'Hope? Are you awake?'

'I am now,' she grumbled.

'Oh, good.'

As the door opened fully, so did Hope's eyes. Bright light flooded into the room from the hall lamp. Summer stood in the doorway in her bare feet and polka-dot pajamas.

'What's wrong?' Hope said. 'Has something happened?'

'No.' Summer padded toward the bed. 'But I'm worried about Gram. Do you think she'll get in trouble because of the tontine?'

Hope rubbed her face and sat up partway, leaning against the pillows. 'I think the whole tontine is trouble.'

'Good lord, yes. I'm amazed that Gram ever wanted to be part of such a thing. It's so macabre.'

'True, but to be fair, it probably seemed harmlessly quirky and bohemian at the time, which is right up Gram's alley. After all, you don't open a mystic shop if you're not a bit quirky and bohemian.'

'So if we've been running the shop for the last five years – more or less – what does that make us?'

Hope smiled. 'Captivatingly unconventional.'

Summer laughed, climbed up on to the bed, and sat on the blanket next to her sister. 'I'm pretty sure that Gary would agree with the *unconventional* part, not so much the *captivating.*'

'Then it's a good thing that dear detective Nate does.'

With a touch of embarrassment, Summer laughed again. 'You're being silly. But while we're on the subject of the police, that's what I'm worried about. Now that Nate knows about the tontine, won't Gram get in trouble for participating in it? Didn't Gerald say that tontines were illegal?'

'In some places they are, apparently. But my guess is that it doesn't apply here, because otherwise the lawyer wouldn't have done the paperwork for the group. It might also depend on the type of tontine. A small, private one is OK, for example. But a big, public one that anyone can join isn't, because there's too much potential for fraud and abuse.'

'That would make sense. Dylan didn't seem to think that there was anything wrong with his tontine, which is obviously private.'

'And Nate was really casual in his response. He didn't act as though there could be legal repercussions. So I don't think that there's anything to be concerned about with regard to Gram. If there does turn out to be a problem later on,' Hope added, 'then you'll just have to convince Nate to look the other way.'

'How am I supposed to do that?' Summer exclaimed.

Hope grinned. 'The old-fashioned way, of course. Bat your eyelashes and coo sweet nothings in his ear when you have that drink you promised him.'

Summer didn't share the smile, and her eyes went down to the blanket. 'Maybe I shouldn't have agreed to that. I'm still married, remember.'

'Now who's being silly?' Hope said. 'It's just a drink. One glass, here at the brownstone, either in the living room or outside on the patio. You haven't committed to a wild night of clubbing or a weekend tryst with the man.'

'Speaking of trysts,' Summer pulled on a loose thread at the corner of the blanket, 'I wonder if Gary and what's-her-name spent the weekend together at the hotel?'

'I don't know. Possibly.' Hope was thoughtful. 'It's odd in a way.'

'Not really.' Summer pulled harder on the thread. 'Gary hasn't been at the house, so he must be staying somewhere else.'

'That's what I mean. You're not staying at the house, and Gary isn't staying at the house, which makes it odd about the card.'

'What card?'

'The Tarot card. The Fool that somebody put in your mail slot.'

Startled, Summer let go of the thread and looked up at her sister. 'I forgot all about the card.'

'I did, too. Then Nate talked about people being fooled by the appearance of wealth, and his choice of words reminded me.'

Summer shook her head. 'I don't agree with him – or Dylan. I still think the murderer must need the money; otherwise, they wouldn't have waited for so many years to start killing members of the tontine.'

'But what if it's not about the money?' Hope said.

'How could it not be about the money? Money is the whole point of the tontine.'

'On the face of it, yes. The problem is the third Fool. If the cards in Roberta's handbag and Marilyn's pocket were meant as some sort of a message in relation to the tontine, then why give a card to you or Gary? You clearly aren't members. Neither of you can get the money. So what's the purpose of it?'

'Maybe it's a mistake,' Summer suggested. 'Maybe the card was intended for someone else. Gram, for instance. Whoever dropped the card through the slot – the killer, presumably – could have thought that Gram was living at my house instead of here or at Morris's.'

Hope was doubtful. 'That seems an unlikely mistake. Everybody knows where Gram lives, and even if not, it isn't hard to figure out.'

'Then maybe it was deliberately designed to confuse us. Maybe the killer was worried that they had given away too much information with the first two cards, and they wanted to throw us off the scent with the third, purposely pointing us in the wrong direction.'

'If that's the case, then their strategy worked, because I'm definitely confused, and I have no clue what direction to go in.'

Summer reflected a moment, then offered a final possibility.

'Maybe we're wrong about everything. Maybe the simplest answer is the correct one. Sylvia or Kirsten is the murderer. The plan is to kill Gram next, followed by either Kirsten or Sylvia, and that's the end of it. Easy-peasy.'

Hope looked at her without speaking.

'I know what you're thinking,' Summer said. 'That I sound horrible. Just as ghoulish and macabre as the tontine. Here I am, sitting on your bed in my pajamas, wishing for a cup of coffee, calmly discussing whether one of Gram's oldest friends plotted to kill the rest.'

'No,' Hope answered. 'I was thinking that maybe the murderer is right about the cards. Maybe we're all fools.'

Half an hour later, coffee mugs in hand, Hope and Summer were standing on the brownstone's third-floor landing, gazing down the hall at the closed door leading up to the attic steps.

'I'm not sure if this is such a good idea,' Summer murmured.

'Probably not,' Hope agreed, in an equally low tone, 'but I don't see that we have much choice. We need that paper.'

'We need that paper.'

'But do we really need to whisper?'

Summer raised an eyebrow at her sister. 'Do you want them to hear us?'

Hope gave a little shrug. 'I would be very surprised if they didn't already know that we're standing down here. They probably also know why. Don't forget, I spent most of the afternoon in the attic searching through stacks of boxes. Then Gerald tried to get up there for the same reason—'

'And he failed, thankfully.' Summer started to take a sip of her coffee and choked. 'Is that his blood on the wall?'

'Yes. Gerald got a couple of cuts in the fall.'

'He's lucky. It could have been a lot worse.'

'It's bad enough,' Hope replied. 'He's in the hospital, and we can't talk to him, which means that he can't tell us who made him take Gram's keys and who he's supposed to meet tomorrow in the spa.'

'Today,' Summer corrected her. 'Today in the spa.'

Hope looked at the pale streaks of sunlight rising through the window at the end of the hall. 'You're right. It's morning.'

'At least that's one point in our favor. The attic is always much safer at dawn than at dusk.'

Acknowledging the truth of the remark, they were both silent for a long minute, listening for any sounds above them.

'It's quiet up there,' Hope said, whispering in spite of herself.

'That's a promising sign,' Summer whispered back at her. 'They must be tired. Interacting with Gerald took a substantial amount of energy for them, especially if they *assisted* in his fall down the stairs.'

'They also slammed the door at the top of the steps when Dylan and I talked about the paper being up there. And there was some growling after Dylan complained about the staircase being dangerous and not in compliance with safety codes. He's in accord with his dad that the attic should be shut off permanently.'

Summer's eyes stretched wide. 'Dylan actually spoke those words?'

'Loud and clear,' Hope confirmed.

'Merciful heaven. Forget my comment earlier about Gerald being lucky. Dylan was the lucky one – lucky that the door at the top of the steps didn't instantly fly back open and a sharp object wasn't flung at his head.'

'I thought the same thing. Needless to say, I switched the subject as fast as I could.' Hope lowered her voice so that it was barely audible. 'I'm worried that Dylan might be starting to take too great an interest in the attic, and also that he might be learning too much, especially considering his remarks just before he and Nate left last night.'

Summer nodded. 'We'll have to be more careful in the future, both in regard to what we tell him and not letting him come up here.'

'Agreed.'

Again they were silent, listening for noises.

'Still quiet,' Summer observed. 'I guess whatever they were moving around in the early hours, they're done now.'

'They were moving things around? I didn't hear that. It must have been during the fifteen minutes that I actually managed to sleep.'

'That's fifteen minutes more than me.'

The sisters shared a tired sigh and each took a hefty drink of coffee.

'Well,' Hope said at last, sighing once more and setting down her mug on the railing, 'procrastinating isn't going to help. There's no indication of activity, and it's light outside. This is as good as it gets.'

With reluctance, Summer concurred. 'Don't stay up there too long. It's better not to find the paper than . . .' She let the sentence trail away unfinished.

'But I have to find the paper. Gram's life might depend on it—'

Hope broke off abruptly. She hadn't meant to say it. She had tried hard not to think it. But the dreadful possibility had finally slipped out.

Summer looked shaken. 'So my guess could be correct? Sylvia or Kirsten is the killer, and the plan is to go after Gram next?'

'Honestly, I don't know. As Dylan and Nate pointed out, Sylvia and Kirsten both had the motive and the opportunity. But I still find it difficult to believe, particularly with regard to Sylvia. Yesterday at brunch when she talked about the tontine and Marilyn and Roberta's deaths, she sounded a lot more obtuse than culpable. She even doubted whether there could be a third victim, because she didn't see what purpose it would serve.'

'If she didn't think that there could be a third victim, then she clearly wasn't the one who put the third Fool through my mail slot.' Summer's brow furrowed. 'Except maybe it was an act at brunch yesterday. Maybe Sylvia was just pretending to be obtuse to keep us from suspecting her.'

'Then it was an awfully convincing act. You might be right, though. At this point, anything is possible. Sylvia could be the one who actually stole Gram's keys. She could also be the one who Gerald is supposed to meet at the spa.' Hope stopped and shook her head. 'No, that doesn't make sense. Gerald wouldn't have been so agitated about meeting his mom. He was desperate about bringing the paper to someone, and he seemed terrified of the consequences if that didn't happen. It's more likely that the person threatened Sylvia, and Gerald was trying to protect her by promising to deliver the paper. That would also explain why he mentioned Gram just before he went unconscious. He was warning me that Gram was in danger, too.'

'Which only leaves Kirsten!' Summer exclaimed. 'The simplest answer really might be the best.'

Hope was hesitant. 'But isn't it almost too simple? Doesn't it feel as though we're missing something?'

'We're missing the paper.'

'So is the murderer, evidently . . .'

And without further ado, Hope stepped into the hall and headed toward the attic door. When she reached it, she paused and glanced back. Summer was sitting on the landing, her knees pulled to her chest.

'You have to be careful.' Summer's voice was shaky. 'We don't know what they were moving around up there. They might have put something at the edge of the steps, and it could come crashing down as soon as you open the door.'

Hope tried to feign a smile, with little success. 'That would be a first. They've never laid a trap for me before.'

'Not for you, but for others,' Summer reminded her.

With that thought in mind, Hope moved to the side of the door and gingerly turned the knob. The door opened an inch. Nothing happened. She opened it further. Still nothing. Hope leaned forward and cautiously looked up the steps.

'The stairs are empty,' she reported. 'The door at the top is closed. There doesn't appear to be any change from last night.' She didn't mention that the streaks of Gerald's blood on the floor at the base of the stairs had dried from dark red to russet brown.

'I have an idea,' Summer said suddenly.

Hope turned to her.

'To speed things up, you could try searching with a pair of dowsing rods. Or a pendulum. The pendulum has always worked for you before.'

'It's worked twice,' Hope clarified. 'Once to find the garage door opener and once to find the television remote.'

'But you were successful both times.'

'And both times I got a long lecture from Gram afterward on how the pendulum isn't a toy and should never be used for frivolous purposes.'

'Finding something as important as the paper can't possibly be considered a frivolous purpose,' Summer protested.

'No, but it's too dangerous taking the pendulum into the attic. The veil is already so thin up there. We can't risk opening up a channel and letting something in.'

Summer shuddered and offered no further argument.

Hope turned back to the staircase. 'Wish me luck.'

'There is no luck when it comes to the attic,' Summer remarked grimly.

Avoiding Gerald's blood, Hope put a tentative foot on the first step. She waited for a response. There was none. She climbed several more steps and waited again. After a minute, she proceeded the remainder of the way up the staircase.

Just as it had appeared from below, the door at the top of the steps was firmly shut. Hope leaned her ear against the wood and listened. The only noise was a faint chirping from the family of finches that roosted in the pine outside the attic window.

Reaching for the knob, Hope gave it a slight jiggle. It moved without resistance. She paused for a moment, remembering Summer's warning about a potential trap. If there was anything perched on the edge of the steps waiting to crash down, she wouldn't be able to avoid it in the narrow stairway. But nothing had ever fallen on her before. She was just going to have to take the chance. With a deep breath and partially closed eyes, Hope turned the knob and swung open the door.

There was no crash. When she reopened her eyes and switched on the light, she found no trap, either. Summer was correct on a different point, however. Things had definitely been moved around during the night. For starters, the stacks of boxes had changed. Some had shrunk, while others had grown. Two of the old willow rocking chairs had shifted from the left corner of the room to the right. And the pair of antique snowshoes that she had told Dylan about were now standing on their tails, leaning against a support beam. But the most noticeable alteration was directly in front of her. Just inside the doorway, only a few inches from Hope's feet, sat a single brown banker's box.

Having never seen the box before, she was quite sure that she was not the one who had placed it there. Hope stepped toward it for a closer look. The cardboard was wrinkled and

misshapen as though it had gotten wet and then dried on multiple
occasions. That didn't surprise her. Over the years, there had
been more than a few leaks in the attic. Some were the natural
result of the brownstone's aging roof and gutters. Others had
come from a more mischievous source when the attic windows
were opened in the middle of rainstorms.

The lid on the box was in such poor condition that flimsy
pieces of cardboard broke off in her hands as she lifted it.
At first glance, the box appeared empty, but when she leaned
down to be certain, she discovered a large manila envelope
at the bottom. The envelope was just as wrinkled and tattered
as the box. It was stamped with a name and address at the
top. The black ink was heavily smeared. Hope picked it up
and squinted at it. She couldn't decipher many of the words,
but the first few were enough.

Law Offices of . . .

Her heart skipped a beat. It turned out that she didn't need
dowsing rods or a pendulum. The attic had found the paper
for her.

Hope looked up, and her eyes traveled slowly around the
room. No shadows moved. No sounds reached her ears except
for the busily chirping finches outside the window.

'Thank you,' she said aloud.

Then, switching off the light and gently closing the door, she
returned to her sister and the third floor, the envelope hugged
in her arms.

TWENTY-THREE

'The print on this first page is too faded,' Summer said, magnifying glass in hand, closely studying the yellowed paper. 'I can hardly make out any of it.'

She and Hope were sitting at the palm-reading table in the front corner of the boutique. The natural lighting was the best in that part of the shop, exactly what they needed for examining a brittle, moisture-stained document.

'The second page is the same way. Except . . . see here at the bottom' – Hope turned the crinkled sheet toward her sister and pointed to the spot – 'the names are smudged, but those are clearly six signatures lines.'

'So it's definitely the tontine!'

They looked at each other across the table and shared a triumphant smile. Unfortunately, neither the smile nor the triumph was long-lived.

'But if we can only read a few intermittent words and some signatures, what good will it do us?' Summer slumped against the back of her chair. 'We were hoping for a grand revelation, weren't we? We don't know anything more now than we did when we got out of bed this morning.'

'We know that when it chooses to, the attic can be remarkably helpful.'

'For a price,' Summer replied dourly. 'Always for a price. It will want something in return. Just give it time. Then we'll learn how much to regret our gratitude.'

'Well, I'm not regretting it yet,' Hope said. 'Regardless of whether we can read the document or not, it's still an advantage for us to have it, because now we can decide if I should bring it to the spa for the meeting.'

'Bring it to the spa for the meeting?' Summer exclaimed, gaping at her.

Hope nodded. 'That's the question. Should I take the pages and pretend that I know what they say, or would it be better to leave them behind as a potential bargaining chip?'

'Have you lost your mind? You want to bargain with a *murderer*?'

'I don't want to, but we might have to. Our options are limited. Gerald was absolutely adamant that I go to the spa and give the paper to the person. Can we really take the chance that he was hallucinating from the pain of his injuries or exaggerating his fear of what might happen if the person doesn't get the paper? Gram's life could be at stake. And possibly also Sylvia's or Kirsten's.'

Summer's expression was grave. 'Even so, it's awfully risky to go to that meeting, Hope. The person has killed twice already.'

'I'll just be extra careful not to eat or drink anything while I'm there.'

'If that was meant as a joke, it isn't remotely humorous,' Summer reproached her. 'Besides, we don't even know for certain whether some food or beverage played a role in the deaths. At this point, it's merely speculation.'

'But it's not speculation that the murderer will in all likelihood be at the spa today, planning on meeting Gerald at noon. This is our best – and maybe only – opportunity to find out who the person is before they kill again.'

Summer offered no rebuttal, because there was none. 'What about Nate? Should we tell him about the meeting?'

Hope considered a moment. 'I'm not sure. On the one hand, it would probably be safer to have the police there. On the other hand, having the police there will probably scare off the murderer, which defeats the whole purpose. What do you think?'

'I think that irrespective of the meeting, we can't let Nate know how we got the paper. He won't understand. And the same goes for Dylan. If Dylan was already getting overly interested in the attic, this will make his curiosity explode. Or – as I said once before – he'll recommend psychiatric treatment.'

'For us or the attic?'

Summer burst out laughing, but she was silenced an instant later by a sudden knocking on the front door of the boutique.

'We don't officially open for another twenty minutes,' Hope

said, checking her watch. 'I don't have an early appointment scheduled. Do you?'

'No. There isn't anything on the calendar.'

The knocking continued.

'Let's just ignore it.' Summer lowered her voice in case their visitor had good hearing. 'Moreover, let's keep the boutique closed this morning. We should get to the spa early, so we can figure out where exactly Gerald was supposed to have his meeting and—'

Hope looked at her in surprise. 'What happened to the meeting being too risky?'

'It is too risky. But you're right about our options being limited. And if we're both there, then it will be much more difficult for the person to sneak up on us or trick us in some way. I'm still wondering whether we should tell Nate about the meeting, though. It might be prudent in the event that—'

Rather than stopping, the knocking grew increasingly louder.

Summer tossed her magnifying glass on the table with annoyance. 'The door is locked, and the sign says we're closed. Can't they take the hint and go away?'

'Maybe it's important. Maybe it's Dylan or Nate . . .' Hope rose from her chair and tiptoed to the window overlooking the sidewalk. She craned her neck, attempting to see the person at the door without being seen in return. 'Nope. Not Dylan or Nate.'

'No?' There was a note of disappointment in Summer's tone. 'Who is it, then?'

Her question was answered a second later when Rosemarie Potter's face pressed against the glass. 'Hope? Is that you in there?'

'Of all the people,' Summer groaned. 'Of all the mornings. Of all the—'

'I hear somebody talking,' Rosemarie continued excitedly. 'It sounds like Summer!'

Summer sank her head into her hands and groaned again.

Hope chuckled. 'You have a distinctive voice, apparently.'

Rosemarie pressed her face harder against the glass, trying to get a better view into the shop. Her cheeks puffed out like a blowfish.

'Lovely,' Summer muttered. 'Now, on top of everything else, we need to wash the windows to remove giant lip prints.'

'Summer?' Rosemarie called once more. 'Hope?'

'I'm afraid we can't avoid it. We'll have to let her in.' With a sigh, Hope started toward the door. 'I'll do a quick reading if that's what she wants, and then let's try to hurry her back out.'

Summer nodded. 'I won't offer her any tea; otherwise, she'll just linger. Maybe you could pretend that you see one of her future husbands at the farmers' market or the pet supply store. That would get her moving.'

Hope threw her sister an amused look before turning the lock and unlatching the door. Rosemarie rushed into the boutique, the wind chimes above the door swinging wildly and her tangerine bird-of-paradise dress flapping around her.

'I'm so glad that you're here!' Rosemarie exclaimed. 'I know it's a bit early to drop by, but I was worried after what happened yesterday. All those police at the house, and none of them would tell me anything . . .'

Restraining a smile, Hope returned to the palm-reading table, reminded that she owed Percy an extra doggie cookie for being so helpfully obstinate by refusing to enter Summer's house the day before. She had the drawer open and was already reaching into the cookie bag when she realized that the pug was absent.

'Where's Percy?' she asked in surprise.

'He's with the groomer for his weekly shampoo and to have his nails clipped.' Rosemarie followed her to the table. 'I got breakfast.'

'At the groomer's?' Summer said with a half-suppressed laugh.

'Oh, no. At the new shop across the street from the groomer's.' Seating herself on one of the empty chairs at the table, Rosemarie deposited a waxed paper bag next to the manila envelope and wrinkled pages. 'They make custom donuts.'

Hope hastily collected the paperwork, both to keep it from possible prying eyes and to protect it from getting any more damaged. 'What are custom donuts?'

'According to the examples on display,' Rosemarie explained, 'they use combinations of donuts to spell out messages for birthdays and other special events.'

Summer was skeptical. 'I like a donut as much as the next girl, but what happened to good old-fashioned cake and ice cream?'

'I said the same thing! There's nothing better than a birthday cake with frosting and candles. But the people at the shop promised me that a single bite of one of their donuts would change my mind forever.'

'And did it?'

'I don't know yet. They didn't offer samples, so I ended up buying a bag of donut holes, figuring that we could all try them together.' Rosemarie leaned forward and opened the top of the bag. 'Voila – breakfast!'

The appealing smell of warm fried dough and cinnamon sugar wafted into the air. Summer's skepticism promptly vanished – along with her memory.

'Thanks, Rosemarie. Would you like a cup of coffee or tea to go with those? I can make a fresh pot of either. But maybe we should eat a couple of the donut holes first. That way we'll know whether tea or coffee would taste best . . .' Summer reached into the bag. 'You want some, too, don't you, Hope?'

'Not one bite!' Dylan hollered. 'NOT ONE BITE!'

Rosemarie nearly tumbled from her chair in shock. Summer's hand froze on the way to her mouth. The envelope and papers that Hope had been discreetly sliding into the drawer fell to the floor.

'Put it down! Put it down *right now*!'

Ordinarily, Dylan bellowing at Summer to release her breakfast as if she were Percy and had just picked up something unsavory from the sidewalk would have caused Summer to bellow in return. But she was too startled to respond. Hope and Rosemarie were too startled, as well. All they could do was stare at Dylan in astonishment. He had apparently arrived on the heels of Rosemarie, but none of them had noticed, perhaps because of the already singing chimes and the collective curiosity over the concept of custom donuts.

Dylan approached the table with quick strides, grabbed the donut hole from Summer's hand, and threw it into the waxed paper bag. Then he picked up the bag and pointed the opening toward Rosemarie. 'You also. Put them in. Hurry up.'

With a bewildered squeak, Rosemarie dropped the pair of donut holes that she had been holding back into the bag. Dylan sealed up the top.

'Now go wash your hands,' he directed.

They didn't move.

Dylan's nostrils flared like an irate alligator. 'Do you want to suffer a torturous death from poisoning? If not, go wash your hands!'

Summer's mouth started to open in reply, but it almost immediately closed again, and without further delay, she swiftly headed toward the rear of the shop. Squeaking a second time, Rosemarie jumped up and raced after her.

'Use soap and rinse thoroughly,' Dylan instructed them.

As Summer and Rosemarie disappeared into the kitchen, Hope remained standing at the table in stunned silence, her mind struggling to process Dylan's words. He turned to her and motioned toward the bag.

'Did you touch any of its contents?'

Hope shook her head.

'And none of you ingested even a crumb?'

She shook her head again.

'Good.' With a relieved exhalation, Dylan tossed the bag on to the floor and settled himself into the chair that Summer had vacated. 'Until these murders are resolved, you and your sister can't eat or drink anything from an outside source, not even one that you fully believe to be harmless. It isn't safe.'

'Does that mean . . .' Hope's voice was ragged. 'It's definite now? Marilyn and Roberta were poisoned?'

Dylan gave an affirmative nod. 'I received the call from the lab this morning, only a few minutes ago, in between seeing patients at my dad's office. The report was the same for both women: strychnine poisoning.'

'Strychnine!' Hope exclaimed in horror. 'My god, that's rat poison.'

'It's frequently used as a rodenticide, but not exclusively,' Dylan said. 'The results are consistent with the symptoms that Marilyn and Roberta exhibited immediately prior to their deaths. Among many other unpleasant effects, strychnine causes severe and extremely painful muscle spasms and, eventually, respiratory failure.'

'So there was no allergy, after all?'

'As a matter of fact, my initial assessment at the community center was correct. Roberta did experience anaphylactic shock. It turns out that she was allergic to aspartame.'

'Aspartame?' Hope frowned. 'I thought aspartame was an artificial sweetener used in things like diet soda and sugar-free yogurt.'

'It is an artificial sweetener,' Dylan confirmed, 'and that's precisely why the murderer chose it. Strychnine is an exceedingly bitter, odorless, white crystalline powder. To mask its bitterness, the murderer added aspartame. That way, neither victim would have tasted anything strange. I doubt the murderer knew that Roberta was allergic to aspartame. Roberta might not have even known herself. It's an uncommon allergy, but by no means rare. Hence, Roberta's – but not Marilyn's – hives, flushing, and facial swelling.'

'Did the lab determine what the strychnine and aspartame were put in?' Hope asked.

'Not yet. And we may never get a definitive answer. All the items on Roberta's plate – the spaghetti, bread, and dessert – came back negative. Marilyn's lemon water also came back negative. Incidentally,' Dylan observed with a slight smile, 'that puts you and Olivia in the clear.'

Hope was not amused by the remark.

'The problem with strychnine,' Dylan continued, 'is that depending on the dose, it can take anywhere between fifteen and sixty minutes after ingestion for symptoms to begin to appear. We know from Olivia's account that Roberta was already ill before she got her plate, and we know from your account that Marilyn was already ill before she got her glass, so they must have consumed the strychnine some time earlier. But it could have been half an hour or an hour earlier, and that's a lot of time, with a lot of potential food and drink options, all of which have disappeared by now, either deliberately or due to ordinary clean-up.'

'But we can be certain that Marilyn and Roberta ingested the strychnine at the spa and at the community center?'

'Without question. Nate confirmed that both women were at their respective locations for at least an hour prior to their deaths. Roberta was busy with her bingo, and Marilyn was busy

with her treatments. We can also be certain of one more thing,'
Dylan added.

'What's that?' Hope said.

The slight smile resurfaced. 'The murderer is a woman.'

Hope's breath caught in her throat. Did Dylan know about
the meeting at the spa? When Gerald had talked about the stolen
keys and the intended meeting, he had repeatedly referred to
the person involved using a female pronoun: She *didn't give
me a choice. You have to bring* her *the paper.* Had he told Dylan
the same thing?

'Why a woman?' Summer asked. In a more leisurely manner
than her exit, she had reappeared from the kitchen, a checkered
dish towel draped over her shoulder. 'Because of the old myth
that poison is a woman's weapon?'

'It is indeed a myth,' Dylan replied. 'Contrary to popular
belief, a greater proportion of poisoners are actually men. But
there are no men connected to this case, aside from Gerald –
who I think we can all agree is not cut out to be a killer – and
your dear husband. So unless you imagine that Gary is cleverly
and systematically working his way through the members of
the tontine in order to disguise his true goal of poisoning you,
we can state with reasonable confidence that the murderer is a
woman.'

Summer paused, as though deliberating whether to laugh or
cry at the idea that Gary could be orchestrating a scheme to
poison her. 'I agree with you,' she said after a moment. 'My
money is still on Kirsten.'

'You've scratched Sylvia off the list?' Dylan inquired.

Hope coughed as a warning to her sister. The conversation
was heading in a dangerous direction. If they explained to
Dylan why they no longer considered Sylvia to be a suspect,
then they would have to explain Gerald's planned meeting,
which would inevitably lead to the admission that they were
suddenly in possession of the papers from the attic, and that
was an explanation they didn't want to make.

Summer must have caught the hint, because she immediately
changed the subject by offering Dylan the dish towel from her
shoulder.

'You touched that piece of donut I was holding,' she reminded him. 'I wasn't sure if you needed to clean your hands, too, so I brought a towel.'

Dylan declined. 'Thanks, but I have to wash my hands when I get back to the office anyway, before seeing the next patient. I'll try not to lick my palms in the interim,' he said drolly.

'Your patients must be getting impatient.' Summer glanced at the clock on the wall, then at her sister. 'The morning is quickly ticking by.'

It was Hope's turn to catch the hint. If they wanted to get to the spa early, they needed to get rid of Dylan soon.

'Strychnine poisoning takes precedence over bursitis and bunions, which is what my morning has consisted of so far,' Dylan responded. 'But you're right, I have kept my dad's patients waiting too long . . .' As he rose from his chair, his gaze went to the floor. 'What are those?'

'Those?' Hope looked down and saw the envelope and accompanying pages that were still lying where she had dropped them at Dylan's unexpected entrance. 'Oh, those are nothing.' Hurriedly scooping them up, she deposited them in the open drawer.

'Nothing?' Dylan questioned.

'Nothing,' Hope repeated, firmly closing the drawer.

His eyes moved across the table, pausing at Summer's magnifying glass. 'It appears as though you've been examining something. Anything of interest?'

Hope struggled for a plausible answer. She could see that he was piecing it together. The yellowed sheets of paper, and the magnifying glass, and Summer's thinly concealed eagerness to get him out of the shop. Dylan may not have known about the meeting, but he was clearly beginning to realize that something was in the works.

To Hope's relief, Rosemarie chose that moment to return from the back of the boutique. She approached the table at which they were all collected with unsteady steps.

'The tea is much appreciated, Summer,' Rosemarie said, sipping from a mug that she held with equally unsteady hands. 'I'm sorry that I got so panicky in the kitchen, about sufficient soap and scrubbing.'

'There's no need to apologize,' Summer replied gently. 'That cup of chamomile will make you feel better.'

Rosemarie nodded. 'I would ask for a refill, but I have to pick up Percy. I'm already late, and I don't want him to think that I'm neglecting him.'

'He could never possibly feel neglected,' Hope assured her. 'Percy knows how much you love him.'

A happy blush spread over Rosemarie's face, and her hands calmed somewhat. But when she set down her mug on the table and started to move toward the front door, her steps were still unsteady. It gave Hope an idea. She could help Rosemarie and, at the same time, push Dylan out of the boutique.

'Percy is at the groomer's the next block over,' she told Dylan. 'Maybe you could walk there with Rosemarie on the way back to your office? Give her one of your strong arms to lean on?'

Rosemarie's blush traveled across to her ears and down to her neck. 'That would be awfully nice, but I don't want to inconvenience you. You must be terribly busy.'

'Never too busy to see my good friend Percy,' Dylan responded gallantly.

'Oh, gosh.' Rosemarie giggled.

Dylan gave her a matching gallant smile and then, turning his head so that Rosemarie couldn't see, he cast Hope a sharp look. Hope blinked at him innocently, pretending that she didn't understand him.

Giggling some more and wishing Hope and Summer a lovely remainder of the day, Rosemarie headed outside. Dylan began to follow her, but when he reached the doorway, he turned back.

'Can I trust you?' he said. 'Or do I have to call Olivia?'

'Why would you need to call Gram?' Hope asked, still blinking innocently.

The sharp look repeated itself. 'To check on you and make sure that you don't do anything reckless.'

'What nonsense,' Summer scoffed. 'Calling our grandmother to check on us as though we're a pair of lost little waifs who can't possibly make rational decisions and fend for ourselves.'

But as she said it, Summer and Hope exchanged a glance, wondering if perhaps Dylan was correct and they were in fact about to do something reckless.

TWENTY-FOUR

After some discussion, they decided to separate. Hope would enter the hotel first, followed by Summer a short while later. Their goal was to keep a low profile and make their arrival as inconspicuous as possible. They didn't know if someone would be watching. Presumably, the murderer was still expecting Gerald to appear for the meeting. News of his injuries couldn't have traveled far overnight. Aside from the calls to Nate and the paramedics, Hope and Summer hadn't told anybody about the attempted burglary and fall down the stairs, not even Gram. And Dylan hadn't told Morris. The only unknown was Sylvia, who might have been notified by the hospital that her son had been admitted.

They had greater difficulty agreeing on what to do with the paperwork for the tontine. Since neither they nor the murderer could read more than a few words of the document, Hope was inclined to simply leave it behind at the boutique. Summer, on the other hand, thought that they had a better chance of reasoning with the murderer if they had the pages with them. Hope was doubtful that a person who had used strychnine to poison Marilyn and Roberta could be reasoned with, but she ultimately yielded when Summer argued that there was no risk in bringing the paper to the meeting and considerable risk in *not* bringing the paper.

All of the excitement with Rosemarie, Dylan, and the donut holes had ended up taking a considerable amount of time, and when Hope and Summer finally arrived at the entrance to Amethyst's cobblestone drive, it wasn't nearly as early as they would have liked.

'We'd better hurry,' Summer said, a few anxious drops of perspiration appearing on her nose. 'It's close to noon, and we still have to figure out where exactly in the spa Gerald was supposed to go.'

'I've been thinking about that. The reception area is far too public, as are the corridors and dressing rooms. Only the treat-ment rooms are private enough for a meeting like this. Which means that either Gerald or the murd—' Hope stopped herself abruptly. Even though there was nobody in close proximity, saying *murderer* aloud in the street probably wasn't the best idea. 'One of them must have a booking in their name.'

Summer nodded. 'Fingers crossed that it's Gerald, because if the other person used an alias, it will be nearly impossible for us to figure out who it is before they realize that Gerald isn't coming and slink off.'

'And fingers crossed that Lisa is working this morning, because she was great at finding Gary's room for Megan and me the other day—' Again, Hope stopped herself, and this time she winced. 'I'm sorry. I shouldn't have brought that up.'

'Don't apologize. I'm glad that you and Megan found Gary's room and saw what you did. As painful as it was for me to hear, I'm a firm believer that it's better to know the truth. And that's why we need to find out the truth about this, too, regard-less of how awful it might be.' Summer paused. 'You don't think – what Dylan said earlier – about Gary working his way through the members of the tontine in order to disguise his true goal of poisoning me . . .'

'Dylan didn't mean that seriously!' Hope exclaimed.

'Are you sure? Because it's possible, isn't it? There's no question about Gary cheating on me, so why couldn't he take it one step further and try to murder me, too? It would save him from a lot of hassle and a potentially messy divorce. He's familiar with the community center and the spa. He also has access to plenty of Tarot cards.'

Hope stared at her.

'It's possible, isn't it?' Summer reiterated.

'Well, yes, in theory,' Hope began hesitantly. 'But let's be honest, it's a pretty complex scheme, and Gary has never been especially clever or motivated. And he couldn't have known about the tontine, because *we* didn't know about the tontine.'

Summer couldn't argue with her on those points. 'I suppose you're right. I suppose I'm just being paranoid. Plus, I doubt that Gary would ever hurt Gram. He always liked Gram.'

'Right now, thankfully – regardless of Gary – Gram is the

safest of all of us,' Hope said. 'She's with Morris, and if Morris hasn't already been notified of Marilyn and Roberta's lab results, I'm sure that he will be shortly. Then he'll probably be even stricter than Dylan and won't let Gram put a morsel in her mouth without running it through half a dozen chemical analyses first.'

Summer chuckled. 'I can see Morris doing exactly that. Speaking of Dylan, he wouldn't actually tattle on us to Gram, would he? I don't want her coming to look for us.'

Hope shook her head. 'No. I think Dylan was just testing us. He could see that we were up to something, and he was trying to work out what it is.'

'Well, fingers crossed that he doesn't work it out – at least not until this horrible meeting is concluded.'

'At the rate we're crossing them,' Hope replied, 'we're going to need more fingers.' And with a wistful smile at her sister, she turned and headed toward the hotel, the manila envelope tucked under her arm.

Any chance for an inconspicuous entrance evaporated the moment that she stepped through Amethyst's glass doors.

'Hello!' Megan called from across the lobby. 'Hope!'

With a large wave in greeting, Megan began to zigzag toward her, cheerfully conversing with various hotel guests along the way. By the time she reached Hope, nearly everybody in the lobby had taken notice of Megan – and, by association, Hope.

'If someone was watching for Gerald,' Hope remarked under her breath, 'then they now know that I'm here. It's a good thing that Summer didn't come inside at the same time.'

As though reading her mind, Megan gave her a quick hug and said, 'I'm glad Summer isn't with you.'

Hope looked at her in surprise.

'I need to warn you.' Megan dropped her voice and directed Hope to the nearest nook off the lobby. 'It's about Gary.'

'Gary?' she asked, her surprise – and apprehension – growing. Did Megan also have some reason to suspect that Gary might be involved in the murders?

'Summer needs to be prepared,' Megan told her. 'Gary might be coming back around. Misty checked out this morning.'

'Oh, is that all?' Hope exhaled with relief. 'You had me worried there for a second.'

It was Megan's turn to show surprise. 'But it's a big deal! Without Little Miss Mystique and her hotel room, Gary will surely return to the house, and if he returns to the house, he'll no doubt attempt to worm his way back into Summer's life.'

'He might try, but he's going to face some stiff competition,' Hope responded with a smile. 'Last night at the brownstone, Nate proposed a date of sorts, and Summer accepted.'

'He did? She did?' Megan questioned excitedly. 'Why didn't I hear about this before?'

'It just happened, and there have been a lot of other things going on . . .' Hope hesitated. For a minute, she was tempted to give Megan a full update regarding Gerald and the attic, the papers tucked under her arm, and the meeting in the spa. But then she decided against it. The explanation would take too long, and even in the nook, they were too exposed. Plus, Hope was already having reservations about the wisdom of her and Summer's plan, and she didn't want Megan to add any further misgivings.

Megan evidently noticed her distraction, because she said, 'You look rushed, so I won't keep you. I have to dash myself. Bridezilla and the wedding planner are back. Now they want to forgo flowers completely and use origami butterflies instead.'

Even with the stress of the impending meeting, Hope had to laugh. 'I'm starting to feel sorry for the groom.'

'Me, too. I have a sneaking suspicion that the marriage won't last much longer than the origami butterflies, which will probably be changed to hydrangeas by tomorrow.' Megan rolled her eyes. 'But I expect to hear all the details about Summer and our favorite detective later. Wine and cheese at the boutique after work, as usual?'

Hope nodded, and Megan hurried out of the nook, blowing her an air kiss in parting. As she watched Megan zigzag back across the lobby the way she had come, Hope wondered with some amusement if Dylan would make a dispensation for the leftovers from the four o'clock wine-and-cheese. She tried to think of what arguments she could use to persuade him, doing all that she could not to focus on the task immediately before her. If she concentrated on Dylan, then she might manage to make it down the staircase to the lower level of the hotel, past the purple orchid on the black marble table, through the double doors into the spa.

Her heart was pounding so hard when she entered the reception area that Hope was sure it could be heard over the rhythmic pitter-patter of raindrops playing as part of the spa's background music. She must have looked as jittery as she felt, because the two ladies lounging on a pair of velvet chairs glanced at her with pitying expressions. One woman had a glass of lemon water in her hand, and when she started to take a sip, Hope almost shouted at her to stop, but she caught herself just in time. She didn't recognize either woman, so there was no reason to believe that the water had been poisoned.

With her usual bun and slim-fitting uniform, Lisa rose from behind the reception desk. 'Hey there, Hope.'

Hope gave a shaky, grateful sigh. 'Hi, Lisa.'

'Do you have an appointment today? I didn't see your name . . .' As Hope approached the desk, Lisa lowered her voice to prevent the ladies from overhearing. 'How are you? I have to confess that I'm not doing so well. I can't quite come to grips with what happened last week. Poor Mrs Smoltz. It's the first death we've ever had at the spa. And I think that word has been spreading about it, because we've had more than the usual number of cancellations over the past few days. Some were without any explanation at all.'

'That's why I'm here, actually,' Hope said. 'Not in regard to a cancellation, but to follow up on something to do with Marilyn. Can you tell me if Gerald Norquist has an appointment scheduled for noon?'

'Gerald Norquist?' Lisa's brow furrowed. 'I don't think so. I don't recall him as a client – and I'm usually pretty good with names – but I'd be happy to take a look.'

'Thanks . . .'

Lisa sat back down at the desk, tucked a couple of loose strands into her bun, and checked the computer. 'It's just as I thought. Gerald doesn't have an appointment. He's never been to the spa.'

Hope frowned.

'Out of curiosity,' Lisa said, 'is he related to Sylvia Norquist?'

'Yes! Sylvia is Gerald's mother. Does she have an appointment?'

Lisa checked the computer again. 'Sylvia has Tuesday evening and Thursday morning booked. Nothing today, though.'

The frown deepened. No Gerald. No Sylvia. Who else might have an appointment? It couldn't be Gary, could it? 'What about Kirsten Willport?' Hope asked.

This time Lisa didn't need to check her computer. 'Kirsten is here right now. She was scheduled for eleven.'

'Which room?'

'The treatment should be nearly over. She'll be out any minute, if you want to—'

'Which room?' Hope pressed her.

Her tone must have been either sufficiently determined or sufficiently desperate, because without further debate, Lisa answered, 'Kirsten is in room nine.'

'Room nine,' Hope echoed. 'I really appreciate this, Lisa. I remember you mentioning last week that tiger's eye helped with your exams. If you want to come by the boutique tomorrow or the next day, I'm sure that we can find you another crystal, or a tea – Summer is excellent with teas – to relieve any lingering stress or nervousness.'

'That would be great! I'll definitely stop by. I don't work on Wednesday afternoon, so . . .' Lisa didn't finish the sentence. Perhaps she sensed Hope's own nervousness, because lowering her voice once more, she said, 'Everything is OK, right? Nothing bad is going to happen again, is it?'

Although Hope would have dearly liked to reassure her, she couldn't. She wasn't confident enough herself. All she could muster was a small, not overly optimistic smile. 'I'm expecting Summer to arrive shortly. Will you tell her about Kirsten's room?'

Lisa responded with an anxious nod.

Hope nodded in return and, taking a deep breath, headed toward the adjoining corridor with the treatment rooms. Under other circumstances, she might have laughed at the irony. Room nine had also been Gary and Misty's room. For the second time in less than a week, she was walking down the same corridor to the same room with the same amount of dread in her steps.

But Hope could see no humor in the perverse situation. Her mind was fixed on one thing: Was Kirsten the murderer?

For better or worse, Hope found the corridor empty. There was no sign of Sean with his housekeeping cart. There were no other spa employees or guests, either. Only the same rhythmic pitter-patter of raindrops as in the reception area, which to Hope, in her agitated state, was beginning to sound more like a jack-hammer than a tranquil drizzle.

Room nine was midway down the corridor, on the left-hand side. She paused when she reached the closed door. Should she knock? Announce her arrival? Call the police? Blockade the entrance? Sean had said that the spa walls were solid and few noises passed through. Hope leaned toward the door and listened. She expected not to hear anything, but to her surprise, somebody inside the room seemed to be talking. The voice was too indistinct to make out any words or even to determine if it belonged to a woman or a man. And then, suddenly, there came a muffled shriek.

Hope grabbed the handle of the door. It wasn't locked, and she hastily swung it open. Last time a giggling, cuddling couple had appeared before her. This time there was no couple, only Kirsten Willport. She wasn't sitting in a chair, or lying on a treatment table, or even simply standing in the room. Kirsten was huddled on the floor, cowering in the far corner, her spa robe wrapped tightly around her. Her face was pale and panicked. Tears of fear were streaming down her divine skin.

Momentarily forgetting why she was there, Hope started to move toward her. 'Kirsten, what's wrong? You look as though—'

'No, no!' Kirsten cried. 'Go back. Go back!' She waved wildly at the door. 'Get out. Get out!'

'But I—'

It was all Hope managed to say before the door slammed shut behind her and the lock clicked. Hope spun around, and when she did, she discovered that Kirsten hadn't been waving at the door. She had been waving at a person standing behind the door.

'How disappointing to see you, Hope,' the person said.

TWENTY-FIVE

For Hope, there was no disappointment. Only extreme confusion. Ever since Gerald had told her about the stolen keys and the intended meeting, she had tried to figure out who would want the papers from the attic. The top suspects had been the remaining members of the tontine. Gram had always been out of the question, of course. But if it wasn't Sylvia or Kirsten, either, then the killer had to be somebody who could access both the community center and the spa, somebody who was aware of the tontine, and somebody who knew enough about everyone involved to deliver a Tarot card to Summer's house and force Gerald to do their bidding. Summer had thought the person *needed* money. Nate had thought the person *wanted* money. And Dylan had gone so far as to suggest that Gary might be using the other murders as a ruse to kill his wife. But the one person who nobody had remotely considered – the one person who didn't seem at all connected to the matter – turned out to be the person standing in front of Hope now.

'Mystique?' Hope said, stunned.

'I prefer Misty, thank you. And if I'm being truthful, there have been times when I've thought about changing it entirely. People tend not to take me seriously after learning my name. My mom claims that she was going through a hippy-dippy, back-to-nature phase when I was born, and she thought Mystique sounded *groovy*.' Misty threw her head back and laughed at Hope's bewildered expression. 'I can see that you weren't expecting me. For what it's worth, I wasn't expecting you, either. I was expecting Sylvia.'

That only staggered Hope more. 'Sylvia? I–I thought . . .' The words came out in a raspy whisper. 'I thought the meeting was with Gerald.'

'The meeting was *arranged* with Gerald,' Misty corrected her. 'But he's such a scaredy-cat that I figured if I threatened his mom, he'd go running to her in a fright, and then she'd show up here in his place. I didn't think that he'd come crying to you instead.'

'He–he didn't come crying to me.' Hope struggled to steady her voice. 'I caught him trying to steal the paper you wanted.'

'Gerald tried to steal it?' Misty laughed harder. 'Maybe he deserves more credit than I've given him. It never occurred to me that he would actually attempt to get the paper.'

Hope's confusion continued to grow. 'But you told Gerald that he had to bring it to you. He was adamant about it. You don't want the paper, after all?'

'No. It was just an excuse. I needed a way to get Sylvia alone – or partly alone – and demanding the paper seemed the best way. You can't imagine how hard it is.' Misty leaned her willowy frame against the door with a weary exhalation.

'What is?'

'Killing people. The first one or two are easy enough. No one suspects you. No one suspects that anything bad will happen. But after a couple of deaths, people start to get nervous. They trust less. They become more wary of strangers. And the ones who worry they might be next on the list' – she pointed at Kirsten – 'get especially careful.'

Hope's shock in regard to Misty had been so great that she had forgotten all about Kirsten. Turning around, she found Kirsten still cowering in the corner.

'Are you feeling all right?' Hope asked her. 'Did you eat or drink anything in the last hour?'

Misty chortled. 'So the police have finally figured out my poison of choice? A wicked combination I put together, isn't it?'

Ignoring her, Hope focused on Kirsten. 'Have you had any food or beverages since you've been here?'

'I–I didn't want to,' Kirsten squeaked in reply. 'But she tried to make me. Right before you came in. She tried to make me drink from that cup.' Her tear-stained eyes went to a red plastic cup in Misty's hand.

'You mean this?' Misty raised the cup slightly. 'It's just water – with a little something extra.' She chortled again.

'Don't worry,' Hope told Kirsten. 'You'll be fine. There are two of us now and only one of her. She can't force you to drink anything.'

'There are two of you now,' Misty agreed, 'but I'm optimistic that you will have the good sense to leave, Hope. This isn't really any of your concern.'

'Not any of my concern?' For the first time since her arrival, Hope's outrage overtook her astonishment. 'You can't honestly think that I'll just walk out the door so you can freely poison Kirsten and then go after Sylvia and my grandmother next!'

Misty frowned. 'I'm not going after your grandmother. Why would I go after your grandmother?'

'Because she's a member of the tontine!'

'Yes, but Olivia is the only one of the group that my aunt ever liked.'

'Your aunt?' Kirsten gave a strangled gasp. 'You're Rebecca's niece?'

There was a knock on the door, followed by an apprehensive voice.

'Hope? Hope, are you in there?'

It was Summer. Hope breathed a sigh of relief. She hastily considered how best to respond, but Misty spoke before she could.

'Summer, dear, is that you?' Misty called to her. 'It sure sounds like you, and your sister's expression confirms it, but I'm afraid that Hope can't come out to play right now. She's too busy trying to convince me not to pour strychnine down Kirsten Willport's throat.'

Kirsten gave another strangled gasp.

If Summer also gasped, the door was too thick to hear it. The handle on the door jiggled, but it didn't turn.

'It's locked,' Hope shouted. 'I'm OK. And Kirsten is OK, too—'

'Not for long,' Misty said.

'Hold on, Hope,' Summer cried. 'I'll get help! I'll call Nate. I'll call Dylan. Just hold on!'

Footsteps thudded down the corridor, away from the room.

'How sweet.' Misty smiled and once more leaned against the door. 'I always wished I had a sister. I feel that I know yours quite well. Gary has certainly talked about her enough. I must say that marrying him was not Summer's wisest decision.'

Hope's gaze narrowed, and some sharp words bubbled on

her tongue. But then it occurred to her that instead of lashing out at Misty, the smarter move would be to remain outwardly calm and prolong the conversation. The longer Misty talked, the sooner help could come, and the better the chance that both she and Kirsten would get out of the room alive and well.

Remembering what Megan had told her upstairs, Hope said, 'I heard that you checked out of the hotel this morning. Does that mean you and Gary have called it quits, or have you two lovebirds decided to set up house together?'

'I checked out this morning,' Misty replied, 'because I was hoping to have my business here concluded this afternoon. And I would have concluded it if you hadn't interrupted me with Kirsten, and if Sylvia had come to the room instead of you as she was supposed to.' Her smile widened. 'But you can't really believe that I would set up house with Gary? What an atrocious thought! Gary Fletcher was a means to an end. Nothing more. I needed someone to give me the inside information on everybody. Their interests and activities. Bingo and spaghetti suppers at the community center. French clay facials at the spa. In that regard, Gary did a marvelous job. He's such a blabbermouth – and so useful at running errands. He got all those Tarot cards for me.'

In spite of her efforts to keep composed, Hope was startled by the admission. Summer had been right about Gary being the one to supply the cards. Did that mean he was also part of the poisoning scheme? Had he actually been intending to kill his wife?

'Was Gary going to poison Summer?' Hope asked in horror. 'Is that why she was given the third card?'

'No. Gary wasn't going to poison anyone. He never would have the stomach' – Misty chuckled at her pun – 'for something like that. He didn't know about my plans. The card at Summer's house wasn't from him. It was from me. I left it there before you caught Gary and me together. I wanted to give Summer a clue about the affair and what a rotten husband she has. I sincerely hope that she doesn't take him back. The man is a fool.'

Hope couldn't contest that. 'And the first two cards? Were Marilyn and Roberta also somehow fools?'

'They thought my Aunt Rebecca was a fool. As did Sylvia and Kirsten.' Misty shot Kirsten a withering look. 'Rebecca was already ill when she suggested the idea of the tontine to the group, but she hadn't been formally diagnosed, and she didn't know how quickly the disease would progress. She wrote about it in her journals, which I have. How those four would snicker and snort that soon there would be one person fewer to share in their precious annuity. How stupid they thought Rebecca was for agreeing to a tontine when she had no chance of outliving the other participants. No one but your grandmother visited my aunt when she got really sick. No one but Olivia thought about anything but the damn money.'

'I'm sorry,' Hope said. Although not with the same degree of resentment and bitterness as Misty, it was her turn to give Kirsten a reproachful glance. 'They should have been kinder.'

Misty shrugged. 'As the old saying goes, revenge is a dish best served cold – or, in this case, with spring water and artificial sweetener in a plastic cup.'

Hope hesitated, wanting to express sympathy for how Rebecca had been treated by her supposed friends, but at the same time wanting to persuade Misty that strychnine poisoning wasn't the best solution.

'I also find consolation in the fact,' Misty went on, 'that those four are the real fools. It was all about the money for them, and yet there is no money.'

'No money?' Hope asked, not understanding.

'Have you not read the tontine? I had assumed from what you said earlier about Gerald and the paper that it's in the envelope you're holding.'

'It is in the envelope,' Hope acknowledged. 'But it was stored in our attic, and the pages have become illegible.'

'Then allow me to enlighten you,' Misty said. 'My aunt had a copy, and it's perfectly clear. Rebecca was brilliant with investments, and at the time that the tontine was formed, interest rates were high. She put the entire amount in government savings bonds, and the pot grew beautifully. After twenty years, the bonds matured and stopped earning interest. No one bothered to reinvest the money, so for the last decade and a half, it's just been sitting there. Instead of increasing, the pot has been steadily shrinking with the annuities being paid every year. When I last checked, it was down to almost nothing, just a few remaining dollars and cents.' She turned to Kirsten with a triumphant grin. 'I bet you didn't know that!'

Kirsten was too hunched in fear to dare utter a syllable, but it was apparent from the surprise now joining the alarm on her face that she had erroneously believed there to be a sizable sum in the tontine.

'Fools, fools, fools . . .' Misty sang gleefully.

She was interrupted by the return of pounding footsteps down the corridor – lots of them – followed by a profusion of pounding on the door.

'Hope! Can you hear me?'

'Are you all right, Hope? Is Kirsten all right?'

'Can either of you reach the door?'

'We need you to give us a sign—'

It was a combination of Dylan, Nate, and Summer, along with a jumble of other voices, all speaking at the same time.

Misty heaved a wistful sigh. 'I suppose now that everyone has arrived, there's no chance of me simply walking out of here.' She started to lift the cup in her hand.

'Oh my god, no!' Hope cried. 'Don't do it! Don't drink it!'

Although it wasn't clear whether they understood Hope's exact words, the group on the other side of the door certainly heard her panicked shout, because they immediately began shouting in return. They were asking questions and demanding answers, but Hope didn't address any of them. In that moment, her attention was solely on Misty.

'You don't need to do it,' Hope told her. 'Please. You don't need to drink the poison.'

'I can see why my aunt liked your grandmother,' Misty said. 'It must run in the family, because I like you, too. It's a shame that we couldn't be friends. I think we would have gotten along well.'

'I'm sure that we would have – I'm sure that we will – but we'll get along even better if you give me the cup.'

Misty shook her head. 'It's nice of you to care. But there's really no need. I have not the least intention of killing myself.'

'Then don't act like you're about to drink strychnine!' Hope snapped. Her substantial relief was mixed with substantial annoyance.

'I wasn't about to drink it. I was planning on pouring it out, in the sink behind Kirsten. They can arrest me, but I'm not going to make it easy for them. There won't be any weeping confessions from me. They have to *prove* that I killed Marilyn and Roberta. And at this point, they've got nothing. No fingerprints, no photos, no evidence whatsoever. No one saw me at the community center, and whether he likes it or not, Gary is my alibi here last week. She' – Misty motioned toward Kirsten – 'is a blubbering witness at best. And you won't be too difficult to discredit. If you testify against me, I'll claim that you're being vindictive because I had an affair with your sister's husband.'

Although she didn't say it, Hope couldn't help being slightly, morbidly impressed. Misty had considered nearly every last detail of her defense.

Misty gave Kirsten a menacing stare. 'Don't imagine that you and Sylvia are safe now. I'll finish what I started. Just you wait.'

The handle on the door shook furiously, and a loud thumping began, as though somebody was hitting the handle with a hard object, trying to break the lock.

'I will make you a deal,' Misty said to Hope. 'First I'll go to the sink and rinse my cup, then you'll go to the door and let them in. You can try to race me, but I wish you wouldn't. I might get nervous and spill something into Kirsten's mouth by accident.'

Hope didn't need to deliberate. 'Agreed.'

With quick feet but a watchful eye directed at Hope, Misty moved from the door to the sink. In one swift movement, she poured the poison down the drain and turned on the faucet full blast to remove any residue in either the sink or the cup. The instant that Kirsten was out of danger, Hope stepped to the door and clicked open the lock.

A crowd came bursting in. There was a minute of chaos, with everyone swarming around Hope. Misty tried to slip away unnoticed, but she only made it as far as the corridor before Nate and a pair of uniformed police officers intercepted her. After repeatedly assuring Dylan that she was unharmed, Hope prevailed on him to use his medical skills to assist Kirsten, who was sobbing hysterically on the floor.

'What a nightmare,' Summer said, standing beside her sister and watching the commotion. 'Thank heaven it's over.'

Hope chose not to dispute her. Instead, she replied, 'I'm hungry. We didn't have any breakfast. Let's go for a long lunch.'

Summer turned to her with wide eyes. 'You're hungry? But you haven't been hungry since . . .'

'After lunch,' Hope went on, 'we should open up the boutique. I'll do a little reading.'

'A reading?' The eyes stretched wider. 'With the Tarot?'

'Of course. The King of Swords' – she gestured toward Nate, reminding Summer of the card that had previously represented him – 'has completed his case. We need to find out what his next adventure will be.'

Summer gave a whoop of excitement. Dylan, who was kneeling next to Kirsten in an attempt to calm her, looked over at them.

'And maybe,' Hope added, her lips curling with a smile, 'I'll be tempted to do a second reading . . . to see if Dylan will win his tontine.'

ACKNOWLEDGMENTS

I am grateful to my astute and discerning editor Carl Smith at Severn House, along with Natasha Bell, Jem Butcher, Katherine Laidler, and Kate Lyall Grant.

I am also grateful to my outstanding agent Kari Stuart at ICM, along with Cat Shook and Jenny Simpson.

And as always, I am grateful to my wonderful family for their boundless love and support.